# Thankful For Friends

DIANE GREENWOOD MUIR

Cover Design Photography: Maxim M. Muir



ISBN: 9798879198249

*Don't miss any books in Diane Greenwood Muir's*

## Bellingwood Series

Diane publishes a new book in this series
on the 25th of March, June, September, and December.
Short stories are published between those dates
and vignettes are written and published each month
in the newsletter.

## Mage's Odyssey

Book 1 – Mage Reborn
Book 2 – Mage Renewed

## Journals

(Paperback only)
Find Joy — A Gratitude Journal
Books are Life — A Reading Journal
Capture Your Memories — A Journal
One Line a Day – Five Year Memory Book

## Re-told Bible Stories

(Kindle only)
Abiding Love — the story of Ruth
Abiding Grace — the story of the Prodigal Son
Abiding Hope — the story of the Good Samaritan

You will find a list of all published works
at nammynools.com

# CONTENTS

# NOTE FROM DIANE

Have you seen the new movie, *Wonka*? Like the original, it uses a favorite song, "Pure Imagination." As Willy Wonka darts around, creating imaginative ways to serve chocolate, I listened to the lyrics.

*Come with me and you'll be in a world of pure imagination. Take a look and you'll see into your imagination.*

Bellingwood is a product of my imagination and you've chosen to travel into it. When you read, you experience what I experience. Our imaginations reveal what the characters look like. One person's ideas are different than anyone else's. I'm often surprised at how you read things into the story I never intended to be there. Your imagination is doing its job.

Bellingwood is also a community. My father, a United Methodist minister, did something unique in every church he pastored. He was a great leader, but one thing he did was build community. Where there was strife, he brought unity. Where financial difficulties had created tension, he eased it by bringing people together to raise funds. He worked with groups who had nothing in common, showing them how to find community.

I was once told that I'd make a great preacher. Nope. While I love to teach what I've learned through a lifetime of study, managing a church is nothing I desire. Drawing people together? That doesn't require a church structure, nor does it require everyone to have the same beliefs. We come together and care for each other, no matter our differences.

Imagination and community. Thank you for being part of Bellingwood.

The team that supports my writing with everything from photography to design work, proofreading, and editing is filled with friends who mean the world to me. Thank you to: Carol Greenwood, Alice Stewart, Eileen Adickes, Fran Neff, Max Muir, Lisa Burton, Nancy Quist, Linda Watson, Amanda Kerner, Rebecca Bauman, and Judy Tew.

Spend time with us at facebook.com/pollygiller.

# CHAPTER ONE

Hurry, hurry! Polly was in a hurry. She needed to get to the school in time for Zachary's Thanksgiving program and she was late. She should have known better than to try to fit in a trip to Boone. Lexi would have done it, but the girl was busy. Very busy.

Lexi and Agnes were madly baking pies, cupcakes, cheesecakes, and cookies, not to mention the huge list of side dishes they were setting in for Lexi's home catering service. When Lexi nearly broke down in tears this morning because she was out of pumpkin, chocolate chips, and butter, Polly told her to set up an online order and she'd pick it up.

Sylvie and Eliseo were out of town and the bakery was up to its ears in orders. Not only that, but Sycamore Catering had more work than it could handle. Which meant that when Polly's friends and those who had already signed on to purchase food from Lexi's little catering venture couldn't get what they needed elsewhere, they called on the poor girl who didn't know how to say no.

The kids all helped when they could, and it was JaRon who stepped up and made an extra effort to be Lexi's helper. Cassidy tried, but even though it was with Agnes, Cassidy just didn't care to be stuck in the kitchen when there were other things she could be doing.

Polly had just unloaded the large grocery order, leaving it to Lexi to figure out where to put things, and now she was hurrying to the elementary school. The program had already started. She was going to be late. And of course, when she pulled up to the entrance of the parking lot, it was full, cars parked on the street. She didn't have time for this. Knowing from experience it would be a very short program, Polly made a quick run through the parking lot, in case a space was overlooked. And by golly, there it was. It was in the teacher's section of the lot, but right now, she didn't care. They were either here, or they weren't. She raced across the lot to the front door, nodded at the security guard, who lifted an eyebrow, and did her best not to cause a scene as she opened the door to the gymnasium.

The last few months had been hard since the Ricker kids moved in. They'd finished renovating space in the basement to make room for everyone, but even more difficult was integrating the strong family unit into the Sturtz household. Amalee, at eighteen, was as much a parent to her younger siblings as anyone. As their grandmother got sicker last year, Amalee rose to the occasion. The kids still looked to her when it came to making important decisions. Teresa was in fifth grade and having the hardest time adjusting. She wanted to so badly, but her heart had been worn down from all the death and changes she'd experienced. Zachary, a third grader, was a happy boy who found a new friend in JaRon. The youngest, Kestra, was the sweetest girl. She loved school, she loved making friends, and she was the first who saw Polly and Henry as parents to the family. It was going to take time for these kids to become fully blended. Fortunately, Amalee was a bright girl who knew that the best thing for her little family was to become part of something bigger. It was safer and the future would offer opportunities she couldn't give to the younger kids.

Zachary's class made its way to the risers. She hadn't missed him. The hardest thing to watch was him peering into the audience, looking for her. Since Polly was standing near the doors with other parents who had come in late, he'd never find her. Then, his face lit up in recognition. Who else was here?

While his class did their part of the Thanksgiving presentation, Polly moved forward until she could see most everyone in the bleachers. How had Henry managed to get here? They'd talked about the program today and he planned to be at a meeting in Ames for something-or-other. But there he was, with his phone's camera focused on Zachary.

Polly's phone buzzed in her pocket. She ignored it. This was more important. Both Henry and Zachary were more important. The phone buzzed again as Zachary recited his lines. He beamed at Henry, then gave her husband a little wave. Polly was almost glad that she hadn't been seen by either of them and was given a chance to watch their interaction.

The class filed off. Mrs. Wallers patted each child on the back as she led them to seats in the bleachers to make room for the next group.

Polly's phone buzzed again. She had two phone calls and now a text from Rebecca. The girl was coming home on Friday for Thanksgiving break. What could be so important today?

Before she could make her way out of the gymnasium to respond to Rebecca, another phone call buzzed in. This time from Sylvie. Polly couldn't answer any of them at this point. She gave her head a quick shake, trying to clear it.

She sent a text to Henry. *"You made it! He saw you."*

*"Where are you?"* he sent back.

*"In a pile of parents at the front door. Rebecca and Sylvie are calling me. How long are you planning to stay?"*

*"I could walk out right now and be happy, but I'm stuck. Looks like another twenty minutes or so."*

Her phone buzzed again. Twice. Another text from Rebecca and this time, a text from Sylvie.

Polly walked into the main foyer, nodded at the guard, then went outside, and headed for her Suburban. She might as well get out before a flood of parents made travel impossible.

She knew better than to try to read texts while walking. Some people were cut out for that type of multi-tasking. Polly was not. At least when it came to walking and doing something other than paying attention to where she was going.

Once she got inside her car, Polly opened her phone. First up, Sylvie's text. She only felt a little guilty that her adult friend took precedence over her adult-type daughter, but Rebecca was forever getting caught up in small things that she believed were terribly, terribly important.

*"I need you,"* Sylvie had sent. *"Andrew has had an accident. Call me, please."*

That would likely be why Rebecca was desperately trying to reach her as well. She checked those texts.

*"Polly! Where are you? I need you. Call me!"* That was the second text. The first one read, *"Andrew is in the hospital. He broke his arm and he's all messed up. I need to go to Iowa City now!"*

This was a type of multi-tasking Polly wasn't prepared for either. She sent a quick text to Rebecca. *"I'm on my way to you. Calling Sylvie right now."* That would calm Rebecca for a few minutes.

She swiped a call open to Sylvie.

"Polly, thank you. I didn't know who else to call."

"What happened? Both you and Rebecca found me."

"Andrew was out last night with a bunch of friends. Downtown Iowa City. A car clipped him. It was going way too fast, and you know how people are."

"What do you mean?"

"Those kids act like pedestrians own the streets, even when the lights tell them cars have the right of way."

"He was in the middle of the street?"

Sylvie sighed. "Yes."

"Had he been drinking?"

"He won't admit that to me. I don't know."

Polly paused. "How come you're just contacting me now?"

"Because the boy that I love and adore lost his phone in the accident. They rushed him to the hospital because he'd hit his head. When they asked him who to call, he couldn't tell them anything."

"Concussion?" Polly asked.

"A small one, but that wasn't the reason. Oh, he could give them names galore, but why would he have a single phone number memorized? They are always available in his phone."

"No phone, no phone numbers."

"Right. One of his buddies finally got into his dorm room and took Andrew's laptop to the hospital. Then he had his address book again."

"It took this long?"

"Now Andrew is ready to get out of the hospital. I talked to a doctor, who said that he'll be fine. They did all the observation while none of us were aware that it was even happening. They've set his arm and he's ready to go home as soon as he's released."

"I'm heading to pick up Rebecca. We'll go get him."

"I'd ask Jason, but that boy is buried since we are gone. I can't ask him to do one more thing. I'm so sorry."

"Don't be sorry. Andrew is my boy, too. He's done with classes for the week?"

"I think so. It's only a couple of days until Thanksgiving break, so he isn't worried about it."

"Rebecca is going to try to get away with cutting out early, too," Polly said with a laugh. "Are you okay?"

"Eliseo offered to find us a way home tonight or tomorrow, but if you're there and Andrew is in Bellingwood, I'll be fine. We never get away like this and honestly, Eliseo is having a relaxing week. Well, he was. I don't want to take that away from him."

"Let me tell Henry and Lexi where I'm going. Then, I'll call Rebecca and soothe her beastly fears. We'll scoop Andrew up and I'll make sure he is as snug as a bug in a rug."

"Make him call me?"

"You bet. Tomorrow, we'll get him a new phone."

"I can't ask you to do that."

"You can't stop me either. The boy will be a basket case without his communication. You're going to be okay?"

"Now that I've talked to you, I'm calming down. You were the only person I could imagine calling."

"Have you talked to Jason and Charlie?"

"Not yet. I didn't want him to feel responsible for one more thing until I knew what was going on. I'll call him now."

"We'll let you know what's happening when we know more."

"Thank you, Polly."

"I love you."

"Oh, I love you, too. And Eliseo says he does, too."

"Poke him for me."

Polly closed her eyes and let her head drop. She had to slow down and think through the next steps. When she looked up, she saw people walking out of the school. She needed to get out of this parking lot. She turned on the Suburban, backed up and drove through, only having to wait for a few cars who had managed to hustle into the driving lanes first. Once she was headed for the highway, she told her phone to call Lexi.

"Lexi's Catering, how may I help you?" an elderly voice said.

"Agnes?" Polly asked.

"This is Mrs. Hill. What comforts can we provide for you?"

"Where's Lexi?"

"Our young caterer has her hands full of bread dough right now."

"Can you put me on speaker?"

"Your wish is my command."

The next thing she heard was, "Polly?" The sound of machines going in the background nearly drowned out Lexi's voice.

"Hey, you guys in good shape? I'm heading to Iowa City."

"You're what?"

"Andrew had an accident. I'm going to pick him up and bring him back to Bellingwood. He was in the hospital last night."

"What happened?"

"Car clipped him. I think it's a broken arm. Maybe a concussion."

"Rebecca must be a mess."

"I haven't talked to her yet. Sylvie and I just spoke."

"That poor mama-heart would be breaking. How awful to be so far away when your boy is hurt."

"She's worried. I'm not sure where we're going to park Andrew tonight, but I thought I'd let you know that I won't be home until later."

"Don't worry about us. As soon as kids come home from school, I have work for them to do. They'll be begging for bedtime tonight, just to escape me."

"You're doing fine, Lexi. Would you like Henry to bring food home for dinner?"

"No," Lexi said, though hesitantly. "I can do it."

"Have him bring home lots of food," Agnes said. "Don't listen to the girl. Her seams are about to give way. And maybe ask him to pick up the girls at their grandma's house."

"Ohhh," Polly said. "That too. I forgot. I'm losing what bits of my mind I have left."

"We're here for you, tweetie-pie," Agnes said. "Take care of your peoples. Bring them home where they're safe. You know, I have an extra bedroom if Andrew needs a place to sleep."

"Thank you," Polly said. She held back the laughter that wanted to burst out at the thought of Andrew spending time with Agnes Hill. He'd claw his way out of her house, broken arm or not.

By now, she hoped that Henry was out of the elementary school building. He wouldn't answer her call if he was still busy.

It had taken nearly a month for the Suburban to be returned, fully restored after having been attacked by a crazy woman with an axe. A month of frustration driving around with Rebecca's small car. Everyone had to participate when it came to toting family members back and forth. But Ray Renaldi with his big black SUV, Amalee with her car, and the rest of the family as well, had done everything possible to make it work. Polly admitted to no one that she had kissed the steering wheel the first time she was back in the driver's seat.

She told the Suburban to call Henry and waited as it rang. Polly was ready to end the call when he answered. "You left."

"I did. I'm on my way to Des Moines and then to Iowa City."

"Sounds like something happened."

"Andrew got clipped by a car last night and ended up in the hospital. Broken arm, slight concussion. At least that's what I got from Sylvie. I haven't talked to Rebecca yet. All I had time to do was assure her that I was on my way to pick her up."

"And then what?"

"I guess I'm bringing Andrew back to our house."

He chuckled. "Where exactly do you intend to put him?"

"Henry, how do I still not have a guest room? I tried. I thought I had succeeded. I failed."

"That's just the way of it, isn't it? We'll figure it out. Would you like me to prepare the office?"

"Do you mind? It could be most of this next week. At least until Sylvie and Eliseo come home. I hate giving up that space, but it's all we have."

"I can work upstairs. Will you have trouble with Rebecca?"

Polly laughed out loud. "You mean, the girl who will be fully packed when I get there, intending to come home and tend to her man? Oh yeah. I'll have trouble. But she only has three days left in the week. She can come home on Friday, just like we planned."

"You're harsh," he replied with a laugh. "Anything else?"

"So many things," Polly said. "Are you okay with picking up the girls from Bill and Marie?"

"I should have said up front that I'd take care of that. Of course. I'm headed up to the elementary school worksite. It's only another couple of miles."

"And dinner. Can you pick up dinner?"

"Pizza?"

"What about barbecue?"

"Sure." Henry hesitated. "I was going to tell you I don't know what people want, but I can make decisions. I'm a big boy."

"If you'd like, Rebecca and I can put together a plan while we drive. She'll call it in for you to pick up."

"Would you? That would make things easier."

"Sure. Did you talk to Zachary after the program?"

"A few minutes." The smile in Henry's voice was obvious. "He asked where you were, and I told him that you had seen the whole thing. He was so proud to find me in the audience."

"I saw his face when he did, Henry. It was the sweetest thing."

"Makes me want to be there for everything. I'm glad I was able to do that for him today."

"Me too. I was late and felt terrible, but you fixed it."

"But you were there. Should I ask why you were late?" he asked.

"Because I thought I had time to pick up supplies for Lexi."

"That girl is making a killing. What a racket."

"I know. Sylvie should leave town more often before a holiday."

"Or not. Do you think Lexi will want to keep doing this after all the insanity is over?"

Polly nodded to herself. "I think she'll want it even more. She's doing something that she loves. She gets to pay Agnes and the kids a little bit for the work they do to help her. Lexi is made for a bigger life than taking care of our home."

"Do you remember that first year with her? You put in a lot of effort and time to give her the confidence that she is showing now."

"All I had to do was remind her who she was. For a girl to have gotten as far as she did on her own without the help of her family, she had all she needed. She didn't lose it when they kidnapped and held her. Those people suppressed her personality, but it was still there. She needed to heal and feel safe. Then she needed to fall in love with her baby girl and from there she found what had been buried."

"Seems like she's found it and immersed herself in the insanity of it," Henry said. "Okay, I need to go since I'm here. Looks like questions are coming my way. I'll pick up the girls. Text me when you have an order placed for dinner. I love you."

"I love you, too. Thank you for covering for me today."

"Doodle, you spend your life covering for others. I can take care of you. Now, go."

She went. Then she took in a breath and girded her loins in preparation for the next phone call. Rebecca would be dramatic about it and there was nothing like a dramatic Rebecca to keep things entertaining. Polly was thankful she didn't have many miles before driving onto the Drake University campus. Drama in person was much easier to manage than over the phone.

Polly told the system to call Rebecca and before it rang a second time, Rebecca answered. "Where are you?"

"Driving to you."

"What did Sylvie tell you?"

"That Andrew had a broken arm and maybe a slight concussion. I'm bringing him home tonight."

"Home, his home? He'll be all alone. I can take off the rest of the week. No one will care."

"Nope."

"Nope, what?"

"Nope to both things. He's staying with us at the house."

"Where? There isn't any room."

Polly needed to stay patient. Rebecca sounded more than a little freaked out. Drama was always high with this one. "Henry is setting up the office."

"But he won't be able to rest. Everyone will be in and out all the time."

"Do you really think that either Sylvie or I would be okay with the two of you living at her house for the next week?"

"Why? I'd be taking care of him. One of these days, you all are going to have to accept that we're together."

"Not the time or place for that conversation. Right now, we're focused on taking care of Andrew and making Sylvie comfortable with the fact that she's not able to be here to take care of him herself."

"I could do it. When we're married, she won't be there to take care of him."

"You aren't coming home with me tonight."

"Yes, I am. Andrew needs me."

"Andrew needs nothing," Polly said. "You need to have him

need you. And when you come home on Friday, he can need you all over the place, but you are going to your classes for the rest of the week, and you will complete all the work necessary before Thanksgiving break. No discussion."

"That's not fair."

"You do know that I could drive right on past and skip picking you up altogether."

"You wouldn't."

"No, I really wouldn't, but you aren't making it easy for me to choose spending the next two hours locked in a car with you."

"It's only an hour and a half."

"Rebecca." Polly voice held a warning.

"How long until you're here?"

"I'm driving into Des Moines as we speak."

"He didn't call me, Polly."

"When he was hurt? He didn't have his phone."

"I know. But …"

"He did what he could when he could. Have a little patience. Andrew is healthy. He's coming home from the hospital. You get to see him and worry over him in person. It's going to be okay."

"But what if it wasn't?"

"What if you turned purple and blew up?"

"What?"

"What-ifs aren't worth the breath used to speak them. What *is* moves you forward."

# CHAPTER TWO

Only half-expecting Rebecca to come out without her bags in tow, Polly was surprised to see her carrying only her backpack and purse. They had heatedly discussed the issue for the last part of the trip. Fortunately, Rebecca hadn't had time to pack. Polly was certain there would be a longer discussion during the drive to Iowa City.

Rebecca got into the front seat of the Suburban, dropped her purse on the floor in front of her, buckled up, and sat back.

"Hello to you," Polly said.

"I hate this."

"Worrying about someone you love?"

"All of it. If we were married, there'd be no question. I'd be the one helping him make decisions and I wouldn't feel like some stupid fifth wheel. We're adults. He signed his own consent forms and everything."

"Will coffee help?"

Rebecca shrugged. "It can't hurt, but this is weird. In everything else, we're together. When it comes to something serious, every adult out there is part of his world and I'm on the sidelines. Like a stupid cheerleader. All I can do is cheer you all on. I can't get onto the field and do anything."

"Okay." Polly wondered how long Rebecca was going to feel sorry for herself when it was Andrew who had been hurt. This was not the time for anyone to take Rebecca to task for her selfishness. She'd figure it out on her own. She always did.

"It's scary, you know?"

"Which part."

"Andrew could have been badly hurt. I mean, much more than he was. I would never have known. He was by himself in a hospital room, and I couldn't be there to hold his good hand. I don't like being so far away from him."

"It's only an hour and a half."

"Plus the time it takes for you to come pick me up. I don't even have my own car here to rush over and be with him."

"Cathy?"

"I could have borrowed her car, but then you said you were on the way."

"How can I make this easier on you?" Polly asked.

"You can't. I know that. I'm only venting."

"Were you able to at least do a video call with him so you could see his face?"

Rebecca burst into tears. "Loving someone is hard work."

"Yes, it is." Polly reached over and took Rebecca's hand. "It doesn't get any easier, even after you are married. And then you add children and more children and friends. Before you know it, all that love just melts you down. When they hurt, you hurt."

"Do you hurt right now?"

"Double. I hurt for you and I'm worried about Andrew. Then, there's Sylvie, who is so far away she can't get here to take care of her baby."

"She's not coming home?"

"Not unless I tell her that she needs to."

"That would be hard."

Sylvie had entered a contest on a lark last spring through one of the companies who supplied baking pans. No one had been more surprised than she was when she actually won the trip to Lake Tahoe. The only problem was that they needed to travel before the end of this year. Between the crazy wedding calendar throughout the summer and fall, and the fact that she didn't dare travel after Thanksgiving, there had been one possibility. Two weeks prior to Thanksgiving. She'd been willing to just skip the whole thing, but once Sal discovered Sylvie was contemplating a cancellation, she rounded up everyone to ensure that for this one week, Sylvie could take a vacation.

Eliseo hadn't been fond of the idea of traveling either, but when Sylvie started getting excited, he set his own plans in motion. It was only a week. People could cover for the two of them.

Their dogs, including Padme, were out at his sister's place being spoiled by his nieces and nephews. Jason was at the barn full-time this week, and Noah had gotten up early every day to help him in the mornings, then dragged his buddies, Miles and Graham, there in the afternoons to help Jason finish the day's work. It had been going well these first few days. No complaints, no worries.

Until now. Polly hoped Sylvie would be able to take another vacation in the future. Hopefully she wasn't superstitious about these things. The woman was pragmatic, but this would make it hard for her. It didn't matter that her boys were adults. She would always be their mother.

"Polly?"

Polly glanced over at Rebecca. "What?"

"You just drove past the coffee shop."

With a chuckle, Polly said, "Oops. There are more."

"Don't worry about it. We can get something later. I'd rather just go find Andrew."

The rest of the trip passed as they talked about everything except Andrew. Rebecca seemed intent on ignoring the conversation. Polly understood. There was nothing they could do and worrying wouldn't get them anywhere.

The university hospital campus was immense, but Rebecca

knew exactly where they were going. When Polly pulled up to the main doors, intending to allow a valet to park the Suburban, Rebecca stopped her.

"What?" Polly asked.

"Let me."

"Let you what?"

"Can we check out of here without you? I'm sure Sylvie has filled out paperwork. Andrew has filled out paperwork. We don't need you, do we? Can Andrew and I just be us for this?"

"I feel like this is some type of joke. You don't want me to come up to his room?"

"Please?"

Polly shook her head, in a mixture of frustration and understanding. If they needed her, Rebecca had a phone. And if Rebecca needed to establish some type of control in this situation, allowing her to do so couldn't hurt anything. "Go on," she said. "They won't let me sit here very long. Call when you're coming out. I'll be back."

"Thank you," Rebecca gushed. "Thank you."

This was going to be a long day. Polly looked at her phone. What she wanted to do was call Henry, just so she could talk to him, but he had taken enough time away from his work today. He'd be there when she got home tonight.

Polly watched Rebecca disappear through the doors, then pulled out. She'd find a quiet place until it was time to gather the kids into the Suburban. She thought back to her life in Boston after graduating from college. The last thing she wanted was her father to hover over her as if she didn't know what she was doing, when in actuality, she had no idea what she was doing. He'd let her make terrible mistakes and it wasn't only because he lived so far away. He would have been there in an instant if she'd allowed it. But she was independent and bull-headed and was doing life her own way. And no one was going to stop her from moving forward.

The first apartment she'd rented was a dump. It wasn't in a dangerous neighborhood, but one that was right on the edge.

When she called her father, he always listened and never judged her for making the decision. It had seemed like a good one at the time. She was trying to save money and not rack up any debt. When she got scared of things happening around her, he never told her that she'd made a mistake, he helped her come up with ways to get through the lease period, making the apartment safer, helping to make her feel comfortable.

She could give to Rebecca what her father had given her. A safe way to become an intelligent adult.

Polly's phone rang, surprising her when she saw Jeff Lyndsay's name on the screen.

"Hello, Jeff," she said. "It's pretty late in the day. Everything okay?"

"I guess."

"What does that mean?"

"It's okay."

"Sycamore House?"

"Everything is fine here. The building is fine, the people are fine, the business is fine."

"You sound grumpy. What's not fine?"

"Me."

"Are you sick?"

"Have I ever called you when I'm sick?"

"No," Polly said, "but there could always be a first time. Are you sick?"

"No. I'm fine. I guess."

"Is Adam okay?"

"He's fine."

"Jeff," Polly said with a small chuckle. "You have to give me something. What's going on?"

"Where are you? Are you at home?"

"No. I'm in Iowa City, picking up Andrew. Do you need me to be in Bellingwood?"

"Not really. I just need to talk to someone."

"Are you quitting?" Polly figured she might as well get the worst questions right out there. He sounded depressed.

"What?" Jeff asked. "No. No, I'm not quitting. It's nothing about your business or my job or anything like that."

"Then, what is making you so gloomy and grumpy."

"My mother."

She should have guessed. If there was one person who could put Jeff over the edge, it was his mother. "What's going on with your mother?"

"I don't know."

"I'm going to need more information."

"She just called me."

"And."

"She wants me to come home for Thanksgiving."

"That's next week. Surely you already have plans for Thanksgiving." Polly had a vague memory of him talking about the holiday, but her mind wasn't focused enough to remember.

"I told you. Adam's mother is making a big deal about the day. She's cooking a whole big meal and we're going to help put up all their Christmas decorations. Then, I was hoping to have a couple of quiet days after that to recharge before our own Christmas insanity starts."

"Right. And out of the blue, your mother wants you to come to Ohio. Did you tell her that you have plans?"

"I've told her and told her."

"So, what's going on?"

"I don't know. She got upset with me when I reminded her that we had already talked about it."

"And you couldn't find out what's going on."

"No. She just kept telling me that I had a responsibility to my family and then she tried guilt. I'm never around because I have a whole life without them. Well, yes, I do. I have for the last ten years. What makes now so different?"

"Something is going on," Polly said.

"But what?"

"Have you talked to your sister or brother?"

"No."

"Have you talked to Adam?"

"I'm not talking to him about this. He's got his own mothering-drama going on. His mom has been calling and emailing and texting every day for the last two weeks whenever she thinks about something else we should do. Families are hard, Polly."

"I know. I'm sorry. I'm thankful I don't have to deal with it, but I listen to Cat and Hayden try to figure out how to take care of everyone on both sides. Her family is insistent that they should have every holiday with the entire family, no matter what."

"But they don't always go back, do they?"

"Nope. And it puts Cat in a tailspin for a couple of days until she gets angry that they push her so hard. She's done a good job of compromising, but they don't want to compromise. They want it all."

"I don't know what I'm supposed to do. That's why I'm calling. I can't talk to anyone else. And you won't let me get away with being an idiot."

"I didn't hire an idiot. I didn't befriend an idiot. You are a smart, resourceful man. You need to call your family and find out why your mother is pressuring you at this late date. Something has come up. But Jeff, be smart about it."

"I don't know what you mean."

"What do you have going on this weekend?"

"Not much, why? I was going to help Adam round up some things that he needs for Thanksgiving Day."

"Are you guys cooking?"

"No. Decorations his mom wants for the outside of the house. She won't let any of us do any of the cooking."

"First, find out what the problem is in Ohio. Second, fly your silly hiney out there this weekend instead of waiting for Thanksgiving. Get it off your plate."

"But …"

Polly interrupted. "No buts. You have unlimited time off – you know that. And you have plenty of money to pay for last-minute plane tickets. If Adam can't go, fine. Go by yourself and be back here on Tuesday so that your plans aren't all a mess."

"I don't want to." He sounded very pouty and whiny.

"That's an entirely different problem. Make the call. Talk to Adam. Schedule the flight. I don't want to see you in Bellingwood this weekend."

"You're a taskmaster."

"Yes. Yes, I am. The sooner you find out what this is all about, the sooner you can relax into the holidays."

"I never relax during the holidays."

"Exactly."

"Are you bringing Andrew back with you?"

"Yes. Until Sylvie and Eliseo are home, he'll stay at our house."

"Because you need one more body in your house."

"He's a good kid and where else would he go?"

"To Jason's house."

"Well, this is how it is going to work. And nope, you don't get to distract me into arguing with you about something silly so you don't have to deal with your family." Polly chuckled. "And just like that, there's the text from Rebecca that they're ready for me to pick them up. Let me know what your plans are."

"You've already made them for me, but I'll talk to you after I have everything scheduled."

"You know I love you, right?"

"That's why I called. Give Andrew my best."

Polly was already swinging out of the space and drove around several buildings to get back to where she could pick up the kids. She hoped nothing awful was happening in Ohio for Jeff, but if his mother was this unreasonable, something was going on. She texted Rebecca to let her know she was ready, then got out and shivered in the chill air. Walking around to the passenger side, Polly opened the back door as well as the front passenger door. She didn't know where Andrew would be most comfortable.

The main doors opened, and an aide pushed a wheelchair toward them. Andrew had blankets wrapped around him and Rebecca's eyes were puffy and red. That made Polly grateful that she'd allowed Rebecca to go in by herself. The girl hated looking weak and emotional, but when she was with Andrew, Rebecca always felt safe.

Polly was a bit shaken by how Andrew looked. He had a black eye, a bandage on his ear and cuts and scrapes on his face. When he took off the blankets to try to stand, he winced at the movement and then smiled at her.

"The other guy looks worse," he said.

"As long as you are alive, that's all that matters." Polly started to go for a hug, but Rebecca stepped forward. "He's kind of broken, Polly."

"Right. I'll just hold his hand. Where do you want to sit, Andrew?"

"If I sit in the front seat, can I lean it back?"

"Absolutely. We want you to be comfortable."

He limped toward the Suburban with Rebecca and the aide both close. It took maneuvering and moaning to get him into the seat, but it finally happened. The aide left and they closed up the car, then Rebecca walked around to the other side with Polly.

"Can we go to his dorm room? His roommate has packed all his stuff and there are guys ready to bring it down."

"Maybe get his pillow and a blanket, too," Polly said. "Anything to make him more comfortable on the ride home."

"He has his happy drugs. He can take another one in a half hour. I thought that would work so we can get him home."

Polly raised an eyebrow.

"I'm coming home tonight," Rebecca said. "I just want to make sure he's settled. Maybe I could take my car back in the morning? Would that be okay?"

"That's a very smart idea," Polly said. She gave Rebecca a quick hug. "Do we need to stop in Des Moines for you to pick up clothes?"

"I have stuff at home. I'll leave early enough to change in my room."

They got in and Polly looked over at Andrew. He was drained. "You're okay with traveling?"

"I don't want to be in the hospital any longer. I'm ready for you to baby me," he replied with a grin. "Mom said you would. Rebecca said you would."

"And I will. Do you want to tell me what happened?"

He closed his eyes and shook his head. "I barely remember. The rest of the guys know the story better than me. We were crossing a street, and some bimbo-chick came barreling toward us. I was not paying attention and all of a sudden, she clipped me and sent me flying across the street. I hit one of those concrete trash can things and that's how I broke my arm. The rest of this is just road rash."

"And two bruised ribs," Rebecca said. "He's limping because the car hit him. Luckily, nothing broke in his leg. It's only a bruise."

"So," Polly said, doing her best to not imagine what had happened to her boy, "is this the same arm you broke years ago?"

Andrew tried to turn to look at Rebecca, but he winced again. "No. Now I have a matching set. Pretty cool, huh?"

"Right. Cool. So, point me to your dorm."

"I have it here," Rebecca said. "I've already texted his roommate. He'll let me in and then we'll bring everything downstairs and load it in the back. Are you sure there isn't anything else you need, Andrew?" She gently touched his shoulder.

"We went over the list a million times today. He even sent me pictures of the room so that I didn't forget what was in there. No, buddy, just because I don't remember everything from last night, doesn't mean I don't remember my stuff." He closed his eyes. "Wait. I did almost forget. Rebecca, there are three small hard drives in the top drawer of my desk. Could you be sure to get those?"

"Of course."

"I have a bunch of papers to edit this weekend." Andrew waved his sling, then said, "Ouch. Don't do that. I'm not sure how I'm going to type, but I'll figure it out. These need to be finished just after the holiday."

"It won't be long until you start feeling more normal," Polly said. "You'll have time."

"Pull up here," Rebecca said, pointing in front of Polly. "I'll be back with a bunch of guys." She chuckled. "Not often I get to say that."

It took longer than the half hour Rebecca had promised Andrew to medicate him again before the car was finally loaded and Polly pulled back out to drive home.

"Rebecca," he whispered.

"Yes?"

"Can we make me comfortable now?"

"Oh my gosh," she said. "I'm sorry. Let me find your medication. Do you want to lie back?"

"Not before I swallow the thing. I'm about done with today."

"We'll get you high and then you can sleep. Polly promises not to go over any big bumps, doesn't she?"

"I do," Polly said.

"Where am I sleeping tonight?" Andrew muttered.

"Lexi and Henry are preparing the office for you. That will be your room for the next few days."

"I don't have to go up or down stairs?"

"Nope. Except to get into the house."

"I can do that many steps. Thank you. You're the best."

"Let's wait until the medication has taken hold and I want to hear you tell me all about how wonderful I am and how much you love Rebecca and me and everybody in your life."

"I wouldn't do that."

"Henry did. It was quite entertaining. What else do I need to know?"

"Oh!" He lifted his arm with his index finger extended. "Ow. They called Mr. Mikkels at the pharmacy with more meds for me. I can give you my credit card. Will you pick it up tomorrow?"

"Of course I will. What else?"

"When I feel better can we go get me a new phone? Mine was destroyed."

"Not lost?"

"Lost. But they found it and it was all smashed and everything. It should be in one of those bags. I have to talk to Mom when I get to your house tonight."

"You can use my phone," Polly said.

"Or mine," Rebecca said.

Polly pointed at Rebecca. "Or Rebecca's. Sylvie will be glad to know that you are out of the hospital and safe in Bellingwood."

"We could call her now," Rebecca said. "If you want to tell her that you've escaped."

Andrew shook his head. "I want to lie here and not think about anything if that's okay."

# CHAPTER THREE

Landing at the Bell House was everything that Polly expected. Poor Andrew had no idea what was coming at him. Polly's family loved visitors. Especially people that they knew well. The only part of the family that wasn't quite as excited were the Ricker kids. They really didn't know him yet. Andrew hadn't been home for long stretches since he left for college in August. Rebecca had made sure to introduce everyone during video sessions when she was home, but that didn't happen nearly enough.

Amalee knew him from her freshman year in high school. He and Rebecca had always been together, but otherwise, that was it.

He'd slept through most of the trip, knocked out by his painkiller as well as the fact that he'd had an exhausting day. Rebecca made sure he was comfortable and even though he was asleep, kept touching him to make sure that the blanket covered his shoulders, or that his now longer and unkempt hair was out of his eyes.

Henry came out when Polly pulled into the driveway. He took one look at Andrew's scrapes and cuts before giving Polly a pained look. "You got really messed up, bud," he said, offering an arm as Andrew sat up in the front seat. "Let's get you inside and situated. Before we move, tell me where you want to land before the onslaught of family is upon you. If you want to go straight to bed, I'll take you to the office. If you want something to eat and some company, we can do the sofas off the kitchen. Family room, living room, your choice."

"Bathroom?" Andrew asked plaintively.

Henry chuckled. "First things first. Okay, then."

"Kitchen sofas after that, if it's okay. I can walk, though. My legs didn't break."

"But you did. Let me help you tonight. Tomorrow you can be on your own."

Andrew relaxed as soon as Henry offered. The kid would be as strong as necessary, but that was one thing about having a strong adult around. When you trusted them and they offered to take over, it was easier to let go and allow them to be in charge.

Henry helped Andrew out of the Suburban and Rebecca stood in front of the steps to make sure he got up and into the house with no problems. Polly smiled and waited until they were inside before pulling into the garage. She popped the back hatch open to start carrying Andrew's things inside, and before she was out of her seat, four boys stood there waiting for instructions.

"Hey there," she said.

Noah looked beat. He'd been working a lot of hours at the barn this week and could only have just gotten home. He would never tell Eliseo how much time he'd put in and he would never complain.

"What do we need to take inside?" he asked.

"Everything." Polly pointed at two laundry bags. "Drop those in the back porch. Caleb, would you go to the front seat and get Andrew's pillow and blanket? And anything else that looks like it needs to come in. Thank you, boys, for coming out to help."

"Zachary is upstairs taking a shower," JaRon said. "He'd be here, too."

She gave him a quick hug. "I know. Did he talk about his program during dinner?"

JaRon shook his head. "No. He didn't say anything until Dad told us that you were there and then had to leave to go get Andrew. Is Andrew going to be okay?"

"Just a broken arm and some scrapes. He'll be fine. Nothing to worry about."

"He looks bad."

"That's because it only happened last night. I promise. A couple of days and he'll look like the old Andrew."

"His hair got long," Elijah said. "I should grow mine out. Maybe braids or something."

"Whatever you want to do, buddy," Polly said, handing him another bag. It felt like Andrew had brought everything from his dorm room. Bag after bag. His backpack was overflowing with books. And just when she thought the world had gone digital. Not so much with the readers in her world.

By the time they were all inside and Andrew's things were sent to the office or to the laundry room, she stopped to look at him parked on the sofa. Delia and Gillian were playing with their toys on the rug in front of the coffee table, both girls checking him out every once in a while.

"Where's Rebecca?" Polly asked.

"She went upstairs to talk to Amalee," Cassidy said. "I'm supposed to be in charge until she comes back. But Andrew says he doesn't need anything."

Andrew shot Polly a weary smile.

"Andrew is worn out," Polly said. "When he comes up with something that he needs, he'll be sure to let you know."

"I will," Andrew said. "I have everything I need right here."

He was covered with a blanket from the back of the sofa, and someone had propped extra pillows behind his head. If there was one thing that Polly had a preponderance of in this house, it was pillows. Throw pillows, bed pillows, body pillows, and more bed pillows. It seemed like she never had enough until suddenly, she had more than she could imagine. It was almost perfection. Blankets and pillows made for a very cozy home.

Rumbling on the back steps caused everyone to turn that way

and Rebecca came into the area, followed by Amalee, Teresa, Zachary and Kestra.

"Amalee," she said. "I want you and your sisters and brother to meet my best friend, Andrew Donovan. I know he looks kind of scary right now ..."

"Hey," Andrew offered a weak protest. "Okay, probably." He grinned at the kids. "I've heard so much about you. I know we've talked a little, but not nearly enough. Rebecca and Polly tell me great things about you. Kestra, I have been meaning to ask. Where did you get your name?"

The little girl was surprised at having been called out. "Daddy."

Her father had been killed in action not long after her birth.

"I have heard that name before, but you'll never guess where," Andrew said.

"*Star Trek*?" Amalee asked. "Dad loved *Star Trek* and that's where it came from. Kestra was Deanna Troi's older sister who died. Do you remember that episode?"

Andrew nodded. "It was sad, but she was a sweet girl, wasn't she?"

"It also means star," Teresa said. "At least that's what Daddy told us. She was his shining star."

Kestra smiled at them. "At night we see the stars. Mommy said I shine like that. Not all the time, but when I need to be seen, I shine bright."

"That sounds like the beginning of a wonderful story," Andrew said. "Do you know that's what I love to do? Write stories?"

"Polly told us," Teresa said. "How do you write a story?"

"It's the easiest and the hardest thing to do all at the same time," Andrew replied. "If you were going to make something up for a story, what kind of character would you want to make up?"

"A dragon?" Zachary asked.

"What color dragon?"

Zachary screwed up his face. "I don't know."

"Is it a good dragon or a bad dragon?"

"A good dragon." Zachary thought for a minute. "A golden dragon."

"So, the biggest dragon in the world. There are lots of other dragons," Andrew said, "but the golden dragon is the king of them all. What's his name?"

He had the kids around him entranced as they all worked to create the character of the golden dragon. He nodded at Rebecca, who took out her phone and started tapping away. Polly looked over her shoulder and saw that Rebecca was taking down notes as fast as possible as the kids talked about the different limitations placed on a dragon. What would stop him from destroying everything? What kinds of things did the dragon love? Since he was so powerful, who or what did he protect?"

Henry took Polly's hand and drew her into the kitchen. Lexi stood behind the counter, stirring a pitcher of fruit juice.

"We're never getting them to bed tonight," Lexi said. "Andrew has enchanted them all."

"At least the littlest will fall asleep on their own and we can carry them upstairs," Polly said. She took Henry's hand. "Thank you for helping get him inside tonight."

"Poor kid looked like a wreck when you drove in. He seems to be doing better now."

"Comfortable and with an audience while he talks about his favorite things. Seems like a perfect way to end his evening," Polly said. "We do need to let Sylvie know that he's here and safe. But it's going to be hard to drag him away to talk to her."

"The kids were nervous about having someone they didn't know well show up to spend a few days in the house," Henry said.

"They've had to meet so many new people these last few months," Polly acknowledged. "I try to make it easy on them, but with all that we have going on, it isn't easy to absorb in a hurry. Oh, Jeff called me while I was in Iowa City. Sounds like he's making a quick trip to Ohio to take care of some family business this weekend."

"Okay?" Henry seemed confused.

"Just wanted you to know, in case I have to spend extra time at Sycamore House."

"That boy never takes time off," Henry said. "I hope this isn't a crisis, but I also hope he learns that the place can exist for a few days without him. No big weddings this weekend?"

"Only a small wedding. Everyone else can handle it. How many people get married the week before Thanksgiving?"

Noah walked back into the kitchen and sat on a stool at the counter. "I'm so tired," he said. "I should be in bed."

"Do you need to take tomorrow off?" Polly asked.

His eyes lit up. "Skip school?"

"No, you silly boy. Skip a day at the barn."

"I can't do that. Jason needs me."

"How can I help you?"

"Give me a day off from school?" Noah was still trying. "I could hang out here when I'm not there and help Andrew."

"Tomorrow is only Wednesday," Polly said. She looked at Henry, who shrugged. "You really want to take the day off? It's only been a few days since Eliseo left."

"I know. Jason said I don't have to be there so early in the morning. He can do it, but I don't want to let him or Eliseo down," Noah said. "And tonight, things got late because we decided to go ahead and start cleaning out the stalls since all of us were there. We didn't want it to get out of control before Eliseo is back."

"That's an interesting decision," Polly said. "Maybe you could have chosen to do those one at a time instead of trying to take it all on at once."

"We only got through half the barn."

"Call Jason," she said. "I want to talk to him about his schedule for the rest of the week."

Noah frowned.

"Call him." She pointed at the charging station on the counter. "We'll figure this out. You aren't in trouble, and neither is he. I just want to figure things out so you aren't quite as exhausted by Friday."

"I'll do it, Mom," Noah said. "You don't have to get involved. I shouldn't have said anything."

"I'm not upset," Polly said. "But I see two young men struggling to keep up with a schedule they believe Eliseo would set for them. That was never his expectation. Call Jason, or I will."

Noah wasn't the kid who usually got ultimatums from Polly. He was so even keeled that he generally saw the reason behind her requests. This wasn't something he wanted to do. But Polly knew what was behind this. Jason didn't need him to work this hard, but Noah couldn't help himself. He took responsibility for too much sometimes.

He gave a helpless glance to Henry, who nodded and said, "Call Jason."

With a long sigh, Noah headed for the charging station and picked up his phone. "If I tell you that I'll go to school without complaint …"

"Call Jason," Polly said.

He swiped the call open and said, "Hey. It's me. Mom wants to talk to you." After a pause, he continued. "I don't know. Something about work. Here." He shoved the phone at Polly.

"Hello, Jason. I have your brother here at the house."

"How is he?" Jason asked. "Do you need anything from us? Charlie could come check on him."

"I'm sure she'll see him at the office in the next couple of days. Sounds like he needs to see Doc Mason anyway."

"Sorry we couldn't keep him here. Neither of us are around enough."

Polly chuckled. "He'd hate to hear you say that he needs someone to watch over him. We won't tell him that. We'll just let him believe he has complete independence while living in the big house."

"Big house? Like a prison?" Jason asked with a laugh.

"Exactly like that. I need to talk to you about what's happening at the barn. You and Noah are putting in a lot of time down there. Eliseo would be unhappy if he knew how many hours you're investing."

"That's on me," Jason said. "I've been taking advantage of Noah. Since he keeps showing up, instead of me working all day there, I've been helping out at Elva's place. Then I come back after school so Noah and I can finish up. That isn't what Noah signed up for and it isn't what Eliseo expects of me. It's just that …"

"Nope. It's one week. Elva and Eliseo both knew what they were asking of you. How do we make this better?"

"Noah helps after school. I can do the rest during the day."

"Good answer."

"I'm sorry," Jason said. "I should have been more aware of the fact that Noah's still in school. I forget sometimes."

"Because you worked your tail off for Eliseo when you were in school. I get that. But you didn't have any other activities."

Noah had lowered his head into his arms on the countertop, embarrassed at his mother's words.

"You're right. I didn't have anything," Jason said. "Just Eliseo and the animals. Charlie has been kind of telling me that I'm taking too much on this week. But it was only for a week."

"I love you, Jason Donovan. Now, I'm going to give the phone back to Noah and the two of you can tell each other how unreasonable I am. It's okay. I get it."

"You aren't, Polly. You're one of the best people in the world. Sometimes I need to remember that I don't have to do everything. I'll call Elva, too. She keeps telling me that she can do it without me for a week. Steve is out there, and her kids are old enough to help. I'm sorry."

"No more apologies. My job is to be the sanity for you sometimes. Here's Noah." She shoved the phone back at him.

He shook his head, said, "I'm sorry, Jason. It's my fault." And he walked out onto the porch.

"What?" Henry asked quietly.

"Jason has been trying to do two jobs this week and allowed Noah to help him. He's not spending his days at the barn, just the times that Noah is available."

Henry nodded in understanding. "Those boys work too hard sometimes."

"It's a good thing until they wipe themselves out. What do you think about Noah taking tomorrow off from school?"

"Is he that worn out?"

"Look at him. I'll bet he hasn't read a single book this week and I'd also bet that he hasn't been doing the work necessary for his classes. He needs to catch up."

"And tomorrow is only Wednesday. I vote we never let Eliseo and Sylvie leave town again," Henry said with a laugh.

Noah came back in, put his phone back in the charger and started to head out of the kitchen.

"Noah," Polly said softly. "Come here."

"What did I do?" he asked.

"Nothing. Your dad and I talked about it and if you want to stay home tomorrow to catch up, that would be fine with us. You can go back on Thursday."

"Really?"

"Really. But you aren't going over to the barn until the afternoon. This is Jason's job, not yours."

"It's kind of mine."

"It's a part-time job for you, not full-time. This is his responsibility. You are there to help him, not to keep up with him."

He closed his eyes, probably trying to be patient with her. "Okay. That's what he said, too."

"You know," Henry said. "We're proud of you."

"Doesn't feel like it."

"You are working too hard because you've taken responsibility for something. You aren't ducking out because you're lazy. Because we're your parents, we want you to know what balance looks like. You can't do it all."

"You guys do," Noah said.

Behind them, Lexi let out a giggle.

"What?" Polly asked.

"He's not wrong. You two do everything. You have this huge family, you have businesses, you keep up with your friends, you do it all."

"Not true," Henry said. "We do our fair share. Polly has you to help at the house. Both of us rely on the older kids to help maintain things with the entire family. She has an entire gamut of employees who take care of her businesses, so she doesn't have to be involved in the nitty gritty of it. I have crews and employees and people everywhere to pick up the slack if something else is going on. We rely on my parents and our friends to be there when we need them. We don't do it all. At least not by ourselves."

"And look at you, Lexi," Polly said. "Here you are in the middle of a baking / cooking frenzy. Are you doing it alone?"

"No."

"The oracle has spoken," Polly said with a grin.

"You're weird, Mom," Noah said. "Elijah isn't going to like this."

"He'll get over it," she said. "He's in the living room, right?"

"He said he had to finish something."

She frowned. "What does that mean?"

"I don't know. Do I look like I pay attention to every word that comes out of his mouth? That would take a lot of time. He never shuts up."

Polly glanced back at the cluster of young kids around Andrew. Caleb must be upstairs in his own room. Since they'd moved him into the room that Jack used to inhabit, he escaped there quite often with his dog, Angel. One day, she walked past and looked in on him and he was fervently working on something at his desk. It couldn't possibly be homework. That would have been too much. When she rapped on his door, he looked up with a big smile. He'd been tracing different car shapes from the magazines. When asked why, he said that the guys were always talking about how cars were designed, and he wanted to get a better feel for them. Then he started tracing motors and engines and various car parts. He was fascinated by how it all worked together. The next day, Henry ordered an engine model kit for him, and Caleb was entranced, spending as much time as he could learning how to assemble the thing.

# CHAPTER FOUR

If Noah was home, he intended to keep a close eye on Andrew. The kids all loved Rebecca's boyfriend. The last few days had gone well. As soon as Rebecca was out of the house, Andrew had let go of all his strength and resolve. By the time Wednesday evening came around, he was better. When he woke up on Thursday, he felt almost like a real boy.

While Polly spent her Thursday morning at the hotel with June Livengood, Andrew and Lexi both managed to wake up late. However, he did what he could to help Lexi work through the multitude of cooking and baking projects she had going. His best bet was to match up the orders and even one-handed, he helped package things for pickup.

Late afternoons at the Bell House had grown busier and busier throughout the week as Lexi's clients stopped in for the dinners or the goodies she'd prepared for them. Polly could tell that she was wearing out, but Lexi was happy. That was all that mattered right now.

Nan Stallings had come over Wednesday evening to help and planned to come back on Friday and Saturday. The girls had become good friends, much to everyone's pleasure. Nan was fun to have around.

Lexi warned Polly that Saturday morning was going to be insane. She'd already lined up Amalee, JaRon, Agnes, Nan, and even Teresa and Cassidy to help. And if anyone could keep that many people on task in a kitchen, it was Lexi. She had a map laid out and using some of their outside tables, would set it up so everyone had a place to work steadily throughout the morning. She could hardly wait.

After Polly finished at the hotel, she ran back to Sycamore House. She hadn't talked to Jeff since he'd called her Tuesday evening and wondered what his plans were for the weekend.

She met Sal on her way in.

"How are things at your asylum?" Sal asked.

Polly laughed. "Crazy. I'm thankful for a big house where we can spread out when necessary. Between adding Andrew to the mix and having Lexi absolutely nuts in the kitchen, I find myself hiding in the living room while Elijah practices. It's about the only quiet place left. When is Mark's family coming into town?"

"Tuesday," Sal said. "And that's when I will relax."

"Because you don't have to worry about making Thanksgiving dinner?"

"And watching the kids, and entertaining Patrick, and cleaning up after everyone. Kathryn is so excited. And the guys are talking to each other all the time about what they're doing for the meals."

"I can't believe they just dig in like that."

"It's some strange brotherly thing. Lisa tells me that it's always been weird like that. I'm on board with it. I told her that we should run away to a spa and let them all have the house."

"You've been working like crazy." Polly had followed Sal into the back office and plopped down in a chair. "And with four kids, too. When are you going to find a proper nanny?"

"When the last of them finally graduates from high school. There is nothing out there that I can find right now. It isn't like I haven't been looking. What is it with these young people? They want a job, but they don't want to work."

"What do you mean by that?"

"No one wants to put in the time. I need someone for at least thirty hours a week. But they don't want weekends or evenings. They don't want to get here too early, and they need a full hour for lunch, and then they can't stay too late because they have things to do. When you get down to it, they'd like to work about four hours a day, but be paid for a full-time job. I'm so frustrated."

"You're not finding the right people. Just the other day, I had to tell Noah that he had to stop killing himself down at the barn." Polly pointed at the pasture. "He was here early and then after school he stayed late. And I think he was there about ten hours on Saturday and another six hours on Sunday."

"What happened then?"

"Noah wiped out Tuesday night and I stepped in."

"Like a good mama should. So, what's up for you today?"

Polly loved the way Sal accepted her. "I need to talk to Jeff."

"Mister Crazy-Pants?"

"What does that mean?"

"He was flying around the office yesterday like a crazed dodo bird."

As an aside, Polly said, "That's a new one. What was he crazed about?"

"His mother. Eliseo and Sylvie are out of town. You are too smart for him. No time. His mother. His mother. His mother."

"Okay, and?"

"What did you say to that man?"

"I told him to deal with it. Go to Ohio and take care of whatever it is that his mother needs. If she's calling him like that, it's obviously something."

They stopped talking when they heard the door open to the addition and then footsteps coming toward them. Cilla stopped in Sal's doorway and smiled when she saw that Polly was there as well. "I didn't see you come in, Polly. How's Andrew?"

"Better," Polly said. "He'll be fine."

"That's good. Rebecca was really worried about him." The two girls had grown close again after Cilla's return to Bellingwood.

Rebecca realized the girl needed a friend more than she herself needed to judge Cilla's past behavior. At the same time, Cilla recognized that what she was going through with the pregnancy wasn't something that her good friends would refuse to accept. Life was sometimes just what it was.

"How is it going today?" Sal asked.

"Pretty good, actually. Thank you for this." Cilla rolled her hand over the growing belly, caressing the soft sweater she wore. Sal's immense wardrobe encompassed many phases of her life and sharing her gorgeous clothes was something she loved to do. It was simply too bad that Polly was not her shape and size, nor were Sal's clothes anything close to Polly's style. But Cilla was thrilled with the day she'd gotten to spend in Sal's closet.

"I'm glad you can enjoy it," Sal said. "You look wonderful."

Cilla smiled. She hadn't yet decided what she planned to do with the baby. She had gone to Des Moines with her mother to speak with an adoption lawyer, but when they returned from that meeting, neither of them was as excited as they should have been.

While mutterings and hopeful thoughts around the neighborhood and among those who knew Polly's friends and family were that Cilla should allow Jon Renaldi, and his wife, Chloe, to adopt Cilla's baby, that was the last thing that would happen. Andrea had put her foot down. She didn't want to spend a lifetime watching someone close to Polly raise her grandchild. If Cilla didn't want to raise the baby, they both wanted it to go to a family who would give it the best life ever, but they didn't want to watch it happen.

"Something going on?" Polly asked.

Cilla shook herself. "Oh. Kristen said you were here and then Jeff wandered out of his office on another tear about his mother and I had to go to the bathroom, so I escaped. He has a weird relationship with her, doesn't he."

"I guess," Polly said with a smile.

"I thought Mom and I were at odds all the time, but I don't panic whenever I have to spend time with her. He's a mess."

"Has he made any decisions about travel?"

"I guess, but he's kind of crazy and I don't know what's going on."

Polly popped up. "I'll be back."

She strode out as Cilla said, "What's going on?"

"Other than Adam, Polly is the only person I know who can deal with Jeff when he's freaking out," Sal responded. "You go, girl!" she called.

Polly walked into the main office, saw that Jeff's door was closed and pointed at it. "He with someone?"

Kristen shook her head. "No. If you give him a minute, he'll be back out here. His mother really has him going this week."

"Don't even bother to announce me." Polly rapped on the door, touched the handle and said, "It's Polly. I'm coming in." She opened the door.

Jeff was lying in a ball on the small sofa in his office. Polly closed the door and said, "What in the world is going on?"

"I don't want to go back. I don't want to deal with this. I'm in hell."

"What happened?"

"Dad."

"What happened to your dad?"

"Mom is completely losing her mind because Dad is losing his." Jeff looked up at her, tears in his eyes. "This is too early. It's going to happen too fast. I don't know what to do."

"What do you mean?" Polly asked, as quietly and calmly as she could.

Jeff sat up straight and then slumped over. "Dad has Alzheimer's. They tested him last spring. And it's advancing fast. Mom says that he might not even know me if I wait to come home at Christmas. They're looking at facilities right now because there is no way she can take care of him."

"Oh, honey, I'm sorry. Have you talked to Adam?"

He nodded. "He'll do whatever I want him to do. If we go to Ohio this weekend, he says he'll talk to his parents, and we don't have to be back in Iowa for Thanksgiving. Polly, this is my dad."

"I know."

"He was always the sane one. What am I going to do with my mother now that he can't balance her?"

"How has she been these last few months?" Polly asked.

Jeff looked at her. "What?"

"Your mother has been dealing with his diagnosis for six or eight months without telling you. Has she gotten worse in your conversations?"

He thought about it. "No. Why wouldn't she have said something?"

"Who knows why people do the things they do or react the way they react. This is a decision your parents are responsible for. You know, because they fully understand what it means and how it will impact everyone's world. They're adults. She is making the best decisions possible. Right now, she has decided to tell you because she wants you to have time with your father before his mind is so far gone that he doesn't remember you."

Those words caused him to break down and sob softly. Polly got up and went to his desk for the box of tissues. She put it in front of him.

"She did that for me?"

"Imagine how hard your last eight months would have been, knowing that your father was deteriorating and being unable to do anything about it."

"I might have gone home more often," he protested.

Polly tilted her head. "Would you have?"

"I don't know. You're right. I feel like she took away my choice, though."

"Jeff, she gave you that time. You talked to your parents on the phone like normal, didn't you?"

He nodded.

"You told them about your life here with Adam and your job and all that you have going on, right?"

"Of course. They always want to know those things."

"And you told them you loved them."

"Most of the time," he said with a small smile. "Dad, yes. Mom, not always. I'm a terrible son."

"Your mother wanted her son to have as many months as possible not living in the place she was living."

"I could have been there for her."

"When she wanted you to come, she called you," Polly said. "Have you made plans yet?"

"Adam and I are leaving tomorrow morning. Once we get there, he'll decide whether he's coming back for his family's Thanksgiving. His mother told us not to worry about it, but I hate to do that to her."

"I'm glad he's going. You shouldn't have to do this alone."

"It's not fair to him. I'm dragging him into my family's craziness."

"He's going because he loves you. You wouldn't avoid being with him if this was happening in his family."

"You're right. I should probably go home to pack. I haven't done anything. Adam took Luna to his mother's house today. They'll spoil her rotten so at least I don't have to worry about that. Polly, it feels like my entire life just turned upside down."

"It will right itself. It will take time and you're going to grieve and weep and be angry and do all the things. But then, one day, this will be part of your daily life."

"I don't want that to be real."

"I understand. But grief and loss and all of that is part of life. It doesn't make sense. It hurts like crazy, we grieve, and we rely on the people who love us to remind us that life is a still a good place to be."

A knock at Jeff's door startled both of them.

"Yes?" he said.

Kristen opened the door. "You wanted me to let you know when Stephanie was back."

"Thanks."

She pulled the door shut and he took Polly's hand. "This is one of those days I'm very thankful to be working for you."

"I love you too," she said. "Whatever time you need, take. We'll figure it out here."

"Mom waited until she knew I had a slow week. It will get

crazy after Thanksgiving, but right now, things are quiet enough for me to leave without stress. I won't stay too long or I'd lose my cool completely. She knows that, too."

"Give your family extra hugs and remember that I love you. If you need to call, even if it's the middle of the night because you need a little sanity in your head, call me." Polly headed for the door.

Jeff stood up and said, "Wait," before she could open it. He walked over and took her in his arms, then held on as if he'd never let go. "I do love you," he whispered. "Thank you."

~~~

Polly sat in her car in front of Marie and Bill's house and closed her eyes. She hadn't expected so much to happen in her day, and she was heading home to more. Just a few moments of quiet before two little girls who loved to make noise got into the Suburban.

Her phone buzzed with a text and she chuckled when reading it.

*"Everything okay out there? Are you not ready for the girls?"*

Marie was wonderful.

*"Here I come,"* Polly replied. She shook herself, turned off the vehicle and headed inside. She'd finally gotten past knocking when she picked up the girls. When they came to visit for other reasons, Polly couldn't help herself. A knock was necessary, no matter that Marie insisted she was welcome to walk right in. What if she walked in on Bill coming around the corner in his underwear? Polly would never live that down. When she'd said that to Henry, his only response was that it would serve Bill right. The man should never be walking around his house in broad daylight in his underwear. At least not with the amount of traffic that occurred out there.

"I'm here," she called out, fully expecting the sounds of little girls in all their excitement to rush at her. There was nothing. "Hello?"
~~~

"We're in the kitchen," Marie called back.

Gillian poked her head out. "Come see what we're making."

When Polly walked in, the table was filled with containers. "What in the world?" she asked.

"Presents for everyone," Delia said. "Grandma said we could give away smiles tonight."

"She did," Polly said, sliding over to give Marie a hug. "What kind of presents do you have?"

"This one's for Daddy," Delia said, holding up a package. Wrapped in brown paper, likely from a grocery bag, Delia had drawn something on there that might look like Henry.

"And what's inside?"

"We can't tell," Gillian said. "Not until you open yours."

"Can I open mine now?"

Both girls looked at her in shock. "No!" Delia exclaimed. "Eat supper first."

"Oh, okay. Is it a yummy present?"

Gillian nodded, a big smile across her face.

"I don't know how you do it, Marie," Polly said. "You take such good care of us."

"Anything to keep the little ones busy while helping them to think about doing things for others. It's not a big deal. We spent more time on the packaging than we did the actual present. They had fun coloring for their family."

"Do you have something for me to take for them?" Polly asked in low tones.

"Already in the box. If you'll help me, we can package these all up. The girls' things are all ready to go. Delia, Gillian, put on your shoes and find your coats. Hurry now."

"If you keep teaching them how to help in the kitchen, Lexi will employ them."

"You tell that girl of yours that if she needs me or Betty, we're both ready to help."

"I think she's got it handled, but I'll let her know. This got big real fast for her. It's a good thing she's so organized."

Marie smiled and continued stacking packages into the box.

"There are a lot of packages here," Polly said with a laugh.

"Yes there are," Marie replied. "We had to make a list so we didn't forget anyone." She pointed at the refrigerator door where Polly saw a rather long list of all the people who lived in the Bell House right now. "Rebecca won't be home tonight, will she? I worried, but thought she was expected tomorrow afternoon."

"Not that I know of, but if something happens, I'll share." Polly winked. "I can always steal Henry's."

"There ya go. Let's get those girls tucked into their spots in the car and you on your way. How were things at Sycamore House today? Henry told me that Jeff is upset about something with his mother."

"His father has Alzheimer's and it's advancing quickly. They're making decisions this week about where he's going to move. His mother worried that if Jeff didn't come home for this holiday, his trip after Christmas will be to see a man who doesn't remember him at all."

"That's fast," Marie said. "Unless it's been in progress for a long time."

"I didn't ask that question," Polly said with a frown. "He was diagnosed last spring. His mother didn't want Jeff to lose a lot of time worrying about something he couldn't fix or control, so she didn't tell him until it became really important."

"That wouldn't sound like a kindness when you're grieving, but it is," Marie said. "How is Jeff approaching it?"

"He's so wound up about everything, nothing makes sense. I tried to tell him that he might not have spent any more time out there because he knew he would only have felt guilty. At least this way, he had a good year and now that he knows, he can make choices."

"What a difficult time, though. The holiday season is a terrible time to make those types of decisions. Every year you remember what happened."

"And for Jeff, it's an incredibly busy time of year. But he's got time right now and he'll go back after Christmas. We'll try to keep him occupied in between so he doesn't plummet into awful grief.

I'll talk to Adam to make sure that I know if something is happening."

"You're a good person to work for."

"I like the idea of keeping my employees. I certainly don't want to do their job," Polly said.

They walked into the living room where the girls were still in the process of putting on their coats.

"I'll take the box to the car," Polly said.

"I'll make sure they're bundled up and their shoes are on the right feet." Marie pointed at Delia's feet. "Looks like we need to change a few things around here. They'll be right out."

# CHAPTER FIVE

Delighted at seeing Andrew in the kitchen before the rest of the kids were downstairs Friday morning, Polly gave him a quick hug. "You're up early."

"I feel good and don't want to sit around all day again. I'm done with that," he said. "Doc Mason said I could drive if I felt good enough. Would you mind taking me to the house before you deliver the girls to their grandmother's?"

That threw Polly. She'd heard Doctor Mason tell him that he could drive, and she knew he hadn't taken any pain medication since late Wednesday night, but she wasn't sure if she was ready for him to be independent.

What she said, though, was, "Sure. You've got time before the kids are all out of the house. Would you like some breakfast?"

"Not right now. I'm going to call and wake Rebecca up and then work on some of the things I haven't done in the last few days. Thank you, and Polly?"

"Yes, honey."

"I'm okay. I'll be fine."

"I love you too," she said with a grin.

He left as feet rumbled down the back steps.

By the time her kids were all out the door and on their way to school, Gillian had made her way downstairs and was chasing Delia through the foyer and into the hallway. It was a favorite running space for the youngest during the winter months.

Andrew followed the two girls into the kitchen on one of their pass-throughs. "What time do we leave?"

"If you help me corral the girls, we can go anytime. Are you in a hurry?"

"I told Mom I'd get the fridge re-stocked. We're going to text about what she needs."

Polly nodded. "Of course, she got rid of everything before she left. She's Sylvie Donovan."

"I want to make sure everything is ready for them to come home. Mom has never done this before, and I want her to feel like she can go on vacation again." He smiled. "I should do it now because once Rebecca is here, I won't focus on anything else."

"You're such a cutie," Polly said with a grin. "Let's get the girls going and we're out of here. Are you going to Boone to get a new phone?"

"Yes," he said, his eyes all dramatic. "At least I had my laptop, but not texting and all that is a real pain. I miss my friends."

"Can I help you with anything?"

Andrew shook his head. "I figure I'm going to be wiped out this evening, but then Rebecca will be here to cater to my every need, right?"

"And this is why I love you. Not only are you cute, but you're smart, too."

When Polly went looking for Delia, she found her sitting in the family room, a brown piece of paper in her hands. "What are you doing, honey?"

Delia looked up. "Nothing." She tried to hide the paper.

"You're doing something. What is that?"

"Nothing." Delia pushed it behind a pillow.

"If it's nothing, then come put your shoes on so we can go to Grandma's house."

Delia looked at the hiding spot, then at Polly, then to the door. She was trying to make a decision. Finally, she snatched the paper, jumped to the floor and ran at Polly, as if to escape her.

Polly let her go past. Little secrets would come out when they did. She didn't need to make a big deal out of something that was probably unimportant in the big scheme of the day. She followed Delia, who dashed to Andrew and stuck the paper into his hand before pulling the sleeve on his good arm so he would bend down as she whispered in his ear. He nodded solemnly.

"Where's Gilly?" Polly asked Delia, who shrugged. "You were just playing with her." Another shrug. "Delia, go find Gilly."

After another shrug, the little girl pushed the door open to the foyer and yelled, "Gil-lee-un!" at the top of her voice.

"Go," Polly said. "Don't yell. Go."

Delia shrugged again and trotted into the foyer, letting the door slam behind her.

"What is that?" Polly asked Andrew.

He held up one of the brown paper wraps from last night's cupcakes that Marie had helped the girls decorate for everyone in the family. They'd done a nice job and packaged them in clear plastic cups to keep them relatively nice, before wrapping the paper around each cupcake. Marie certainly knew how to make good use of all the time the girls were at her house. They were never bored.

"Whose is it?" Polly asked.

"I don't know, but she said something about taking it back so she could make a cupcake for Rebecca. It bothered her that I got something, and Rebecca wasn't here to get hers."

"Crazy little girl," Polly said. "Okay, you keep hiding it from me and help her remember to take it to Marie."

"On it. Andrew the master-spy is on the job." He tucked the paper into the top of his cast.

Delia and Gillian raced into the kitchen.

"Found her," Delia said.

"Yes, you did. Thank you. Shoes, girls. On your feet. I'll help you with your coats. Let's get moving."

~~~

The door on the porch slammed open and Rebecca rushed in. "Where is he?"

"Where is who?" Polly asked. The kitchen was busy again. Once the kids were home from school, they'd scattered for a few minutes until those who had tasks assigned from Lexi returned to start working. There were a couple of hours before dinner was on the table and Friday evening life at the Bell House usually meant a party, or if no one else was around, pizza. Henry was already handling the pizza pickup. He should be here soon.

"Andrew! I haven't been able to reach him all day. He said he was getting his new phone and I should have heard from him by now." Rebecca was in a frenzy. "Is he here?"

Polly was confused. She hadn't actually known what time Andrew planned to come back, but he'd had a list of things he wanted to do today, and she also would not have been surprised if he'd taken a nap in his own bed. Even though things weren't quite as chaotic during the day here, there was still plenty going on with Lexi's customers showing up and her work in the kitchen. She'd spread out onto tables all over the kitchen and things that were easily packed up, were set up in the foyer.

"I dropped him at his house this morning. He said that when he was ready, he'd drive back here so he could have his car. He probably fell asleep in the silence of his house."

"Did he leave his laptop here?"

"I don't know," Polly said. She pointed down the hallway. "If anyone has permission to go through his things, you do. It's all in the office."

Rebecca hadn't brought anything into the house, which meant that her car was packed with clothing, books, random stuff that needed to come home, and whatever else she could cram in there. Letting her have a car in Des Moines the few days before break may have become a genius idea. She could pack herself up and haul it all home. With her new room in the basement, the best part
~~~

was that if she didn't want to haul it through the kitchen, she could get there by taking the stairs down to what was now Lexi's basement storeroom, then through the tunnel, into the old moonshiner's office, and then to her room.

The old office had pretty much turned into a playroom for all the kids. With Noah, Elijah, and sometimes Rebecca living down there, the other kids loved having a place near them. Or at least near their older siblings' rooms.

Gone was the crazy racing track that they'd strung up everywhere throughout the basement. It had been hard seeing that come down, but the buildout had been successful. It had gone quickly too. Henry had asked Heath and Hayden for as much help as they could give him and they'd even employed Noah and Caleb to work. Elijah was useless. Unless you believed that entertainment and pranks were useful while construction was going on. He was glad to carry tools back and forth and fetch food and drinks, but getting his hands dirty, much less sawdust on his clothes, was not what that boy wanted to do.

When Polly pointed out that playing baseball was much dirtier, he declared that his baseball uniform was made for such things. His regular clothes were not.

Rebecca had yet to fully embrace her new room. The walls were painted eggshell just as the boys' room was. However, she'd managed to fling her clothing and belongings all over, covering every horizontal space she could find. If nothing else, that made it very much her room.

They'd had a big party the first weekend she came home. Noah and Elijah settled into the new room, while Kestra and Teresa were happy in the boys' old room upstairs. Caleb had moved into Jack's old room in the servant's wing, and Zachary was looking forward to sharing the room with JaRon and as many dogs as would show up. Amalee couldn't believe that she had such an amazing room to live in. She spent as much time in it as possible, astounded that she had the opportunity to decorate it as she pleased without worrying if her siblings would be left out and not have enough.

Her decorating scheme had ended up being royal blues, purples and shades of gold. She'd left the walls as Rebecca had painted them. It was still a work in process. Polly, Rebecca, and Amalee had several discussions about the fact that it didn't matter if Amalee was graduating in May. This was her room for as long as she wanted it. If it was one year, if it was five years, she should move in and take over.

The party had started upstairs. The entire family participated in the parade of rooms. Polly knew they would never be as clean as they were that first week, so she'd taken pictures of each child in their new space. Even those who hadn't moved or changed spaces were part of the celebration.

Then, Henry and Polly tacked a nameplate for each child on the wall beside their door. Jack had cut them for her out at the woodshop. They went from room to room, Henry hanging the nameplates and then the parade went to the basement. They'd attached nameplates to the wall outside Lexi's apartment so she knew just how important she was to the family. At least that was Polly's plan. She still wasn't prepared for Lexi to ever leave her.

After celebrating the basement rooms, they'd come back upstairs and had a big welcome home cake with ice cream, which made it the best part of everyone's day.

Now, if she could just keep herself from having to find another part of the house to transform into rooms for more children.

Polly and Henry had talked about the attic, but because it was so beastly hot up there in the summer, he wanted to spend more time investigating ways to ameliorate that problem. Along with the problem of all the junk that was still up there. During the summer, even though Polly's craft room had a small window air conditioning unit, the attic was no fun. She had a heater for the winter and that wasn't a great deal of fun either. It was insulated, but none of the ductwork had been aimed that way, so none of the household's regular heating and air conditioning worked as it did elsewhere. It was a storage unit and not much more.

Rebecca and Henry came into the kitchen at the same time. He was not prepared for the onslaught of panic from his daughter.

"His laptop is there. He has no way of contacting me. What happened to him?" Rebecca pleaded.

By now, her worry had stirred up the rest of the family.

"I have to find him," she said. "What if he's hurt? What if he had a car wreck? What if he fell down?"

"What's going on?" Henry asked, concern written across his face.

Polly was worried, now, too. Andrew had planned to be here by the time Rebecca got home from college. "Andrew isn't here."

"Okay? What does that mean?"

"I dropped him at his house this morning. He was going to do some grocery shopping for Sylvie, buy a new phone, and I don't know what else. Rebecca is right, though. He should be here by now."

Henry walked through the kitchen to the dining room and dropped the pizzas on the table. "JaRon, you're in charge of dinner," he said. "Get paper plates and chips out of the pantry. Feed people. Polly, Rebecca, my truck. We'll find Andrew."

Rebecca put her coat back on and Polly grabbed hers as she followed them. She turned to Lexi. "I'm sorry."

"We'll be okay. Cassidy and Mrs. Agnes will be here in a minute. We'll manage it all. Call me when you know something."

Polly nodded and ran outside, shivering at the temperature. She hadn't planned to be doing this tonight.

Fortunately, Henry's truck was still warm. Rebecca had already climbed into the front passenger seat, which made Henry chuckle. He held the door behind his for Polly as she climbed up and in. "Little girl's all in a frenzy?" he asked.

"I hope for no reason, but thank you for responding."

"First thing, we should go to his house, right?" Henry asked.

Rebecca nodded. "He just doesn't do this. He always lets me know what he's doing and where he's going."

"You must have been a mess on Tuesday," Polly said.

"Well, he told me he was going out with his friends. I knew that, so I wasn't too worried. And then, Tuesday was a crazy day with classes. I just ran and ran and ran until I settled down and he reached me. Then, I panicked. I shouldn't have been so selfish that day. If I'd just checked up on him …" Her voice trailed off.

"There was nothing you could have done," Henry said. "Luckily, Andrew is a smart boy and he figured out how to contact everyone to let them know where he was."

"Then why hasn't he called us today?" Rebecca wailed.

"We're going to find out," Henry said.

Polly reached forward and put her hand on Rebecca's shoulder. "He's okay."

"You can't know that," Rebecca said. She shrugged out of Polly's grip and then dropped her head into her hands. "What have I done? I brought you. What if he's dead?"

"Rebecca," Henry scolded. "Stop it with the overdramatic stuff. You know better."

Rebecca turned to Polly. "I'm sorry. That wasn't nice."

Polly didn't want to tell her that she'd had the thought about the same time. She was definitely holding back when it came time to enter the house. Henry and Rebecca could go first.

Henry pulled into the driveway and Rebecca burst from the truck. She looked into the garage and said, "His car is still here. At least it isn't a car accident." Then she bolted for the back gate.

"You go," Polly said to him. "I'm not getting anywhere near this until I'm needed. Hurry. Don't let her do this by herself."

He nodded, got out and jogged through the gate into the back yard. Polly got out and followed them, hanging back.

The back door was locked, which surprised everyone, but Rebecca had a key and soon she and Henry were inside. Polly was nearly at the back steps when she heard Rebecca scream, "Andrew!"

She rushed forward and opened the door. That was when she heard Andrew say in a rough voice, "Rebecca, please go into the other room. I need Henry, not you right now. Please?"

"What happened?" Rebecca cried. "Who did this to you?"

Polly was done waiting. Andrew was alive. She pushed forward through the kitchen, which looked like it had been used by a family of fifteen for weeks. Sylvie had not left it like this.

Andrew was on the floor of the dining room, his legs outstretched and zip-tied to the legs of the dining room table. She could tell that he'd jerked things around, trying to escape, but had been unable due to his positioning. His good arm had been zip-tied to the legs of Sylvie's very heavy sideboard.

"I'm calling Chief Wallers," she said. "You can tell us what happened, but I'm calling him first."

"I know," Andrew said with a sigh. "I know. Rebecca, it's really bad around me right now and I don't want you to see me like this."

That was understandable. He'd had a long day and neither his bowels nor his bladder had made it through the day without release.

"Go get him a blanket," Polly said, tapping Rebecca's shoulder. "Cover him up first."

"Can you cut these off me?" Andrew asked Henry.

"You bet," Henry said. "But I hate to say it, they might need pictures of this. Are you hurt anywhere? Your head? Anything else broken?"

Polly had called the police department and since it was still business hours, Mindy answered.

"Mindy, I need Chief Wallers at the Donovan's house. Something has happened to Andrew. I don't know what. He hasn't told us anything yet. Maybe send an ambulance unless they're out on something else. He doesn't look like he's been hurt, but I'd like them to check him out."

"What else can you tell me?" Mindy asked.

"He's been attacked in his house. He's tied to the dining room table." Polly couldn't focus on her words, she was so focused on Andrew. "I want to release him. He needs the relief."

"Ken is nearly there," Mindy said. That made sense. The office wasn't that far. "Go ahead and release Andrew but be careful about what you touch. Are there signs of a break-in?"

"I really don't know anything yet," Polly said. "We just found him like this. I'm going to say yes, but I don't know."

"Ken should be almost there. I'll get rescue on its way."

"Thanks."

"Cut him out," Polly said to Henry. "Ken's almost here."

At her words, a sharp rap sounded at the front door. Then, she heard it open and Rebecca talking to Ken Wallers as the two of them came through into the dining room.

Ken stood in the doorway, almost in shock, when he took in the scene happening on the floor. "What in the world happened?"

"It's a long story," Andrew said, accepting the blanket from Rebecca. He tried to sit up, but his muscles didn't work. Henry scooted around his back and supported him as he sat upright, then wrapped the blanket around the boy's torso, draping it across his legs.

"Rebecca," Henry said. "Go upstairs and find some fresh clothes for him. I don't care if they're shorts or what. We're going to get him into a warm shower and clean him up before he starts talking. He's been through it."

"How long have you been here?" Polly asked.

"Since you dropped me off," Andrew replied. "They hit me when I stood in the kitchen looking at the mess they made." He peeled back his shirt. "I had just taken off my coat and all of a sudden, I felt something awful hit me. They tased me!"

"Who is they?" Ken asked. "Anyone you recognize?"

"No. I was so surprised that the kitchen looked like it looks and then I couldn't believe it when these two guys came in and the one didn't say a word. He just tased me. I've never felt anything like it. It was awful. I really did pee my pants the first time right there. Then they dragged me in here, cuffed me to everything and while I was here, they packed stuff up. I could hear that, but I couldn't say a word. My mouth wouldn't work. Then, they left."

"Chief?" Henry asked. He had Andrew standing by this point. Polly had stepped in to get Andrew's other side. "Can we let him clean up and relax for a few minutes before going through everything?"

"Sure. The ambulance will be here in a few minutes. Andrew, did they hit you with anything else?"

"No, once I was down, I stayed down. I wasn't about to resist. I didn't want someone to hit me over the head and give me another concussion or try to re-break my arm. I've been through enough this week. But I did see that one of them had a gun. He was ready to use it if I resisted. Not this boy. I'm not that dumb."

"Go ahead. Clean up. I'm going to call Sheriff Merritt and get his unit up here. I don't know what's going on, but this can't be good."

# CHAPTER SIX

Andrew sat on the edge of the sofa with Rebecca right next to him. She wasn't letting go and Polly couldn't blame her. She wanted to take his other side and hold both of them tightly to her.

Aaron and Tab both showed up at the house with Alan Dressen's crew to look at the scene. The paramedics had come and gone after checking Andrew thoroughly. Mostly what he needed was food and water. He was on his second glass of water as he talked with Tab Hudson.

"What do you think?" Polly asked. "Squatters? Heard that Sylvie and Eliseo were on vacation, and they moved in, not thinking anyone would show up until the weekend?"

"Sounds like it," Tab said.

"They made a mess of everything," Andrew said, looking around. Carpets needed to be cleaned because the pair had tracked in mud and leaves, not bothering to clean anything up. They'd slept in every single bed in the house, used towels and left them lying on the floors. The place was filthy. Once the techs were finished, Polly was coming back and calling everyone she knew to help her. She couldn't allow Sylvie and Eliseo to return to this.

"I can't believe no one noticed," Polly said. "It isn't like the neighbors didn't know the house would be empty."

Alan Dressen bent over the back of the sofa and reached behind Sylvie's drapes, yanking an opened heavy-duty trash bag from the window. "All over," he said. "They came in and closed this place down so they could stay here."

"But how did they get in and out? This is ridiculous. If it happened in my neighborhood, people would have noticed," Polly said.

"They didn't park in the driveway," Andrew said. "You pulled in to drop me off, and we didn't think anything was wrong."

"I know. I'm just angry."

"We'll talk to the neighbors. See if anyone has doorbell cameras that might have seen a strange car parked nearby. If they were only out and about after dark, you really threw them off today, Andrew," Aaron said. "Would you be able to look around and tell us if anything significant is missing?"

Andrew's eyebrows shot up. "My brain must be mush. I didn't think about that. Rebecca, I want to check Mom's jewelry box. She has some nice pieces. Otherwise, I don't know what else would be worth stealing. It's all just our stuff. Normal, everyday stuff."

Rebecca waited for him to stand up, then took his hand again as they headed for his mother's bedroom. Tab followed.

When Polly heard the groan, she realized that the jewelry box had been ransacked.

Rebecca came back out. "They wrecked Sylvie's shoes and her clothes. Why would they do that?"

"Eliseo's stuff?"

"It's been slashed up, too. What are people thinking?"

"At least they didn't get to the furniture," Henry said. "What do we do next? I don't feel good about leaving the house empty tonight, but I don't want anyone to be here in case they come back."

"Mom doesn't know," Andrew breathed out. "Did you call her, Polly?"

Polly shook her head. She'd been so caught up in everything

that making a call to give Sylvie news like this was the last thing she wanted to face. "Do you want me to call her?"

"I should," Andrew said. "I hate that she will come home to this, though."

"She won't," Polly said.

"Not at all," Aaron said. "The minute that we release the house, Lydia will be here with a crew, ready to clean and scrub until there is no trace of anyone else.

Andrew visibly relaxed. "And I have to call Jason."

"He's going to want to stay here tonight," Polly said. "You can't let him."

Rebecca looks at her. "He could if we all stayed and had a big cleaning party."

Henry scowled.

"You don't have to stay," Rebecca said to Polly. "We could just call a bunch of friends who are home for break. It would be fun. Like a sleepover, but for a good cause. And if Officer Bradford drove by a few times or even just texted me or something ..." She looked at Chief Wallers. "Because you aren't on patrol tonight, right?"

"She's good at this," Ken said to Polly with a grin.

"Kayla and Quentin would come. Cilla would come over. I'll bet Barrett would come. Amalee? She'd love this. What do you think, Polly? Henry?"

The two looked at each other. It would solve the issue of having someone in the house. And no squatter, even with a gun or a taser, would want to be part of a big-kid college slumber party. It would also be a good start on the cleanup. Polly didn't believe they'd finish the job, nor do it as thoroughly as she might, but that was a problem for tomorrow.

"That plan sounds as good as any," Henry said.

"But I want regular texts from you," Polly said. "I will check when I'm up wandering the house in the middle of the night, and if I don't see something, I'll be driving over."

"You know I'll do it," Rebecca said. "We might go to sleep, but we'll leave all the lights on and make sure everything is locked."

"I need to check that basement door," Henry said. "Andrew, what about extra keys. Do you think they have one for the house now?"

"Poor Mrs. Donovan will come home to a brand-new life," Ken Wallers said. "I can get a locksmith here tomorrow."

"We'll put things in front of the doors so no one can get in," Rebecca said.

Aaron chuckled. "She has an answer for everything."

Alan Dressen walked in. "I'm not sure what to think, boss. This place isn't usually such a mess, I'm sure, but we could be here for days and not uncover much more. We've taken fingerprints off the dishes and things that look as if they were obviously used. One of the towels in the upstairs bathroom has some blood on it."

"How much blood?" Aaron asked.

"Like a bloody nose, blood. We bagged that, too. Andrew, I'd like you to show me toothbrushes and hairbrushes. Things like that."

"If it's upstairs, it's not ours. Jason has been gone forever now, and I don't leave much here. Mom can't stand it if I don't change my toothbrush regularly, so she cleans me out when I leave for the semester."

Alan sent a nod to his team, one of whom went back upstairs. "And we need whatever you can give us in the way of a description."

Andrew sighed. "It was really fast. They had hoodies on. No logos or anything. And they were wearing medical masks. Not like balaclavas or anything like that."

"Medical masks hide just as much as anything else and they're ubiquitous these days," Alan said. "How tall do you think?"

Andrew beckoned him to follow and led him out to the kitchen. "I don't have a clue," he said. "I wasn't upright and alert once they walked in on me. One of them was about here." He pointed at a spot on the end cupboard. "That's how Mom measured us when we got older. She wasn't big on marking up walls after we grew up. The other one. I think he had darker hair. Oh, this one was brown hair. About the color of Polly's. The other one was shorter, but maybe only a couple of inches. And darker hair, like I said. They wore black sweatpants and beat up tennis shoes. I barely noticed those, but since I was on the floor, I probably should have paid better attention."

"Any thoughts on how old they might be?"

Andrew blew out a breath. "I call myself a writer. You'd think I'd be more observant."

"You'd just been tased," Aaron said with a wry chuckle. "You're doing fine."

Rebecca came back into the main area from Sylvie's bedroom. "People are on board," she said. "Andrew, you need to talk to your brother, but Cilla and Kayla will be here. I called Barrett. He thought it would be cool and wondered if he should bring things. Quentin is at work, but Kayla said he'd come later. They're all really freaked out."

Andrew nodded. Polly watched his face as he processed all the information blowing at him. He hadn't been able to do anything alone since they arrived, and he was slowly becoming overwhelmed.

"Rebecca," she said. "Come with me to the pantry. Let's see what kind of cleaning supplies Sylvie has available. If we need to bring some from the house, we can ask Amalee or Lexi to put it on the porch."

"Okay," Rebecca said, though she sounded confused. "You gonna be okay, Andrew?"

He nodded and made his way back to the sofa, then dropped into it.

"I should be there with him," Rebecca said. "He's not okay."

"He's overwhelmed," Polly said. "A lot is coming at him, and he hasn't been able to do the two things that he knows he should do."

"What's that?"

"Call his mother. He's terrified of that phone call because he knows she will worry about him and the house and she'll try to come home early. He did everything in his power after the accident on Tuesday to stop her from doing just that. And then he has to call his brother, who will be upset because he didn't call the minute he got off the floor. Andrew is probably also embarrassed by all the attention. What do you believe he is thinking of whenever anyone looks at him?"

"I don't know. That he was attacked and his house was messed up?" Rebecca asked.

"Think about yourself in this situation. What would be the one thing you focused on above all else. The most embarrassing part of his day. Would you be wondering if everyone else keeps thinking about that every time they look at you?"

"But we aren't," Rebecca said the words, then stopped and looked at Polly. "I totally would be worried about that."

"He didn't want you near him because it made him look weak."

"He was attacked. Why wouldn't he?"

"If you lost control of your bladder or bowels, would you want Andrew hanging close enough to notice or smell it?"

Rebecca sagged. "I don't care that it happened to him, but yes, I'd care if it happened to me. How do I get past that with him?"

"You don't. You can't help his embarrassment at the situation. I'm glad Henry was here to help, but it's going to take time for Andrew to face the fact that his future father-in-law saw him as a victim."

"Henry doesn't think of him that way, does he?"

"Again, not what anyone else thinks, but what Andrew is thinking. So, go slow. Maybe don't talk about those things at all with your friends."

"I would never."

"Yes, you would. Because you want to make it a no-big-deal thing and you want Andrew to see it that way. When he's ready to look at it and tell the story, let it be his story to tell. It might take some time, but I know that boy. He'll be able to laugh at himself one of these days. Just not today."

"Are we really here looking for cleaning supplies?" Rebecca asked. "Or did you bring me in here to give me a talkin'-to?"

She was grinning when Polly looked up. "Both," Polly said.

"You are amazing at organization and moving from one point to the next. I watched Andrew start to shut down when you talked about calling everyone and getting things started. He needed a break from the motion of the day."

"What should we do about food tonight?"

"Why not pizza and junk food? Enough junk food to get you through the next fourteen hours."

"Things are closing."

Polly frowned. "What do you mean?" It was only about six o'clock.

"Groceries and stuff."

"There is a perfectly good convenience store where you can buy everything you need except pizza. You can even get pizza there, but you know I love Pizzazz."

"We're broke college kids."

Polly laughed out loud. "Oh, how I love you. You know darn well that I will fund this little adventure of yours." She sighed, took out a credit card and handed it over. "Keep the receipts. I don't care what you spend."

"I don't know what we need to clean either," Rebecca said. "What if we find something that doesn't belong here?"

"Ask Mr. Dressen. He'll know what you should do."

"Should I go home with you and bring Amalee back in my car? We could pick up cleaning stuff you think I might need. I don't know where to start."

"You don't yet. You will in a few minutes."

"I just want Andrew to feel like he's safe here. This is going to shake them all up for a while. Remember when that kid was breaking into homes in our neighborhood? It took a while to feel like our house was only ours again."

"It will take time. Why don't you offer Andrew your phone so he can make the calls he needs while everyone is still here. Henry and I will take you home and you can wrangle Amalee and supplies before coming back. When the others get here, make sure someone stays with Andrew while you shop for food." Polly put her finger up. "The main reason Andrew came over this morning was that he wanted to stock the refrigerator for his mother. Talk to him about that. We can make it happen this weekend."

Rebecca nodded. "At least we have a plan, right?"

"The start of one." Polly gave her a quick hug. "I'm glad you pushed us to hurry over here."

"I'm glad you listened to me."

~~~

"You okay?" Henry asked once they were finally in bed.

"I think so," Polly replied.

The rest of their evening had been a lot. Rebecca and Amalee hurried back out of the house without much explanation. Rebecca didn't want to waste time and Amalee was only on a mission to give her friend the help she needed. Of course, the others wanted to go back to the Donovan's house with them to see what had happened, but not tonight. Which meant that questions were peppered to Henry and Polly throughout most of the evening. All while Lexi tried to keep her crew on task.

"We should have called Ray," Henry said.

"He left on Wednesday for Boston." Polly chuckled. "Can you imagine him attempting to tell his mother that he was staying in Bellingwood for Thanksgiving?"

"Speaking of traveling, did you hear anything from Jeff today?"

"No, and I probably won't. He will be wrapped up with all his family stuff and the last person he'll think about is me. Unless, of course, he loses his mind and needs someone to talk him in off the ledge. He'll be fine, though. Adam will be there and he's as steady as they come.

"What do you think about squatters landing at Sylvie's house?" Henry asked.

"We have a problem in town, and I don't know what it means. It's scary, especially with so many people planning to travel this next week."

"That's what I was thinking. Poor Sylvie and Eliseo. If there
~~~

had been any possibility of them getting earlier flights, they would have been home tomorrow. Polly, I hate the idea of one of my kids getting stuck in something like that and being unable to help them."

"I'm just glad we were able to be there for Andrew. Are you okay with everything? You got stuck with the worst of the cleanup."

"He tried not to be ashamed of what he'd done, and I tried to make it as innocuous as possible. I gave him what privacy I could, but that poor kid had been strapped in such an awful position for so long, he could barely keep his legs underneath him. He asked me to throw out his clothes. I did. Is that okay?"

"Absolutely. He'll never want to see those things again."

"I wouldn't either." Henry turned to face her. "The kids are safe enough over there, aren't they?"

"Would you want to run up against Rebecca tonight after the week she's had worrying about Andrew? I'd be more afraid for whoever it was who spent the last week in that house. She wouldn't hold back."

"You're right. What a strange thing to have happen. I know it does, but not in Bellingwood and not to our friends."

"Thanks for working on that basement door. At least we knew how they got in. I hope Tab is able to find some hint of the vehicle they were driving."

"How do you think they knew the house would be empty?"

"Who knows. It isn't like people in Bellingwood are tight-lipped about people's comings and goings. And Sylvie taking her first ever big vacation? That's going to be a hot topic all over town. For that matter, they could have been in the coffee shop and overheard her talking about it to nearly everyone there. She was terrified and excited, all at the same time. I think she asked every customer she knew about flying and how to pack for a trip like this. On and on."

"When did it become unsafe to talk to your friends about the things you look forward to?" Henry asked.

A small knock at the door had them both sitting up straight.

"Come in," Polly said.

"We're scared," Kestra said, holding Teresa's hand. The girls looked scared.

"About what?"

"About someone coming into the house. Can we …"

Teresa shook her head. "I'm sorry. We shouldn't bother you. We go into Amalee's room sometimes when we're really scared. She lets us sleep in her bed with her."

"And Amalee isn't here tonight." Polly looked at Henry. He just smiled and scooted over to the edge of the bed. She scooted along with him. "Tell you what," she said. "I'm surprised that Obiwan didn't show up in your room to help you feel safe. He's usually pretty good about that."

"He's in with JaRon and Zachary. They're nervous too," Teresa said.

"Did you bring your pillows?" Polly asked.

Kestra looked up at her, her eyes shining. Unshed tears gave way to a bright smile. "I'll get them."

"It's perfectly fine," Polly said. "You can sleep with us tonight. We have a very big bed. I think there will be room for the two of you."

"If you just want Kestra …" Teresa started.

"I want both of you," Polly replied.

Kestra bounded back in, thrust a pillow in Teresa's arms and then ran to Polly's side of the bed. "This is a big bed. Amalee's isn't this big."

Fortunately, they'd purchased a queen size bed for Amalee. The girls would never have fit together on one of the extra twin beds they had in the attic.

"Come on, Teresa. It's really soft, too," Kestra said. She snuggled up to Polly, who wrapped her arms around the little girl and pulled her in close.

Polly thought her heart would nearly break. None of her other kids had ever done this and there were times she wondered if she'd missed out on something special.

"Before you two get all comfortable," Henry said, sitting

upright, "do you need to go to the bathroom again? I'd hate for anything weird to happen."

Kestra giggled. "I went before bedtime. I never get up in the middle of the night."

"Are you sure?" he asked, a smile on his face. "Are you really, really sure?"

"We should go try," Teresa said. "Let's do it before we climb under the covers." She took Kestra's hand, and the two girls ran off to use the bathroom.

Once Noah and Elijah moved to the basement, the bathrooms up here were much easier to clean. It was amazing the mess those boys could create. And Amalee was a bit of a clean freak. Nothing like Rebecca, so when she saw something out of order in the bathrooms, she simply made it right. She was wonderful about running small loads of the children's laundry and doing everything she could to be helpful.

Henry ran for their bathroom. "I needed one more break tonight and didn't think the girls needed to see my skinny legs."

"Hey," Polly said. "I like those skinny legs. But since I'm going to be trapped between you and the girls, maybe I should take care of a few things, too." She started to follow him in, but he closed the door on her. She leaned against the door frame and waited. This was going to be an interesting night.

# CHAPTER SEVEN

Yielding finally, Polly got out of bed, hoping not to disturb Kestra, who was a snuggler. At some point in the middle of the night, Henry had left the room. She had no idea where he ended up, but he wasn't sleeping either. Adding two girls to their bed wasn't as much uncomfortable as it was odd. They'd never experienced anything like it, and both were conscious of trying to stay quiet so the girls wouldn't wake up.

On top of that, Polly couldn't stop thinking about how they'd found Andrew. Her mind worked on every aspect of the situation, wondering who it was that had chosen Sylvie's house to squat in and why, hoping that the kids were safe, and thinking about Sylvie's reactions. Everything that could float through Polly's mind, did.

She had heard from Rebecca several times until the texts stopped coming about three-thirty. Hopefully, that meant everyone had crashed and slept through the rest of the night.

Kestra, like Luke and Leia, moved to her warm body every time Polly moved. The cats hadn't minded having two extra warm bodies in the bed, and as she watched, Luke was lying atop the blankets between Teresa's legs. They knew a good thing when they found it.

Kestra looked up and whispered, "Is it time to get up?"

"You go ahead and snuggle back in with your sister," Polly said. "It's Saturday. We're not in a hurry today."

"I love you," the sleepy voice said as Kestra turned to get closer to Teresa.

"I love you, too." The girl was so easy with her affection. Polly hoped she never lost that. She chose her clothing for the day and went into the bathroom to shower and get ready.

When she got downstairs, she found Henry on the sofa in the back of the kitchen with his tablet. "I'm sorry you didn't sleep last night," Polly said.

"I ended up in the family room. I probably slept better than you in the long run. Are we going to have to get used to this?"

"Doubt it. They'll always choose Amalee. Yesterday was a strange day with lots to worry about and then their big sister was gone."

"It was adorable, but I'm not used to extra humans around when I sleep. It was enough for me to learn how to be asleep with you in my bed," he said.

She laughed. "I get it. Sharing my sleep-space was never a big turn-on for me. You're lucky I like you. Have you done anything about breakfast for yourself?"

"Not yet. What do you think we should do?"

"What I want to do is call Sweet Beans and have someone cater a big breakfast here, but I'll settle for toast and coffee."

"And for the kids?"

"Dry cereal and hard tack."

"Not awake yet, are you?"

"Nope. A shower didn't get me there either. And I don't know what the day is going to bring. I know Lexi has her day in the kitchen planned, but I'm not sure what to do about Sylvie's house. The kids shouldn't have to hang out there because they're worried someone will break in. They have other things to do. Andrew is likely still a mess …"

"That boy has had a rough week. I hope Rebecca pampers him a little today."

Polly nodded and wandered to the coffee pot. At least it was full. She'd need a lot of this stuff today. She took out her phone and checked the messages.

Not much yet, but there was one from Rebecca. *"We're coming home. Everybody else is gone. Do you think it's okay to leave Andrew's house now?"*

Polly glanced at the time. Rebecca had sent it while she was in the shower. *"Come home any time. We'll figure it out. You all need a break."*

"Rebecca is headed here," she said to Henry. "She's worried about whether it's safe to leave the house."

"No one is going back there," he said. "The squatters were surprised to have a homeowner show up and now they don't feel confident that it's a safe hideout."

"I'm going to reach out to Lydia and see what she thinks about helping me clean up. Ken said something about a locksmith coming to change the locks. Someone should be there for that. I'm just not ready to get started yet."

"Lydia is awake."

Polly sighed. "She gets up too early in the morning for me."

"You get up early."

"Because I have to. When our house is empty of young 'uns, I'm sleeping in every day."

He just looked at her and smiled.

"Now that the three big kids are coming home, I should do something for breakfast." Polly opened the refrigerator door and shook her head. "I have no idea what Lexi has going on in here. Containers everywhere and not a morsel to eat."

"I could go to the convenience store and buy breakfast pizzas."

"We just had pizza last night," Polly protested.

"And how awful is that?" he asked, heading for the door. "How many do you think?"

"I can't even begin to count right now," Polly said. "I'll text you in a minute. You're okay with this?"

"Today? I'm okay with anything. Let's not disturb Lexi's organization, while at the same time, make it easy on us. The kids will love it."

"They will. Thank you." Polly gave him a quick kiss. And maybe some of their donuts, too?"

He chuckled. "Of course."

Rebecca, Andrew, and Amalee showed up as Polly was carrying paper plates and napkins into the dining room. There was no reason to make today's breakfast any more work than it needed to be.

The three of them looked exhausted, and poor Andrew looked as if he'd been run over by a truck. The bruises on his face weren't yet faded and were an attractive mixture of purple, green, and yellow. His eyes told the story of exhaustion along with worry and fear.

"Henry's bringing back breakfast pizza," Polly said. "You can stay up and eat or you can try to get a few hours of sleep and we'll have food when you come alive again. Your choice."

Amalee looked toward the back steps. "I told Lexi I'd work for her today, but I need more sleep."

"Then, go. The girls are in my bed if you're looking for them. If you'd like to crawl in with them, feel free."

"Your bed?" Amalee asked, shocked.

"They were upset last night with everything that had happened and since you weren't here …"

"I'm so sorry. I'll tell them not to do that."

"No," Polly said. "It was fine. They needed reassurance and it made me happy that they were comfortable finding it with us. I just didn't want you to worry about where they were if you looked in their room."

"They sleep with me sometimes," Amalee said.

"That's what Teresa told me," Polly replied. "It's really okay. Both things are okay. I'm not upset or concerned. You go find some sleep. Lexi knows where you were last night, so she'll see you when she sees you. Don't worry."

Amalee nodded and headed for the back stairs.

Andrew was already moving down the hall. "I'll be back later," he said. "I just need more sleep."

"I love you," Rebecca called after him."

"You too," he replied.

"He didn't sleep," she said to Polly. "I don't think he slept a single minute. He couldn't settle down. Sometimes he'd almost drop off and then something kicked in and he was sitting up and moving around again."

"He had a terrible scare yesterday," Polly said.

"I know. I just wish I could have calmed him down. I hate to leave him alone right now, but that bed in there won't hold both of us, so I might as well just go down to my room."

Polly's eyebrows shot up and Rebecca chuckled. "Like you don't know that we've slept in the same bed together."

"But not when Henry is around."

"I think this would be the only weekend Henry might not get too upset about it," Rebecca said. "Andrew's so broken right now, the last thing he's thinking about is anything but sleep and rest. I really need to take him to Boone to get a phone today. This is killing him."

"You two will figure it out. If you need me, I'm available. How does the house look?"

"It's better. We didn't do deep cleaning. Just picked stuff up and straightened things. I think Jason ran the dishwasher a couple of times so the kitchen looks pretty good. Charlie was doing laundry. Sheets and towels and stuff. They left about two o'clock. Both of them have to work today. Kayla and Quentin left at, like, five o'clock this morning because she had to get a little sleep. She has an early shift."

"And Cilla?"

"I dropped her off. She was a lot of help. It was good for her to be around all of us this morning. Barrett left when we did. It was good to see them."

"So, if I contact Lydia, there would still be plenty to do at Sylvie's house?"

Rebecca nodded. "I hoped you'd say that. Yes. If you weren't going over, I was going to have to find someone to go back with me. Counters and tables and all that need to be scrubbed down and the rooms need to be vacuumed. There was so much mess everywhere. We had to clean up spots on the floor where they'd just left their food out. It was awful."

"Did you find anything that they left? Anything that wasn't familiar to Andrew?"

"Some clothes and stuff. We put those all in a paper bag. I don't know if you want to call Chief Wallers for it."

"But nothing that could tell us who they were?"

"Nope."

"Okay. Do you want to wait for breakfast, or go to bed?"

"I should just go to bed. I won't be able to sleep, but at least I'll give it a try. Should I be more worried about Andrew?"

Polly gave her a quick hug. "Honey, I don't think anyone could worry more about Andrew than you are. Go rest. We'll keep an eye on him until you wake up."

"Thanks." Rebecca headed for the stairs going to the basement. Polly heard her talking to someone and assumed it had to be Noah, so she wasn't surprised when he walked into the kitchen.

"Is everything okay?" he asked.

"I think so. Henry's picking up breakfast pizza. He'll be back in a bit with it. How are you this morning?"

"Okay. Jason texted. We're going to get a late start. I guess he was over at his mom's house late last night cleaning. Mom, is that whole thing weird or what?"

"It's weird," Polly said. "But sometimes weird stuff happens."

"Andrew ..." He shook his head. "I don't know what I would have done, being tied up in my own house and not able to do anything about it. I think I'm going to be glad when Eliseo is back and life returns to normal. This has been a strange week."

Polly nodded. "It really has. I'm not a huge fan of my friends and family being out of place, but travel is good for some people, so I let them leave and wait for them to come back."

He sat down at the island. "Obiwan slept with me last night."

"I wondered where he might end up."

"He tells me when I'm worried about something. I finally figured that out. If Obiwan shows up, that means I'm upset."

"About Andrew or something else?"

"I think Andrew. I just kept seeing him all helpless. I don't know what I'd do if that happened to me."

"You would wait for us to show up, just like he did."

"I kept thinking about what was going through his head all day. Wondering why nobody came to rescue him. Worrying about the bad people coming back. What if he never got out of it? I mean, Sylvie and Eliseo aren't coming back until Sunday. That's no food or water for all that time. If it had happened anywhere but in Bellingwood, he could have died."

Polly rubbed Noah's back. "No what ifs," she said. "We deal with what is. Remember?"

"But."

"But you read novels where the worst things happen so the hero can get the bad guys. How about you remember that while there are plenty of heroes around us, those awful awful things don't happen like they do in stories. Fiction is different than reality."

"I know that, but it makes my imagination do weird things."

"I understand. You are safe with us as your family. I promise I will always wonder what's happening to you."

"Were you worried about Andrew?"

Polly smiled. "I didn't have to be. He had Rebecca to do that for him."

"I hope I find someone as cool as her."

"I hope you do, too."

~~~

"That feels better." Lydia sat down at the table in Sylvie's kitchen. Andy Specek and Polly dropped dirty rags into a bucket sitting by the back door before joining her.

"I hope we got everything," Andy said. "So many tiny spots where dirt and filth show up."
~~~

Polly chuckled. "At least we know that Sylvie is a clean person."

"We probably know more about her than she would have wanted us to know," Lydia said.

The three of them had worked for about five hours and even though there had been laughter and camaraderie, they'd been on a mission. Bathrooms were scrubbed clean, and Polly had run a carpet cleaner over every bit of carpeting she could find. Beds were remade, the kitchen had received a strong scouring and even dirt in the basement had been swept up. They'd washed and folded the shredded clothing, just in case Sylvie wanted to make rags. At least she'd know what needed to be replaced.

The kids had done a great job overnight. It didn't look the same when Polly had walked back in. All she wanted to do was make certain that nothing remained of the illicit visitors. Even yet, she wondered what Sylvie and Eliseo might find.

Ken Wallers had stopped by about one o'clock with the locksmith. The only news he had was that two other homes had been occupied in the weeks before the squatters landed at Sylvie's house. Each of those had been vacant for less than three days, so not only had the damage been much less, but no one had been hurt since they'd stuck to a known schedule. He couldn't give them anything else. He didn't have anything else and he hadn't heard if there had been another break-in after the squatters left Andrew yesterday.

No one was saying much about how dangerous those two might be, but the fact that they owned a Taser and that Andrew had seen a gun on one of them made Polly shudder when she thought about it. She didn't need to find the results of something happening with that weapon.

Lydia smiled and pointed out the window. Andrew and Rebecca were coming up the back walk. He was smiling and pointing back in at them.

When they came inside, his mouth dropped open. "This is amazing," he said. "I can't believe what you got done."

Lydia got up and hugged him, loosely, but she hugged him all the same. "I am so sorry about your week, dear. You've been through it."

"I keep telling Rebecca that at some point it will be nothing more than a story I retell for the entertainment value, but I'm not there quite yet. Maybe when some of this goes away." He swept his hand around his face.

Rebecca hadn't let go of his other hand yet, but when Lydia moved to embrace her, she took it. "And you. Nothing worse than having to let other people care for someone you love, is there?"

"Not really," Rebecca said. "I guess you know that better than anyone, though."

"Oh, my sweet girl. Whether it's my husband, my children, grandchildren, or my friends, I have difficulty not sticking my nose in to do everything I can to make the pain go away."

"Did you get your new phone, Andrew?" Polly asked.

He patted his back pocket. "I'm back in the real world again. Do you ladies mind if we look around? I want to be sure that the place is ready for Mom and Eliseo to come home. I know we didn't get groceries into the refrigerator …" He opened the refrigerator door, closed it, then opened it again. "What's this?"

"I picked up a few things and Lydia did what Lydia does," Polly said. "Soup, a casserole, and some potatoes and vegetables. Until Sylvie can figure out what it is she wants in the house, she at least has food to eat."

"Unbelievable." Andrew's eyes shimmered and Rebecca turned him to walk out of the kitchen.

She looked back with a smile and mouthed, "Thank you."

"He looks like hell," Andy said. "That boy has been through the wringer. Did they find out who hit him in Iowa City?"

"We haven't heard anything," Polly said.

"I'll never understand why people would do that."

Polly nodded. "There are many things I don't understand about people."

Rebecca and Andrew returned to the kitchen.

"I can't believe what you all have done," he said. "Thank you. How can I repay you?"

"I have an idea," Lydia said. "Stay out of harm's way. That would be very helpful to all of us."

"If I could, I would," he said. "Though I'm beginning to understand more about Polly after this week."

"What does that mean?" Polly asked.

"You always say that things aren't your fault. That you just happen to walk into something, and it all goes crazy. I did nothing out of the ordinary this week. Nothing. And it all went crazy."

"Justified," Polly said. "What are you two up to now?"

"We're going home," Rebecca said. "Andrew wanted to look at the house before his mom came back, but it's been a long day. I know that I need a nap."

"Have you talked to Jason today?" Polly asked.

"A couple of times," Andrew said. "I'm glad he came over last night so that he could see I was still in one piece. He's worried about me. Just because he's all big and strong and tough, he thinks I can't take a little pain."

"You're his younger brother. And Jason is all about protecting people who need it," Polly said. "Call him and see if he and Charlie would like to come over for dinner. It won't be normal, but we'll scrounge up whatever Lexi has been setting aside."

"Yeah?" Andrew asked.

"He could see that you're in better shape now than you were last night," Rebecca said. "We'll do that. When are you coming home, Polly?"

"We're about out of here." Polly patted the pocket in her jeans. "Here, Andrew. These should go to you. New house keys."

"Thanks. That makes me feel a ton better about leaving the house empty tonight."

"Aaron says that between him and the Bellingwood police, they'll drive by and make sure everything is okay," Lydia said. "No need for you to worry. He's pretty sure they've moved on to emptier pastures by now."

"Wish I knew who they were," Andrew said. "Nothing was familiar about them."

# CHAPTER EIGHT

Since Bellingwood still had school the first two and a half days of the week, she didn't have a reason to be at home, so Monday morning, Polly was in the office at Sycamore House. Lexi had a few things left to complete before her stint of pre-holiday cooking and baking was finished, but she'd gotten through most everything by the end of Sunday evening.

Sylvie and Eliseo had returned home yesterday afternoon. Andrew, Rebecca, Jason, and Charlie were there to welcome them and to assure them that everything was okay. From what Polly heard, Sylvie didn't let go of Andrew's hand the entire time. She'd barely looked at the house, even though she knew that people had spent hours cleaning up after the squatters had been there. Nothing was more important than the safety of her boys.

On top of her worry was a pile of exhaustion. Generally, the only thing a person wants to do when returning from vacation is to take a day of rest. And she needed one. So did Eliseo, but right now, Polly watched as he walked through the pasture with the horses and donkeys, touching each of them over and over. That was his safe place.

The building was empty as usual, though Rachel and her crew were working on holiday catering they needed to finish. Jeff was in Ohio. No one had heard much from him once he got there. He hadn't given Kristen any idea what day he'd be back, only that he'd be in the office next Tuesday at the latest. It was strange not having him here. Even when he didn't work on Mondays, his presence was made known by all the work he had scheduled around the place.

She was working through reports from last week and turned back to her computer. So much had happened, it was time to finally focus on the various businesses.

A knock at her door startled Polly and she looked up to find Rebecca coming into the office.

"Good morning," Polly said. "What are you doing here?"

"It's nearly lunch," Rebecca said. "I wondered if you wanted to take me out."

"Take you out? I could probably find it in myself to do that. Where do you want to go?"

Rebecca smiled. "Where do you think? Sweet Beans! That new Christmas pop-up beside the thrift store opened this morning and I want to see what they're selling."

"Where's Andrew this morning?"

That elicited another smile. "At Sweet Beans. He's working."

"What? Why is he working?"

"Vacations. Gayla is gone this week. He said he'd cover her hours. They tried to make him stay away since his arm is broken, but he said he could do it and so he is. He wants to stick close to his mother, too. She was pretty worried yesterday."

"She's been worried all week, I'm sure," Polly said. "How did you know about this Christmas pop-up store?" She gathered her stuff and put it into her tote bag. How in the world had she gotten to be this person? It was much easier when she could fit things into her pockets. You don't do that with multiple children in your life, though. If she dug through this bag, she'd find cars and candy and toys and probably even a pair of underwear. She didn't want to dig that deep.

With a laugh, Rebecca shook her head. "You really don't pay attention to social media. It's been all over the online Bellingwood town page."

"Okay. Who's doing it?"

"No one really knows."

"That sounds ominous."

"Or mysterious. It's not anyone local. They posted pictures of inventory. It's cute. And Christmassy and the prices look good."

"One of those fly-by-night deals?"

"I don't know, Polly. Why don't we go check it out?"

"It's not like we need more Christmas stuff. We have boxes and boxes and boxes in the attic."

"What is up with you? We love shopping for Christmas stuff."

Polly stood up and headed for the door. "Just giving you trouble. Of course, I want to check the place out. But I know how much you love Christmas and poking at you is where I am today."

"That's not nice." Rebecca stuck out her tongue. "Should I ask Cilla if she wants to go with us?"

"If you want."

"Since you were poking, I thought maybe you'd poke back about that. Let's just do us."

"Do you want to leave your car here or meet me up there?"

"I'll meet you. We might have two carloads of stuff to take home after we shop."

Polly rolled her eyes as she held the door open for Rebecca to go outside. "Crazy girl. Shop first or lunch first?"

"Shop first. I'm really feeling it," Rebecca said.

"I'll meet you there." Polly hadn't bothered to tell Kristen that she was leaving, so she sent a quick text once she was in the Suburban, then followed Rebecca downtown. They could have walked. It was only a few blocks, but the temperature was cold today. Up and down and all over the place. One day it was pleasant, the next frigid. Complaining didn't make it better, but it was hard not to succumb to a whiny attitude about it. Like anyone had control over the weather.

Polly parked in front of Ray Renaldi's soon-to-come gym. Papers still covered the windows so no one could see inside. More and more equipment had arrived, and he'd been busy renovating his apartment and the basement, but he wasn't ready to open anything yet. With all the hoopla around making New Year's resolutions, he thought that January or February might be a perfect time to introduce his style of fitness to Bellingwood. The thing was, it didn't matter. Though Ray would never be one to allow anything less than success, he hadn't brought a gym to town to open a prosperous business. He brought it to town to give cover to transferring some of his security business and his team to the Midwest. While the business would always be based in Boston, he was looking forward to expanding into areas they'd never had access to before.

Jon would continue daily operations at home in Boston. Since so much of their work was done online, there was no reason for anyone to be stuck in one spot. Ray had expressed how weary he was of living in a large city. The more time he spent with Polly and her family, the more he fell in love with the quiet simplicity of life in small-town Iowa. Even when Polly's crazy antics were at play.

Rebecca had parked near Sweet Beans and walked toward the Christmas pop-up called "Merry Times." Overnight, the windows and door had been transformed with decorations and signs. Tall banners stood outside, blowing in the wind, welcoming shoppers.

This was the week when Bellingwood's downtown would begin its transformation. Autumn displays would give way to holiday celebrations. By Friday, the place would look like a Christmas wonderland. By Saturday, so would Polly's house.

"What do you think?" Rebecca asked, pointing at the garish decorations welcoming them to Merry Times.

"I think I can't see anything on the inside," Polly replied.

"Then let's go in."

"You're very excited about this."

"I'm curious," Rebecca replied. "Aren't you?"

"I'm getting there."

Rebecca opened the door and Polly walked in. She didn't know what it was that she had expected. Rebecca's "Hmph" behind her echoed her thoughts exactly. Long tables were filled with brown boxes. On most stacks, a box had been opened to show what was inside the rest of them. If you trusted that to be true.

There was a large Christmas tree on one side of the room that had been decorated with lights and a few ornaments. More stacks of brown boxes with a computer-generated sign saying "Lights" sat in front of the tree. Other signs described the color of the lights. The ornaments on the tree could be found in even more piles of small boxes scattered on a table nearby.

Two different nutcrackers sat atop another stack of boxes at the back of the room. Artificial trees filled the other side of the room – in colors Polly couldn't imagine using – some flocked, others filled with lights. Wreaths of all sorts covered a wall, and a small collection of Nativity scenes were piled on a table at the front.

"There's a lot here," Rebecca said in a low tone.

"I'm not sure where to even start."

"May I help you find something?" A young man had crept up behind them. Rebecca and Polly had been so engaged in looking around they hadn't heard him approach.

"Are those all the decorations you have?" Rebecca recovered fast and pointed to the decorated Christmas tree.

"We have plain colored balls back here," he said. "Icicles and tinsel and stars and all that stuff. We just haven't had time to get it all out and onto the tree. We're working as fast as we can to be ready for everyone."

They followed him to a pile of boxes that were yet to be opened and arranged, but as Polly looked closer, she could see that the boxes were self-explanatory. "Where are you from?" she asked the young man.

He blinked, clearly not expecting that question. "Uhh, the Chicago area."

"Really. And you came all the way to Bellingwood."

"We're opening Christmas shops in many communities for the holiday season. This one is mine."

"That's interesting. So, someone shipped all this here and you are selling it?"

He nodded. "It's a great gig. When the season is over, they'll come in, pack everything up, and then we get a commission on what we sold. We're paid a regular salary, but it's up to us to make the sales."

"That's interesting," Rebecca said. She smiled, offering her brightest eyes. "Have you done this before?"

"No, this is my first year, but I've heard good things about it."

"What if I wanted to get involved?"

"Really? I'd get a huge commission if I found someone else who wanted to join the team. Let me get you a business card." He took off toward the center of the room where two registers had been set on a table.

"What are you doing?" Polly asked.

"Just curious. Does this seem as weird to you as it does to me?"

"I don't know. We've had things like this here before. Especially around Christmas."

"They're paying him to set up a store and maintain it. Then, he'll get a commission? Bet they show a loss rather than a profit so they don't have to do that," Rebecca said.

"My goodness, but you aren't very trusting."

"Nope. Where do all these things come from?"

Polly pointed at a box. "China. Says so right there."

The young man was back. "This is the card. They do another setup in late January. It stays open until Easter, so it hits all those holidays. You know, Valentine's Day, St. Patrick's, and then Easter. There's a summer setup for the fourth of July, but the biggest one is Christmas."

"No doubt," Rebecca turned the card over. "Mike Little?"

"That's me," he said.

"Are you the only one doing this?"

"There's another guy and his wife in town," Mike said. "They're out for lunch right now. She's in charge of decorating. We still have a lot of work to do, but we only got into the building on Thursday."

"You've done all this in four days?"

"The shipment came in on Friday. You should have seen it. A huge semi and they just kept unloading pallet after pallet of boxes. I've never seen so much. What you see here is only the first part of what they pulled out. But it was all organized and labeled so we could get started right away."

Rebecca tapped the card against the fingers of her other hand. "This is really interesting. Thank you."

"Are you looking for something specific today?"

"Not yet. We haven't started decorating yet, but I've got some ideas. When I'm ready we'll be back. It was nice to meet you ..." Rebecca hesitated, then smiled. "Mike? Right?"

He smiled back and put his hand out. "Let me give you my phone number. If you're looking for something specific, call me. I'll tell you if we have it."

"That would be great." Rebecca handed over the card and waited for him to write down his number. After he gave it back, she handed it to Polly. "Hold that for me, would you?"

Polly took it and watched as Rebecca put her hand out. Mike shook it and smiled.

The bell on the front door rang and he looked up. "Thanks for coming in. I hope we see you again."

The couple that walked in weren't familiar, but Mike walked quickly toward them. "Monty. Linda. How was lunch?"

"Fine," the woman said. "Did you get any more of those trees unboxed?"

"Some," he said. "But I've had a couple of customers."

Polly and Rebecca walked past the three. Polly smiled and said, "Welcome to Bellingwood. I hope you all have a successful season."

The woman gave her a half-smile. "Thank you. Didn't you find anything you wanted today?"

"Not yet, but like I just told your partner here," Rebecca said, "I haven't started decorating. We just wanted to get some ideas. We'll be back."

"Good," the man said. "Come back any time."

Polly pushed the door open and even though it was chilly, took a long breath of the fresh air. She realized that a cloying evergreen scent had permeated the warm air of the store. The door closed and she said, "That was interesting. What was up with you and all the questions?"

"I thought it was interesting," Rebecca said.

"I know better. You were thinking more than that. It's almost as if you were my doppelganger, sniffing out a mystery."

Rebecca put out her hand. "Give me the card."

Polly gave it to her. "What?"

"It's an import / export business out of Chicago."

"So?"

"In Bellingwood and other small towns."

"So?"

"So, sounds like a good mystery story to me. How about you?"

"What could you possibly mean by that?"

"Just a feeling."

"When did you get that feeling?"

"The minute I opened the door. I know that people like cheap holiday décor, but that stuff is over the top cheap. It's cheaper than what you find in any of those dollar stores, but it costs more." Rebecca shook her head. "I don't know what I'm trying to say. I got a weird feeling when I walked in. Maybe it's nothing. I can't believe you didn't feel anything was off." Rebecca handed back the card. "Stick this in your bag, would you?"

"Maybe you were sucking all the weird feelings out of the air and I couldn't get to them," Polly shoved the card in her bag, as they stopped in front of the door to Sweet Beans.

Rebecca pointed at it. "Should I hold the door for you while you have your special relationship with the store?"

"Whatever." Polly opened the door, allowed Rebecca to enter first, then stopped for her personal happy moment. It never took long, especially on a chilly day, but it was worth it.

"What do you want?" Rebecca asked as they walked toward the counter.

"A sandwich. Soup. Coffee. And a cupcake," Polly said.

"That's almost specific," Rebecca said.

"You choose for me. I'll eat anything. I want to see Sylvie."

Andrew had come up and beamed at them. "Hi," he said. Polly could have sworn that he was blushing. Rebecca still had that effect on him after all this time. It was so stinking sweet.

"Is your mom in the bakery?" she asked.

He nodded. "Can you believe it? She's crazy, but she said she had a lot of things to work on. What are you doing here?"

"Rebecca is buying me lunch. I'll be back."

As Polly walked away, she heard, "I missed waking up to you in the same house," from Rebecca. Kids these days. She rounded the corner and heard conversation coming from the bakery. When she arrived at the door, she saw that everyone was working today.

Marta was the first to see her. "Polly! How are you? Did you see that we have our girl back safe and sound?"

Sylvie looked up from a large batch of bread dough she was cutting into shapes. "I'll be done with this in a second. Then I can talk. How are you?"

Polly was smart enough to stay in the doorway. When these women needed to move, they did so in a hurry and the last thing she wanted to do was be the one who tipped a tray of some type of baked good onto the floor. They had enough of their own trouble.

"I'm good. Rebecca and I just stopped into that Christmas store."

"What's it called?" Marta asked. "Merry Time? What kind of things do they have in there? I've seen some of the posts online. Looks like you could find almost anything you want to decorate for Christmas. Ohhh, I wonder if they have those blow-up Santas?"

"I didn't see any," Polly said, "but I wouldn't be surprised. There's a lot of inventory."

Sylvie slid the tray into a cart and stripped off the plastic gloves as she walked toward Polly. Then she brushed at her apron. "I'm kind of a mess. It feels good, but I'm too messy to hug you. And all I want to do is hug the stuffing out of you for taking such good care of my boy last week." Her eyes filled. "I don't know what I would have done without you. Eliseo says we owe you something special. If you hadn't been here, I would have dragged him back to Iowa Tuesday night."

"You owe me nothing," Polly said. She slid an arm around Sylvie's shoulders. "How's that for a hug?"

"Not nearly big enough, but it will do for now."

"You know, he's my boy, too," Polly said. "And Rebecca insists that he's her boy."

"They're pretty cute together," Sylvie said with a smile. "She is very protective of him. I heard from her a million times, keeping me up to date on how he was doing. Smart, too. Even if he'd had his phone, he wouldn't have been that communicative."

"How was it being back in your own bed?"

"Heavenly." Sylvie rolled her eyes upward. "I was in my house with my boy just upstairs and my dog at the end of the bed. Perfection. Speaking of that. All the cleaning and everything you all did. The house was cleaner and nicer than I'd left it. I didn't expect to come home to fresh sheets on the bed, but there they were. Everything was so clean. Thank you. Have you heard anything more about the people who were squatting there?"

"Not yet," Polly said. "Have you talked to Chief Wallers or the sheriff?"

Sylvie shook her head. "Not after last week. That's okay. I felt safe enough there, knowing that the locks had all been changed. Eliseo talked about putting in a security system. I told him to wait until Ray comes back to town. He might have a better idea of what we should look for." She chuckled. "Mostly, I just wanted to give us some time to live with this before we go off half-cocked and make a huge purchase without giving it thought. All weekend, Eliseo talked about calling someone this morning so we could have it installed before Thanksgiving."

"Can you blame him?"

"Not really, but I don't know. Nothing like this has ever happened before. Why do we think it will happen again?" Sylvie shrugged. "But then, I don't know if I'll ever convince Eliseo or even myself to leave for a week again. The vacation was nice, but it was a lot of work. Is that what vacations always are? Days of preparing your world so you can be gone, and then complete exhaustion when you come back? Just for a few days of sitting beside pretty landscapes? It was nice and all, but wow."

"I'm not the best person to advise you on vacations," Polly said. "I like my creature comforts and those include all my friends and family. And especially my house, my animals, and my own bed."

"Andrew wants to travel with Rebecca whenever she lets him. He knows that her time with Beryl is special and important, but he wants to see the world, too. He says that meeting new people and seeing new places will be good for him when he's writing his stories."

"They're young and ready to go," Polly said. "They will figure it out. Maybe not until they have better jobs and can afford it, but they'll go and see."

"I was thinking about doing that for his Christmas gift," Sylvie said.

"Doing what?"

"Giving him a trip somewhere. I can probably only afford something in the United States, but he needs to go do something crazy."

"What about New York City?" Polly asked. "We could send the two kids there over their spring break. They usually hit about the same time."

Sylvie's eyes lit up. "That would be fun. Rebecca is used to traveling. I wouldn't be scared to let him go with her."

"And New York City isn't that far from Boston. If something came up, friends are out there to help."

"Let's keep talking about this," Sylvie said. "I'll mention it to Eliseo. What a fun gift that would be."

# CHAPTER NINE

Polly was surprised to find the driveway at her house filled with cars. Amalee's car was parked on the street, as was Rebecca's. What was going on? Polly had to drive past the house, and rather than park on the street, sent a quick text to Sal.

*"Would you mind if I parked in your driveway? My place is inundated with vehicles."* She pulled into a spot that wouldn't be in the way of either Sal or Mark's cars.

*"What's going on?"* Sal sent back. Then, *"Of course you can. Do you need to come in for a visit? I have coffee."*

*"I need to find out what's going on first. Talk to you in a bit."* Since Polly had stopped not far from the gate that led to her own yard, rather than attempting to negotiate whatever craziness was happening out front, she headed through the back yard. When she got to the glass doors leading into the kitchen, she peered in. There were people everywhere. People she recognized, but lots of them.

She opened the door, walked in and found Doug Randall sitting on the sofa beside JJ Roberts. "Hey guys," she said, heading that way. It seemed to be a safe space in the middle of chaos.

"Hey, Polly." Both young men stood up. Doug put his hand out.

She shook it and then scowled. "What is going on here?"

"Just hanging out," Doug said.

"In my kitchen."

"It's as good a place as any, don't you think?" he asked with a grin.

"Why aren't you at work?" She pointed at JJ. "And you. Why aren't you at the winery? Did you bring me something to drink? How long have you been here?"

JJ made a point of looking at his watch. "About ten minutes. No big deal. Dani is watching the shop until I get back."

"Again. Why are you here? Is Tab around?"

"She's at work in Boone."

"And Anita?" Polly asked Doug.

"At work."

"I'm so very confused."

"We're picking up supper. But we're doing it early tonight."

"Okay. Why?"

"Because it's ready. Lexi and her crew are packing everything up. She sent out an announcement this weekend that if we wanted dinners this week, they needed to be picked up before five o'clock. So, here we are."

"Every single one of her clients is here," Polly said.

"Before five o'clock, if you'll notice," JJ said, tapping his watch. "I was under strict orders to not be late, so here I am."

"Okay. I think I understand. Sit." Polly pointed at the sofa. "This is weird."

Lexi had steadily grown her take-out meal service, but this looked like more than her normal amount of daily customers. She usually had three or four orders to add to the meal she made for the family and pickup was fast and steady. This was something else.

Polly wandered into the main part of the kitchen where Elijah, Amalee, JaRon, Rebecca, Agnes, and even Cassidy were madly packing containers into boxes and labeling them.

"Hi, Polly." Francesca Mellado stepped up to her. "Dinner looks wonderful tonight."

"Not surprising. Good to see you."

Jody Gordon stood off to the side, holding a glass of water. "I offered to help, but I think they have plenty of people at the island. Man, I appreciate these meals on crazy days like this. We're doing everything to get ready to leave town as soon as Rick is finished Wednesday afternoon. I just don't have time to cook. Lexi is a treasure."

"She is definitely that," Polly said.

Rebecca broke through the group with a box and walked over to Doug Randall. "Here you go. Sorry you had to wait."

"No big deal," Doug said. He tapped a small package. "What's in here?"

"Those cookies Anita likes. Lexi made up a couple of extra batches this weekend."

"I'm a hero," he said. He looked at the group in the kitchen. "Do you mind if I leave through the back yard?"

Rebecca nodded and shooed him away. "JJ, your box is almost finished. Do you think Tab would like cookies or would you like a couple of pieces of pumpkin cheesecake?"

He lifted his eyebrows. "Cheesecake for sure. You guys are going to turn me into a hero, too. This is amazing. Thank you."

Polly grabbed Rebecca's arm and stopped her. "What is happening here?" she whispered.

"Out of control Thanksgiving prep," Rebecca whispered back. "Lexi feels terrible. She did not expect this many people today. Don't say anything, okay?"

Polly nodded. Two other people left the house and then Francesca and Jody both received their boxes and were gone. Mark Ogden walked in.

"Wow," he said. "You're doing a brisk business today, Miss Lexi."

Lexi looked up from labeling a package, saw him, then saw Polly. She shrank into herself. "It's been a crazy day. I'll have yours packed in a minute."

"Got it," Amalee said, holding up a slip of paper. "The only thing I need is the cheesecake. "Four pieces, Mr. Ogden? No. Five, right?" She peered at the paper again. "Right. Five. Just a second and you'll be ready."

Elijah slid a final piece of cheesecake into a container, stripped off his plastic gloves and turned around. "I should have provided entertainment for the crowd tonight."

"Soothe the savage beasts," Agnes said. She set a container into Amalee's box and another into a different box. "That's for Mr. JJ."

Rebecca took it to JJ. "Thank you for waiting."

"Thank you. Are you sure that Lexi wants to do this tomorrow and Wednesday?" JJ asked. "We can make other arrangements."

"Have you already placed your orders?" Rebecca asked.

He nodded.

"Don't you dare change anything. Lexi's head would explode," Rebecca said.

He chuckled. "How's Andrew? Tab said he had a rough Friday."

"He's better now. Worked at Sweet Beans all day."

"Good. Tell Lexi that I'm bringing her gifts in the form of liquid refreshment tomorrow. Maybe she'll find a way to relax over the weekend. And tell her thank you again."

"I will," Rebecca said.

The kitchen had begun to clear out. Then Alistair Greyson walked in. "I'm late. Nan will have my head. And after she told me how hard Lexi was working," he said. He looked around. "Polly! I haven't seen you in forever. How are you?"

"I'm good, Grey. How are you doing? Busy?"

"Busy enough. Been working with your wife," Grey said to Mark. "Making plans for the hockey rink at the community center. I think it's wonderful that she pushed that through. It would be good to have a permanent location."

"You're still teaching?" Polly asked.

"I am. Just the youngsters. They continue to be impressed that an old man like me can skate around a rink and hit a puck." He chuckled. "Somedays, I'm still impressed that I can do that."

"You aren't that old."

"I'm old enough. How are you doing with all the additional life in your space?" he asked.

"Happy," Polly said. "However, as I look around, I see that I'm missing a few kids. I should find out where they are."

Amalee handed Mark a box. "Thank you," she said politely.

"Thank you, Amalee." Mark nodded. "I'm out of your hair. Sal told me I didn't dare stay too long since this is your home. I'm obedient to my good wife."

"My Suburban is in your driveway. I think I left enough room for you to get around it."

"I already did," he said. "I walked into the house and Sal told me to scurry my behind over. She also told me to tell you that if you want to talk, she's got the wine. I'll be glad when Mom shows up tomorrow."

"Thanks," Polly said with a smile. He walked away and she said, "Amalee, where are your sisters and brother?"

"In the family room. I put on a movie for them."

"Good enough."

JaRon came over with another box and handed it to Grey. "Here you go, sir. All ready for you."

"Thanks, JaRon. Are you planning to skate this winter?"

"I don't know." JaRon looked at Polly. "We haven't talked about it."

"I'd love to have you join us."

"I'm not very coordinated."

"If you're interested, I'd be glad to give you some lessons. Have your mom call me." Alistair put out his hand to Polly. "We appreciate the sanity of these meals. Now that I see what we're doing to your household, I appreciate it even more."

"Things will settle in a few short moments," Polly said. "Then, normal chaos will return."

"Thanks again. Lexi?"

She looked up.

"Thank you for this. Nan said she'd call you later this week, okay?"

Lexi gave him a weary smile. "Sounds great." She looked around the kitchen after Grey was gone and Polly saw Lexi's lower lip tremble.

"Hey kids," Polly said. "Any of you that want to make an extra five dollars helps with clean-up. And you'll get that money today."

Everyone looked at Lexi, then back to Polly.

"We've got this," Rebecca said. "Clean and neat in a jiffy."

"A jiffy?" Agnes said. "Who says that anymore?"

"I said it." Rebecca bumped the older woman with her hip. "Either sit and give orders or get moving, lady."

"No respect," Agnes sputtered. "None at all."

Polly put her hand on Lexi's arm. "Come with me."

By the time they got to the office, tears poured from Lexi's eyes. "I'm so sorry. I messed it all up. I thought I could handle it and everything is out of control. I've made a mess of your supper and the kitchen, and I don't know if I can do two more days and you came home early and saw what a poor job I'm doing. I'm so sorry."

"Whoa," Polly said. "There is nothing to be sorry for."

"But I ran out of food. I'm supposed to supplement our dinner, not sell it all." Lexi's voice was going up in pitch as her emotions took over.

Polly pulled her into a tight hug and let Lexi sob on her shoulder. "Oh, my sweet girl. I'm proud of you, not upset with you."

"But I messed up bad. This was horrible."

"It wasn't horrible. Everyone left here thinking about how wonderful you are, and how successful you are, and how you made their lives better. That's a win."

"Not if I can't manage my real job. It's a failure."

"Not a failure. A mistake. Not really even that if we think about it. You had a very successful day. Did you sleep last night?"

Lexi stepped back and gave an uncomfortable laugh. "I haven't slept in days."

"Lexi, you poor thing. No wonder you feel out of control."

"I know. And I know better, but just about the time I'm ready to drift off, I think about one more thing that needs to be done."

"Do you have a notepad by your bed?"

"I know I should, but ..." She looked so forlorn. "Sometimes I try to type notes in my phone, but I'm usually so wasted, I can't even do that."

"Could you take a nap now?"

Lexi shook her head, slumping even more. "Gillian will be home soon, and I need to figure out something else for dinner. I'm sorry."

"Nope. No sorries from you. You've been a hero for long enough. It ends now. Go upstairs. In fact, go through the foyer so you don't even look at the kitchen. Lie down on your bed. I will wake you in two hours. Dinner will be on the table, and you can see your daughter then. You have no more responsibilities today."

"But ..."

"But nothing. Where are your menus for tomorrow and Wednesday?"

Lexi seemed perplexed by the question. "What? Why?"

"So I don't cook food you're planning to use."

"I have copies of the menus hanging on the door of the pantry."

"You know what?" Polly asked. "I'll make it simple and fast. We're going to have a big breakfast tonight. Pancakes, waffles, eggs, sausage, bacon. Everything breakfast. The kids will love it. You'll get a nap and when you wake up, you can eat and then begin processing on what you need for the next two days."

"And Thanksgiving meal," Lexi said with a sigh.

"Are you tired of cooking yet?"

Lexi smiled. "A little."

"We'll figure it out. And as much as I can be here, I'm on board. You have not screwed this up. A growth spurt is a good thing, but first you have to negotiate your way through it."

"Are you sure you aren't mad?"

"I am the farthest thing from mad. I'm so proud of you I could pop."

"How did I get so lucky?" Lexi asked. She jumped from the seat she'd taken and threw her arms around Polly. "Thank you."

"Thank you," Polly said. "Now go. Shut out what you can and try to rest. Two hours and then you can think about it all again."

~~~

No matter how hard she had tried, the kitchen that Lexi had worked to keep clean was a disaster by the time the family finished dinner. Breakfast had been a great idea, but Polly and Henry managed to turn it into a free-for-all, without even thinking about what they were doing. They'd pulled food from the refrigerator, the freezer in the house, and then because Polly didn't think they had enough bacon, she'd sent JaRon to the freezer in the garage for more. She'd had to send Rebecca for more eggs and flour because when Henry mentioned pancakes, a roar of appreciation went up. The last thing Polly wanted to do was use the flour in the pantry. She didn't know how close Lexi was keeping inventory.

With no expectation of eating again, Andrew showed up while the family was still at the table. He'd stayed late working at the coffee shop, helping to clean up after a busy day. More pancakes and eggs were whipped up to feed the boy. He was willing to eat. College food was pretty good, but he told them over and over how much he appreciated home-cooked meals. So, Polly fed him.

"You guys stopped into the Christmas pop-up store thingie, didn't you?" he asked.

"What is that place?" Noah piped up. "They have all sorts of weird stuff in the windows. A pig in a Santa suit? What's that about?"

"You should have seen the pigs in the dumpster," Andrew said. "Like a whole pallet of the things. And they'd all been unboxed and stuff. These kids were just dumping them. If you're looking for plastic pigs and stuffed cows with sleighbells on their collars, the dumpster is where you can find them."

"I've heard about people dumpster thrifting and reselling what
~~~

they find," Rebecca said. "Do you think anyone would buy those weird things?"

Polly scowled at her. "No."

"What? All you have to do is create a market. If people think it's a crazy idea, they'll spend money."

"Pet Rock," Henry muttered.

Elijah blinked and stared at his father. "What is a pet rock?"

"A marketing ploy back in the old days," Henry said. "Someone came up with the idea. He packaged rocks as if they were alive. The boxes had breathing holes, and there were instructions on how to care for the rocks. He made a million dollars."

"People were really that dumb?"

"They weren't dumb. That wasn't it. It was more about the fact that if their friends thought it was funny, they did too. People bought pet rocks and laughed at themselves for doing it."

"So, a pig and a cow," Rebecca said. "Those are cuter than rocks. Right? All we have to do is convince people that everybody either wants one or already has one."

"If those things are in the dumpster, I'd bet that decision is already made," Polly said. "We are not becoming a rescue site for dumpster thrifting. Got it?"

"What about your house?" Rebecca asked Andrew, shooting Polly a wink.

Polly nodded. "If Sylvie wants that garbage lying around, that's her business."

"She'd kill us," Andrew said. "Me for sure. You, probably. I still think it's weird."

"What?" Rebecca asked.

"Pigs and cows in the dumpster. They haven't even been open a day and already they're tossing out inventory."

"We should go see what else is in there. Is the store closed?"

"I want to go," Elijah said. "Can I go, Mom?"

"You still have school tomorrow. I'm almost positive you haven't done any homework yet."

"But it's like a vacation week. No one cares."

"They care," Henry said. "I can't stop the college kids from being dopes, but I can stop you."

"What about me?" Agnes asked. "Am I a kid or an adult?"

Henry started to open his mouth, closed it, opened it again, and then turned to Polly. "She doesn't know?"

Agnes cackled. "I was only checking to see if you knew. Is it theft if they dig a cow out of the dumpster?"

"I don't think so," Andrew said. "Isn't that how police get their clues? That's how I write the story. Once it's in a dumpster, it's no longer owned by anyone. Do you want a cow?"

"And a pig."

"I want a cow," Cassidy said.

Delia put her hand up. "Me too."

Kestra and Teresa looked perplexed.

"Do you want a cow or pig?" Rebecca asked the girls.

"Can we?"

Polly chuckled. "Of course. Amalee?"

"I wouldn't hate having a pig in a Santa hat. It sounds funny."

"Piggie," Gillian said. "And cow."

"Boys?" Polly looked at the five young boys at her table. Noah shrugged as if he didn't care. Elijah said, "Both for me, please." JaRon and Caleb didn't know what to say and Zachary looked at the floor. Cute wasn't something they were about to admit they wanted. She smiled at Rebecca, who nodded.

"This can't be happening," Henry said. "Are you two really going to dig through a dumpster?"

"Not like I'm a stranger to that alley," Andrew said. "We'll look and see if anything is clean enough to bring home."

"Polly?" Henry said. "Stop them?"

"I think a cow in a red scarf would be cute," Polly said.

Henry slapped his hand against his forehead. "This household has lost its senses. Andrew. Rebecca, get out of here before things get worse. But you're on KP duty tomorrow night."

The two jumped out of their seats and headed for the door.

"Did you hear me?" Henry asked.

Rebecca stopped. "Sorry. Yes. Deal. We'll clean up tomorrow.

See ya!"

"Cassidy, if you are walking Mrs. Agnes home, you're off duty tonight, too. Elijah, since you seem to have so much extra energy, you, Caleb, and Zachary will clear the table. Amalee, you and Teresa will fill the dishwasher. Kestra, you will help Polly and me put food away. If everyone moves fast and finishes their evening work, we might have a surprise when the kids come back with whatever livestock they are able to dig up." He shook his head. "Livestock. In Christmas clothing. I've never heard of such a thing."

The noise of everyone moving to get to their chores and finish them was more than Polly had heard in a while. They were excited about those silly animals, even if they did come from a dumpster. Good heavens, she hoped there was nothing wrong with them.

# CHAPTER TEN

Little mattered except Henry's promise of a fun celebration and the hope for crazy stuffed animals, but the kids tore into their chores. The table was cleared in record time and kids were off to complete homework and music practice and even a little additional cleanup, knowing that no adult would allow them to go to bed if the family room and living room were destroyed. Noah kept the library in good shape. The boy wasn't much for messy spaces when he wanted to think and read.

"What do you have for the party?" Polly asked Henry.

"I should tell you to wait and see, but I need to warm things up. I'll be right back."

She frowned as he walked outside.

"What's that about?" Lexi asked. She closed the dishwasher, latched it, and turned it on. "Thank you for dinner tonight. And the nap. I feel like I can make it through two more days. Are you sure you are okay with all this?"

"I am fine with it. How about you?" Polly asked. She had ideas on how to streamline the pickup process, but didn't want to bring those up until Lexi had a chance to think through things. The girl was as creative as she was organized, and it would be better for Lexi to make changes than for Polly to make suggestions.

"I fell asleep trying to organize my thoughts around a better way for people to pick up their food. I thought I had it all together and then today exploded and suddenly there were people in my kitchen." Lexi took in a breath. "Your kitchen. Sorry."

"It's our kitchen. Did you come up with anything?"

"I'd like to think that people would choose a time and stick to that time, but that's ridiculous."

Polly burst out laughing. "It certainly is. They'll apologize for being late or being early, but they won't be on time. It's easier to accept that than be angry about it."

"I thought about investing in hot and cold carriers that they could pick up from a cute kiosk Henry or Heath could build, but they'll never remember to return the carriers, even if we ask them to do a deposit or buy them on their own."

"Smart girl, and the kiosk idea is a good one," Polly said.

"Really?"

"It would take some thought for Henry to figure out how to insulate it. Do you not want to see your customers face to face?"

Lexi pointed at the window and said, with a sheepish grin on her face. "I could wave to them?"

The back door opened, setting off the normal dog and small children race to see who it was. Henry came in carrying a box and two large grocery paper bags.

"What do you have for us?" Polly asked.

He set the box on the counter, causing Gillian and Delia to scramble up into the stools. Polly pulled out a box labeled *Strawberry Rhubarb*.

"Pie? You bought pies? I love you."

"I was in Dallas Center having lunch with a client at that pantry place. They had homemade pies for sale and I couldn't help myself. While I was in the neighborhood, I made it worse by stopping at the creamery south of Woodward and bought ice cream for the pie. I didn't know when we'd have the party, but now is as good a time as any."

Polly nodded. Thanksgiving was only a few days away, which meant there would be homemade ice cream and pies that came from Marie and Betty. This was a different type of treat. She gave him a quick kiss. "You can act on those types of thoughts any time you want. I love it."

Lexi had pulled out the other three pies. You didn't only buy one pie for this family. They could get by with three, but four was better. Henry had purchased a cherry, an apple, a red raspberry, and the strawberry rhubarb.

He took the ice cream out to the freezer and as he unpacked it, he said, "I bought different flavors of ice cream, too. Mostly vanilla, a quart of chocolate, but there's a pint of egg-nog and one of pumpkin spice." He poked his head around the corner and grinned. "For the more sophisticated palate."

"That would be mine," Polly said.

"And maybe mine, too?" Lexi asked.

"You'll have to prove yourself," Polly replied. "I can't go only on your word, you know. We'll do a taste test to see. Hide those, Henry."

He nodded and stepped back as the noise from barking dogs and children hitting the floor running preceded the entrance of Rebecca and Andrew into the house.

"You aren't carrying much," Polly said, pointing to the single black trash bag in Andrew's hand.

"It's all been destroyed. We brought these home so we could prove that we weren't lying. Everyone will be disappointed." Rebecca took in the pies on the counter. "At least we have pie. But this was just mean."

"What's going on?"

Rebecca opened the trash bag and gently dug in, then pulled out what had to have been the pig, covered in yellow and orange spray paint. "They destroyed everything. Why would they do that?"

"To keep dumpster thrifters from taking inventory they don't want to sell." Henry shrugged. "No big loss. Not only is that thing a pig, but it's a poorly created thing and looks awful. Why would they allow that into their inventory in the first place? Only because of the snout can you see that it might have been a pig at one time in someone's imagination."

The rest of the family had been trickling into the kitchen and Elijah was the first one to speak. "That isn't what it looked like when you saw them, was it, Andrew?"

Andrew shook his head. "Nope. They've been messed up on purpose."

"To destroy a little boy's heart and soul?" Elijah asked, grasping at his chest in mock consternation.

"That's exactly it," Polly said. "Have you all finished your work for the evening? Henry brought pie and ice cream home."

"From where?" Zachary asked.

"From a meeting with a client," Henry said.

"Did they give it to you?"

Henry shook his head. "No, we were at a place where I could buy it and I thought it would be fun to surprise you all." He went back out to the freezer and brought in containers of ice cream. "If you talk Noah and Elijah into bringing out the bowls, we'll serve up the good stuff."

Amalee smiled at Polly as she gathered up spoons and forks. "We never ever did anything like this before. It's really crazy here sometimes."

"Good crazy, though, right?" Polly asked.

Amalee set down the utensils and wrapped her arms around Polly's waist. "The best kind of crazy. Thank you."

"Wait until Thanksgiving Day. Then, you'll see what crazy really looks like."

"I can't wait." She realized things were moving forward and rushed to put a spoon and fork in each bowl as the kids made their pie selection and headed back into the dining room.

"Couldn't you at least call and ask?" Elijah asked Polly. "Please? We're having so much fun."

He'd been begging all day for her to get them out of the last two days of school before Thanksgiving, no matter that they would be out at one o'clock on Wednesday.

"I love you, my ever-hopeful boy, but you are going to school tomorrow and Wednesday. Then, and only then, will you be free from the awful restraints they put on you at the horrible place you love to attend."

"I don't love it."

"Seriously?" Amalee asked. "You are like bright and shiny when you get there. You talk to everyone, and you run to your classes so you can say hello to the teachers." She turned to Polly. "Don't let him fool you. He loves it. By the time he's a senior, he'll be running the whole school."

"That's not fair," Elijah said with a mock pout.

"What's not fair?" Polly asked.

"There are traitors in my presence. Her ..." He pointed at Amalee. "She's a traitor. Telling my secrets to the enemy."

Polly surprised everyone by rushing at Elijah and tackling him to the kitchen floor. She took him down as gently as possible, but the shock of it all had him laughing until he was out of control.

Once he was down, she tickled his sides until he was curled into a fetal position, the only words coming out of his mouth, "Stop. I can't breathe."

"Enemy? I'm your enemy?"

"Friend. Uncle. Can't breathe. Help me!"

She looked up at the crowd – and her family was a crowd – that had gathered in shock. "What?" she asked. "Can't a girl get a good wrestle around the house these days?"

Delia wriggled away from Henry's hand, who was as surprised as anyone, but still laughed, and at the last minute, she jumped toward Polly and Elijah. "I wrestle!"

Polly had released Elijah who was just then trying to sit up straight. He reached out and grabbed the little girl, tucked her in tight and gave her a raspberry on her neck.

"Slobber!" Delia yelled through her laughter. "He slobbered!"

"I'll slobber again," Elijah said and got her cheek.

Polly put her hand up toward Henry, who reached for it and pulled her to a standing position.

"What was that about?" he asked.

"A family who was really trying to focus on the pie and ice cream and not the loss of expected gifts. This will be their memory of tonight instead."

"It's definitely a memory. You're a nut. You don't wrestle."

"Maybe I should change it up a little," she said. They walked around the back of the island, and she hugged him. "The kids are getting older, and I want them to know and understand how comfortable they can be in their own skin. Sometimes affection comes in a wrestling match, sometimes it's a hug, sometimes it's a smooch on the cheek or a ruffle of the hair."

~~~

"Teresa, would you help me empty the dishwasher?" Polly asked.

They'd laughed and eaten nearly all the pie and most of the ice cream. Her kids were never going to sleep tonight, and it was her fault. But she wouldn't trade the evening for anything. The only one that didn't easily join in the fun was Teresa. She'd laughed and smiled, but held back, watching from a distance, never participating.

Teresa hadn't found her way into the family mix yet. She was there, but never had she gone all-in with anything. Polly had tried her regular wiles, but to no avail. She understood that it would take time. It had been less than four months and there had been more changes in that little girl's life than anyone should have to face.

Both Lexi and Henry shot her a look, but Polly nodded, knowing they'd give her the time she needed. For the next few minutes, the kitchen was a-bustle with everyone dropping off dishes, receiving directions for heading to bed, and the nightly protests around bedtime. It was chaos, but soon it all died down. Henry took Delia upstairs with him to keep an eye on the transfer of daytime to nighttime activities.

It was still strange to have her boys in the basement. Polly felt fortunate that she had good kids. They'd given the two oldest
~~~

boys more freedom this year, and so far, they hadn't abused it. Noah loved spending time in the library, while Elijah could barely tear himself away from the pianos in the living room. He tried to convince Amalee that she should start playing the piano again. She'd taken lessons as a child but gave them up in junior high. Elijah wanted someone in the family to play so they could do duets on the two pianos.

"Did you ever learn how to play the piano?" Polly asked Teresa.

"I started, but then Grammy couldn't afford it with all four of us. She thought Amalee was going to be the musician."

"Really. Did you like playing?"

Teresa shrugged as she took another plate out of the dishwasher. "It was okay. I probably wasn't very good."

"Would you like to try again?"

"Lessons? They're very expensive."

"What if you started with Elijah teaching you? He could help you start again."

Teresa stared at Polly, with a look that suggested Polly might have finally grown that third eye. "Elijah? He'd do that? But he's so good. I'm nothing."

"Let me talk to him. You're right. He is a really good pianist. We'll see if he's any good as a teacher. Would you want to try it?"

"It might be okay."

Polly smiled. Her crazy boy might be the person to get around Teresa's frightened little heart. "What do you think about the big holiday coming up? You know, we could have more than thirty people here on Thursday. Is that scary?"

Teresa stopped to think about it. She frowned, put the plate on the stack she'd been building, then said, "You haven't chosen anyone to be the turkey-bearer, or the seed planter."

"I don't know about these."

"I thought everybody did them. We always picked every year who would do the presentations. You haven't done that yet. Do you do it on Thursday morning?"

Polly was at a loss.

"And then there's the Native American helper. Me and Kestra and Zachary always did one of the parts. Amalee was too busy helping Grammy cook."

"Tell me about the Native American helper. What do you know about that?"

"Everybody knows they helped the early white people live through that terrible winter, right?"

"Yes."

"But did you know that they helped black slaves on the underground railroad? That's why Grammy celebrated them at Thanksgiving. They were willing to help everyone have a better life."

"I didn't know that. Thank you. We need to celebrate that one for sure. What is the seed planter about?"

"The five kernels of corn. Someone gets to pass them out and they start the thanksgiving meal. Before anyone eats anything, they take a kernel, say something they're thankful for, and then eat it. Five things to be thankful for."

"We do that one. Is it okay if we use candy corn?"

Teresa's eyes lit up. "That would taste a lot better."

"And the turkey bearer?"

"That person carries a leg from the turkey and pronounces that times are better, and we have a feast before us to celebrate a good year and a happy harvest."

"Teresa, these are fantastic traditions. You did them in your family?"

"Every year."

"Would it be okay if we add them to our family?"

She looked at her hands. "Yes, but only if you want to."

"We'll need more seed planters because thirty people will be here, is that okay?"

"That would be fun."

"Would you be the Native American helper and tell everyone about how they helped not only the white people who came to start a new life, but also former slaves who were escaping to start their new lives?"

"Me? In front of all those people?"

"I'll be right there to help," Polly said. "You can sit at my table and when it's time, you can tell the story. If you want to write it down, you can do that, too."

"Zachary likes being the turkey bearer. He always holds the leg up really high and parades around the room until someone tells him that it's time to eat."

"Then, I'll ask Zachary to do it this year. And Kestra can be the seed planter at one table. We'll get someone from every table to be a seed planter. Thank you for telling me about your traditions. After Thanksgiving, we will sit down together and talk about other traditions your family has so that you don't have to miss out on them."

"You should see what we do on Christmas Eve."

Polly put up a finger. "Later. I'll never remember if you tell me right now. And besides, we need to get these dishes put away so that you can get some sleep before school tomorrow."

"Are you really going to talk to Elijah about giving me piano lessons? Will he get mad because I don't know very much?"

"Not if he's the Elijah I think he is," Polly said. "He'll be excited to know someone who wants to learn."

The two of them continued to put away the dishes and then fill the dishwasher with the dessert dishes and glasses. By the time they were finished, it was nine-fifteen, only a little past Teresa's bedtime.

"You head upstairs," Polly said. "Thank you for your help and for trusting me with your traditions. I'm excited to add them to our feast." She closed the dishwasher door.

Teresa stepped forward with hesitation, then threw it off and wrapped her arms around Polly. "Thank you." She broke away and ran for the stairs.

"I love you, too," Polly whispered. She looked around, saw that it was good, and headed down the hallway.

Noah was safely ensconced in his favorite chair, his legs draped over the side with a blanket wrapped around him and a book in hand. She waved, then stopped. It was an iconic image of the boy and Polly quietly took out her phone, then slipped back into the doorway and snapped a quick picture.

"What was that for?" he asked. No one was ever surprised by her taking pictures of them.

"You're adorable."

"Great. I'm adorable. I'm supposed to be cool and laconic."

"Never laconic, but I'll give you cool," Polly said. "Go back to what you're doing."

"What did you want with Teresa? She isn't in trouble, is she?"

"Not at all. I only wanted to connect with her. You want to follow me into the living room? I'm going to ask Elijah to do me a favor."

"This I gotta see. He's frustrated right now."

"Why?"

"Can't you hear him? The same line over and over and over again. He's trying to get it under his fingers, and he keeps changing the fingering. I don't love these practice sessions. They get really boring."

"Let's interrupt him, then." Polly grinned. "I shouldn't. I should let him do his work, but maybe this will give him confidence."

"What are you doing?" Noah unfolded himself from the blanket and the chair and stood up. Her boy was over six foot now and still quite lanky, making him look even taller.

"You'll see."

They walked down the hallway. She could have gone through the bathroom in the library, but she'd startled Elijah more than once by doing that, so using the main entrance made more sense. Polly rapped on the door and walked in, then smiled. Elijah had the classic look of a musician intent on learning his piece. His face was flush with concentration. He'd been dragging his hands through his hair. It was a mess. When she entered, he had one hand up in the air, just about to bring it down to the piano keys.

He looked up, startled. "What? Am I too loud?"

"Not at all. I want to talk to you about something else."

"And you brought Noah? Am I in trouble again?"

"No, Elijah. I'm offering you an opportunity to be a hero."

The door opened again and Henry walked in. "I heard voices, so I figured it was safe to come in. What's up?"

"I was just about to talk Elijah into being a hero."

"Do I get a superhero suit?"

"How about a promise of your own tuxedo. Your growth spurts have slowed. Is that enough?"

"Really?"

What he didn't know was that she and Henry had the tuxedo upstairs in their closet. The entire clan was gathering for family portraits on Sunday afternoon and Polly wanted photos with Elijah in his new tux at the piano. Debbie and Chris Johns, the photographers who rented the office space beneath Jeff Lyndsay's apartment, had worked with Polly and Henry and their family for several years now. They always did beautiful work.

"Really. But that's not this conversation. Have you ever thought about teaching piano lessons?"

"Mr. Specek says it's a good way to make money, but I don't have time right now."

"You'd have time to teach one lesson, wouldn't you?"

He frowned. "To who?"

"Whom," Noah corrected.

Even Polly rolled her eyes at that one.

"Well, it is," he protested.

"Anyway," Polly said. "Teresa took a few lessons until money ran out. She sounds interested. I'd like you to start with her and see if she really does have any interest and find out how much she knows. What do you think?"

"I never thought about that. You'd let me teach her?"

"I'd let you try."

"Do or do not. There is no try," Elijah intoned.

"I'd let you start. You need patience ..."

He pointed his thumb down. "Fail. Elijah."

"You can do it. I don't want her to be scared. You need to research the best way to teach a beginning student."

His thumb went up. "I could do that. Mr. Specek would help."

"And you need to make her love it."

"I love it. Everybody should."

"Okay, we have a beginning. What I want is you to be a hero in this. Make it a wonderful experience for Teresa. She idolizes you a little bit, so keep your cool, be encouraging, and let's see what happens."

He gave her a wicked look. "Are you paying me?"

"Of course. That's the incentive."

# CHAPTER ELEVEN

Usually on the first day of a holiday break, everyone got up late. First day of freedom and all. Since their Thanksgiving dinner wouldn't happen until later in the day, she wasn't worried about early morning wake-up calls.

But that wasn't the way her family worked. Anything to disrupt expectations. However, they quickly learned that to wander into the kitchen, no matter the reason, would earn them a task. She had a million things to complete. When you had a family the size of hers, spreading them out meant that things happened much more quickly.

JaRon and Amalee had declared themselves kitchen helpers for the day, while the rest of her kids had run from the idea. That only meant that they were responsible for cleaning the house and preparing the foyer for a party.

Henry had prepared the eight-pound boneless ham to slow-cook on the grill and Lexi had the turkey in the main oven. With nearly forty people coming, all with a side dish, there really wasn't that much more to cook, but Lexi insisted on cheesecakes to go with the pies that Aunt Betty was bringing.

The last couple of days had been insane for her. She'd made more cheesecakes than ever before, because why wouldn't people want something amazing for their holiday dinner? She had refused a few requests for Thanksgiving side dishes, since those weren't on her menu plan for the week. That startled a few of her random customers, but after a long talk with Polly, she realized that she'd already set down the rules and needed to stick to them as closely as possible.

"You remember I'm going to Andrew's at eleven-thirty, right?" Rebecca asked. She had poked her head into the kitchen from a foyer door, intentionally hiding the rest of her body from Polly.

"Why are you hiding?"

"I don't want to get caught in your unyielding web of tasks. No other reason. We're decorating tables in here. Don't make me do something else."

"Okay," Polly said with a grin. "Keep up the good work. Tell me when I can come look."

"Not for a while. Can you believe that tomorrow we'll start decorating for Christmas?" Rebecca's eyes shone. "I can hardly wait. This house makes it fun. There are so many possibilities in every room."

"I'm glad I raised a Christmas-fanatic," Polly said.

Rebecca started to open the door a little more, then stopped herself. "Nope. No conversation will tempt me into your trap. I'm busy."

"Who is helping you?"

"Oh, I have the best helpers," Rebecca said. "Cassidy, Teresa, Delia, and Gillian. The older girls are mostly trying to keep track of the little ones. It's entertaining."

"Take video and pictures," Lexi called from the porch where she was digging out more cream cheese.

"On it." Rebecca disappeared and Polly shook her head.

"What's next?" Polly asked Lexi.

"If JaRon would come out here and help me bring in all this frozen orange juice, we could get that going."

"All this frozen orange juice?" Polly asked.

Lexi came around the corner, her arms filled with one-pound boxes of cream cheese. She did not mess around. "Virgin mimosas. We're going to have tons of appetizers thanks to Marie and Lonnie, so I thought we'd make something the kids could enjoy." She stopped and stared at the pantry. "Oh, we need the plastic champagne flutes. Amalee, I have no idea where those have hidden themselves. I bought them weeks ago when they were on sale. Could you look?"

"In here?" Amalee headed for the pantry.

"I truly have no idea. Good luck."

JaRon had been smarter than Lexi and took a large bowl with him to the freezer. He returned with cans and cans of orange juice. "All of this?" he asked.

"It's going to taste so wonderful," Lexi replied, "that won't be enough. But it will have to do. Can you run out to the garage and get the drink dispenser?" She shook her head. "Nope. Gonna ask someone else to do that. You start at the sink and open those cans." Turning to Polly, she asked, "Which kid is available for errands around the house?"

"Elijah is cleaning his side of his room," Polly said. "I'll send him." She was prepared to escape the chaos of the kitchen for a few minutes, even if it was to enter the dungeon of chaos that was Elijah and Noah's room. Not that Noah's side was that awful. His looked more like the guard room for Elijah's dungeon. They'd put quite a bit of lighting into the room, but Elijah sometimes acted like a cave monster. For that matter, so did Noah. They both liked having a dark room with light aimed directly at whatever they were working on.

Rebecca, on the other hand, walked past their room and simply reached in to flip on all their lights, generally evoking a tortured yell from one or the other of the boys. She loved light. The basement might not have been the best choice for her, but Henry had purchased sunlight bulbs and added a ton of fixtures for her. The small white lights in the crown moulding at the top of her room were on most of the time and she'd strung white Christmas lights around her mirror and her dresser and every other piece of furniture where it made sense. Her room, when clean, was a joyful place to be. Whenever Rebecca was home, Polly loved spending time down there talking to her daughter.

She walked down the steps as quietly as possible, hoping to surprise Elijah at whatever he was doing. He wouldn't have heard her anyway since he had his earbuds in and was flashing his fingers through the air as if he were playing the piano. Polly stood in the doorway waiting for him to realize she was there.

"Mom!" He yanked the earbuds out. "You scared me."

"By what?" she asked. "Standing here? I'm awfully scary, though, aren't I!"

He lifted his arms, curled his fingers and roared. "I'm a scary Polly-monster."

"Mama-monster to you, bud," Polly said. "I'm not seeing a lot of cleaning being done in here. What'cha been up to?"

"I found this cool new channel. All the music I want to learn how to play. Problem is, I can't sit still, and I can't focus on anything else, so I dance around and play it in my head."

She laughed. "I know I should be angry that you haven't done what I asked of you, but that's pretty cool. How about this. Put your phone and its phenomenal playlist down. I need you to do something for Lexi. Then, come back and either choose a different music channel or leave the phone on your bed until you have all of your clothes taken upstairs and in the washing machine, your bed made, your stacks of music sheets you've printed out in order, and run the vacuum. Then, you can go back to what you were listening to."

"Maybe I could play in the living room instead?"

"After those things are done, we'd all appreciate your playing. We always do."

"You won't make me clean the living room?"

"I didn't say that. But maybe I can help you with it. First, go to the garage and bring in the big drink dispensers."

"Where do I put them?"

"On the table in the foyer. We'll wash them from there. Then, come back in and do three things. Clothes into the washing machine, make your bed, stack your music. Oh, four things. And vacuum your floor. If you keep moving, you'll have those done in a half hour. Right?"

"That isn't very long, is it?"

"Exactly." Polly opened her arms and Elijah walked in for a hug. Every time. That boy would take affection from her without question. It was another one of her favorite things about him.

~~~

One great thing about families is that in Polly's world, at least, they didn't ring the doorbell, sending dogs into paroxysms of barking and forcing someone to break away from the middle of something to let them in. Her family just walked in, no matter whether it was the front door, the side door or in through the patio doors at the back of the house. Not that anyone really did that. But they all knew it was perfectly acceptable.

Marie and Jessie Locke were arranging food on the long tables in the foyer. Lexi had printed out beautiful cards for where things should go. That was another thing Polly was grateful for. Not a single soul in this group would consider correcting or rearranging what Lexi's plan called for. It didn't matter that they had a better plan, this wasn't their house. When she was in the middle of presenting a huge meal, that wasn't the time. And in the end? None of it was all that important.

Will Kellar had been torn from the noise and chaos by Henry and Hayden. He didn't know what to do with himself. Will's first instinct was to hover over Lexi, ensuring that she had all the help she might need. After her second "Move, please," he'd slunk into the foyer, his tail between his legs. Henry rescued him, and after putting their cold weather gear on, the three headed out to the patio to be real men and do the grilling thing. What they really did was stand around being cold and staring at the grill which was doing the work. The ham was almost ready to come in, so at least they had good reason to be outside other than avoiding Lexi.

The tables in the foyer were beautiful. Rebecca was one of
~~~

Polly's favorite decorators. They'd collected fall-colored leaves from the back yard and from Sycamore House before Eliseo mulched all the sycamore leaves. Those big, beautiful leaves might be a pain for people who had to deal with them, but they were beautiful. Flameless candles, and small cornucopias filled with autumnal garland filled things out.

Polly had wandered through all the rooms on the main level where people had taken up residence. Agnes was in the family room with Jack and his sister, Jill, Bill, Dick, Dave and Lonnie Swenson, and their two youngest. While they all thought they were watching a football game, Agnes was truly regaling them with tales of her days running the restaurant in Boone. As Polly got the story from Lonnie, who tried to escape, all Bill had done was ask what her favorite Thanksgiving side dish was. Agnes had started out by telling him that it was Carlos, one of her servers, and then the story spun off.

Noah had an enraptured group of children sitting on the floor in the library as he told stories. He was essentially reading to them, but for this he couldn't sit still. He wandered around the room, bringing to life character after character. Andrew stood and watched the whole thing and waved for Polly to follow him down the hallway.

"What's up?" she asked.

"Interesting thoughts in my head," Andrew replied. "I know that Noah is as interested in books as I am, maybe even more so. But the way we approach words on the page is different. He tells stories. I write stories and that's how I approach those words that float around in my head. Do you think Noah wants to be a writer?"

"He's never really expressed an interest in it," Polly said.

"That makes sense. I love writing stories, but Noah loves getting caught up in the stories that have been written. Did you see what he was doing in there? He brought life to every character and those kids were entranced. They will know more about those books than I ever did because he took them deep into the story."

"It's pretty cool."

"That's not a big enough word, Polly. It's bigger than that. Noah is amazing. Do you know what he wants to do with his life? Because manual labor isn't for that boy."

"Unless he needs to make money to support his book addiction."

Andrew glared at her. "Like you'd ever let that happen."

"I will do my best to keep that reality from him. Why are you asking?"

"I don't know. I just know that there are professors at the university who don't understand the books they want us to learn like Noah does. It's as if when he reads a book, he absorbs it. Not only that, he's able to pour it back out so that other people understand it as he does. I hope he goes into teaching."

"What about you and teaching?"

Andrew pointed at himself. "Me? A teacher? I would tell the students to go write a story and if they didn't, I'd flunk 'em. Besides, it would take away too much time from my own writing."

"Everything takes away time from your writing now, doesn't it?"

"And I don't like it, but I don't have the power to flunk people. That, and all those papers I edit give me enough money to keep living."

"How are you feeling?" Polly pointed at his arm. "And your face looks pretty good."

"The surface injuries have all gotten better. The arm doesn't hurt. I'll be glad when the cast is off. This is annoying on so many levels."

"I don't even want to know," Polly said.

"You're weird."

"And you love me." She pushed open the door to the living room and blinked. She looked back into the hallway and then into the living room again. Elijah was at the piano, Heath was on the floor with Caleb and Molly Locke. Agnes was seated in front of the fireplace like she'd never been anywhere else.

"Is there a second Mrs. Agnes in my house?" Polly asked.

"Just the one," Agnes replied. "But I feel forgotten and left out. Did you even put me on the list? I didn't see my name up there."

"The list on my refrigerator?" Polly asked. "Your name isn't on it? That doesn't seem right. Did you erase it?"

"Why would I do that? It's your list, not mine. If you want to forget about the best thing that ever happened to you, that's your problem. I'll keep showing up because that is what I do. I appreciate the good things in life. Like you and your family. I won't be angry because you don't appreciate me enough to remember me. I'll simply turn it around and love you even more."

Polly nodded. "Of course you will. Let's be clear, though. Just because your name isn't written on a list, doesn't mean your name isn't written on my heart."

"Oh," Agnes said. "Nice response. Your points are back in the positive realm again. You scored big-time with that one."

Henry walked into the living room. "Fifteen minutes. That came from Lexi. Little ones and big ones should wash their hands and find their way into the foyer. Polly?"

"What can I do?" she asked.

He took her hand. "Take my hand and guide me through the rest of our lives?"

"If you insist," she said, holding on. "Nothing else?"

"I've announced it to every room. Are we missing anyone?"

"I can put it out over the intercom, but that's a little intrusive. Let's see who shows up."

"Am I carving the turkey today?"

"Would you? I thought we'd talked about it, but I'm running on pure adrenaline at this point."

"Maybe we did. Dad asked."

"Not Bill. I want you to do it. This is your house and your family. Okay? We'll have you cut the first slice before the kids' traditions begin, then Lexi can take it into the kitchen and slice it to the platter with the electric knife."

"I could do that, too."

"No, the kids need you to be part of their celebration. Let's see who we have in the foyer."

Kids of all ages, adults, and various and sundry animals had passed through the foyer after they cleaned up. By the time Polly and Henry got there, the room was buzzing with noise and laughter.

"If you could all take your seats," Polly yelled. "You'll find place holders. Hopefully they still make sense. I'm definitely hoping no prankster has …" She watched Marie frown. "… changed things around. Who's the culprit?"

"This could be fun," Marie said. "I'm sitting between Cat and Delia. That works for me."

Polly shrugged. "Find your place holder and take a seat. If it doesn't work for you, we'll fix it. You're right, Marie. This could be fun." Seriously with the capers around here. And no one was grinning to themselves or pointing at another. The prankster could be anyone.

She continued after the tables were filled. How had they managed that without chasing people through the house? She'd take it. "Henry will carve the first slice of the turkey and while Lexi manages the rest in the kitchen, we have some new traditions to honor in this family. Teresa?"

Teresa stood up and read the prepared piece she and Polly had written about how Native Americans had not only helped the white settlers in the earliest years, but how they had been a big part of the Underground Railroad, ensuring that many black slaves found freedom. Applause accompanied her return to her seat between Dave Swenson and Agnes. Agnes gave her a hug, while others reached out to pat her hand as she went past them. This was a wonderful introduction to the big family gatherings she was now part of.

Polly called Kestra to stand beside her. "There are small dishes at each place setting filled with five pieces of candy corn. Tradition tells us that the early settlers had only five kernels of corn to eat. Kestra, would you like to explain how this works?"

Kestra opened her mouth, then shut it, looked down and shook her head. Polly didn't hesitate. "Take your dish, figure out who will start and then go around your table, telling something you are thankful for, one kernel at a time. After we're finished, we have one last presentation and dinner will be served."

It took time, but soon, the chatter died down and people looked at Polly expectantly. She nodded at Zachary who lifted a large turkey leg in the air and walked around the room, weaving in and about tables. He called out, "Let the blessings of the harvest descend upon our family."

Lexi had purchased the largest turkey leg she could find, and he was grinning like crazy as people picked up their champagne flutes and toasted him as he passed. Polly loved her family. They took care of everyone, even silly wonderful children who loved to show off.

# CHAPTER TWELVE

So much for peace and quiet following the long day of Thanksgiving festivities. It was not to be. Not with Rebecca in charge. Today was the day that Christmas burst onto the scene at the Bell House.

The nice thing was that Polly didn't have to be involved. Rebecca managed the entirety of the decorating madness. None of the kids were nearly as offended at Rebecca asking them to do things. Had Polly been delivering orders to run back and forth to the attic, the garage, and the basement, there might have been open rebellion.

They'd left the tables up in the foyer and those were now covered with boxes and tubs. Artificial Christmas trees in their original packaging, some of which were new this year, stood against the wall to the kitchen. Rebecca claimed a brightly colored quilted Santa's hat she found at the new craft store this fall. She fully admitted to being out of control and embraced it wholeheartedly.

Some of the older members of the family had offered to help, but Rebecca made sure that she'd wrangled her siblings before she announced that today was an immediate-family day. Besides, they all had their own homes to decorate. She then offered to decorate for anyone who was willing to pay her. Christmas would be expensive this year since she wasn't currently employed.

Andrew would be here later. He was working this morning, so Noah and Elijah were in charge of bringing boxes in from the garage and the basement. These were new decorations and trees. When Polly thought back to those first spare years they'd lived in this monster house, she found it to be a wonder. But it had been theirs and they were happy to be together.

Elijah walked past her with another box, and she stopped him.

"What did I do this time?"

"Put the box down."

He set it down and looked at her. "What?"

Polly pulled him into a tight hug and felt emotions well up inside her. "I am so happy that you and your brother moved in and let us love you."

"Me too. What's going on?"

"That first Christmas you were here. Did you know that you were my Christmas present from Henry?"

He smiled. "Kinda. We were such a mess, though. Scared out of our minds that we'd lose another home and have to move back in with our old family. I was sure they were going to kill me someday."

Polly nodded. "But you were here with us."

"If Mr. Dunston hadn't been the one to assure us that you really did mean it, I was going to run away. I told Noah that we could run if it was terrible. He didn't want to. He wanted to be here so bad. We thought we would be in your old apartment and didn't know what to think when we drove up to this big place! I kept asking Mr. Dunston if it was real. How could anyone who lived in a house like this want me and Noah? We were scrawny little niggers."

Polly shuddered. That was the second time she'd heard that word this week and it made her want to vomit. "Who said that to you? Surely not the people who had taken you in before us?"

"Oh no. Not them. Mostly the big kids back at the apartment. That's what they called everyone. Truth is, we were scrawny."

"You still eat more than anyone I've ever known," Polly said, tugging him back in for another hug. "You can eat and eat and eat. I guess scrawny did fit you back then. You were such little boys. And now look at you. Growing up with big lives in front of you and a mama who is emotional over the memory of the day you showed up in her life."

"Do you remember how we shared that room with Hayden and Heath? And how Obiwan never let us sleep alone? And do you remember that day we spilled juice all over the carpet in there?"

Polly tilted her head. "You spilled juice?"

"Gotcha. We didn't, but I thought I'd check to see if you were paying attention."

Rebecca chose that moment to walk in. "There you are. I was looking everywhere for that box."

"Really? This one single box?" Elijah asked.

"I really wondered where you were. I thought you had escaped my clutches." She rubbed her hands together. "You are mine for the day and I will use you until you drop dead from exhaustion."

"Don't they call that slavery, Mom?"

Polly put her hands up. "I am staying away from that conversation, but Elijah, you have to stop pushing those buttons with us. I'm serious. Okay?"

"What buttons?"

She scowled. "Don't mess with me."

He had the grace to look ashamed. "I'll stop. Sorry."

"Look at you being all grown up and doing your best to avoid cleaning a bathroom." Rebecca slung her arm around Elijah's shoulder. "Now get in there and get your unpacking on." She bent down and picked up the box, then set it in Elijah's arms. "I'll be right back." As he left the kitchen, she turned on Polly. "Don't be interrupting my workers, woman." As Elijah closed the door, Rebecca laughed. "I have so much fun with them. I hope they're having fun, too. I love this big family."

"So far, I've heard no complaints," Polly said. "Would you like me to talk to Lexi about a mid-morning snack?"

"That would be awesome. We're going to try to be organized, but first I have to open all the boxes so we can see what we have. I'd like to start upstairs because that will be the smallest amount of decorating. Then, down here, it's going to be as if Santa's elves threw up Christmas. Are you ready?"

"I'm ready for whatever you give to me. The poinsettias for the stairway will be here this afternoon. But you know Dad and Grandpa won't have the tree until tomorrow, right?"

"Second best day ever," Rebecca said. "When the big tree goes up and the white lights come on and Christmas becomes real! You know what I mean."

"I do. Henry's just thankful you aren't pushing him to bring that tree home today."

"It always comes in on Saturday. I wouldn't break that tradition. I'm all about creating new traditions. You should know that."

"Right," Polly said. "I'm going to see what Lexi wants me to work on for snacks."

"After yesterday, I think we'll all pop if we see any more food."

"Y'all wanted breakfast. I believe that we'll be just fine. Go on back to your servants. Sounds like they need you." What Polly didn't say to her was that she wanted a little more time to herself so she could quietly drink coffee. She refilled the mug, snagged her phone, and headed for the sofas at the back of the kitchen. Henry was out with his father, Dick, Hayden, and Heath cutting down the large pine tree that Rebecca had chosen earlier this week for the foyer. Once it was down, they had ten pine trees to plant in the woods behind Bill and Marie's house. It would take twenty-five to thirty years for those trees to grow into a tree the size that was needed, but they'd been doing the work for a long time.

Ben Seafold, whose dream was to run a Christmas tree farm, had several years of hard work ahead of him before his dreams came true. He'd planted this year, but when he told Polly that it would take a minimum of seven years and that was after the four years the trees had been living in a nursery, she gasped. That was a lot of dreaming and hoping and planning. He insisted he was retired and had all the time in the world. He loved his new home up north of Bellingwood. Once they cleared out the murder mess across the road from where he now lived, he'd accepted responsibility and purchased that land as well. Ben cleared the brush, opened the entrance way, and cleared a large patch of ground where he planned to build a house that would turn into a Christmas village every year.

His beard was growing out and mostly white by this point. Ben was about to become Bellingwood's Santa Claus. His jovial nature and big old belly laugh made him the perfect candidate. His desire to transform those woods into something beautiful and joyous was contagious around town. People couldn't wait to see what he did, and he'd had plenty of offers to help with whatever he needed.

Bill Sturtz thought that having a small train travel the perimeter through the village would be fun, and the two men, along with JaRon, Caleb, and Dick Mercer were deep into plans for the thing. JaRon wanted it to be reminiscent of the Polar Express. If he had anything to say about it, that would happen.

It would take a few years, but Ben had patience like nothing Polly had ever seen. This was going to come together. Before anyone knew it, Bellingwood might be known for its year-round Christmas celebration.

Lexi didn't see Polly when she came down the steps. Polly watched her blearily look around, trying to identify the source of all the noise. Still in her robe and slippers, Lexi stumbled across the room to the coffee pot and poured herself a cup, moaning out loud when she took the first sip. "There's my life," Lexi said softly.

"I'm back here," Polly said. She didn't want Lexi to go any further with whatever conversation she was about to have with her cup of coffee. "Did you have a good evening?"

After dinner at the Bell House, Gillian, Lexi, and Will headed out to visit his parents. They hadn't made plans to have another

Thanksgiving meal, but Lexi took a pumpkin cheesecake as her gift to them. They got back to Bellingwood later than Polly was willing to stay up and wait. But Lexi, like everyone else, was happy to text Polly, no matter the time, simply to let her know that she was home safe. It was such a small thing, but gave Polly and Henry peace of mind, knowing their nestlings were where they belonged.

"It was nice," Lexi said. "Thank you for rescuing me from an excited Gillian this morning. Is she in there with the others?" She nodded toward the foyer while walking over to join Polly. Putting the coffee cup on the table, she dropped onto the other end of the sofa and dragged a blanket over herself before picking it back up. "I am not awake yet. Still chilly and I know this kitchen has heated floors and you've got the heat up."

"Give yourself a minute. What do you think about a morning snack for the kids?"

That made Lexi shudder. "More cooking?"

"No," Polly said with a laugh. "I was going to recommend we pull out leftover ice cream, cookies from the freezer, and whatever other desserts we have in the house."

"We need fruit and vegetables after this week," Lexi said.

"Okay, instead I'll slice apples and oranges."

"You won't get away with it. The kids are all on vacation. They'll whine."

"You're confusing me."

"Because I'm confused. The dessert thing is fine. Probably easier, too."

Rebecca pushed a door open and looked around. "Polly, where are you?"

"Back here. What's up?"

"I can't find any of the blue lights. I thought we bought, like, ten packages of blue lights. Where are they?"

"I don't remember buying blue lights," Polly said. "Are you sure?"

"Look at this face." Rebecca ran her index finger around her face. "Does it look like the face who wouldn't remember asking about blue lights?" She put the finger up. "Don't say anything. I'm sure it's my fault. What am I going to do?"

"You're going to give me ten dollars so I can get a coffee at Sweet Beans, and then you're going to ask me nicely to head to the hardware store and buy blue lights for you."

"Polly, would you please go to the hardware store and buy blue lights for me? And would you consider buying your own coffee at Sweet Beans, and maybe send my boy home with one for me since I'm a broke college girl?"

Lexi laughed.

"She's laughing at me," Rebecca said. "I have one day to get this house decorated and she's laughing. It feels mean."

"I am mean," Lexi said. "Mean and rotten and I'm barely into my first cup of coffee. That's all you get from me until I start the second cup. Live with it."

Polly leaned forward, set her cup down and hauled herself up from the sofa. "Argh. Yesterday really wore me out. Okay, Becky-girl ..."

Rebecca brought her hand up into a fist. "Where did *that* come from?"

"Figure a new name for bad behavior. Do you want anything else while I'm out and about?"

"You're going to ask Andrew to bring us the good stuff." Rebecca pointed back and forth between her and Lexi. "She's going to need a lot of the good stuff to get through the day after the week she's had. And then you're going to get ten packages of blue lights and some more greenery garland and we need some clear crystal balls for the tree in the upstairs hallway."

"The tree upstairs?" Lexi asked. "Is that my tree?"

"Don't you have one?" Rebecca asked, her eyes showing the panic erupting from her heart. "I wasn't even thinking about decorating your space."

"Just kidding. Gillian and I are all over it. We're going to do a little intimate family thing after the crazy has finished in the household. I told her to steal little bits of decorations ..."

"Is that where the blue lights went?" Rebecca demanded.

"Dope. I never told her to do that. You forgot the lights all on your own," Lexi said. She got up. "And I'm off for my second cup. I can feel the meanness fade away while the snarky is about to take its place."

"I'll be back in a while," Polly said. "No kids, no reason to hurry, just Polly Giller, out and about in the wild streets of Bellingwood." She headed for the porch and snagged her keys from the hook on the way. "Don't wait up!"

~~~

"Thank you!" Polly waved at Paul Bradford as she walked back outside the hardware store. Temperatures were no longer in the fifties, and she was glad she'd worn her heavy coat. There was barely enough time between her house and the downtown area for her Suburban to warm up, but she'd live.

Simon Gardner was standing in his doorway, and she waved at him, then smiled when he held up the paw of his cat, Crystal, to wave back at her.

Coffee and a conversation with Andrew, and she would be finished with the hard work for the day. She drove down the street, then turned north and parked by the side door of Sweet Beans. The place was busy, but then, that made sense. Everyone was out today. Even the hardware store had been busy.

She made her usual stop inside the door, enjoying the scents and sounds of the place. Andrew waved from a table he was wiping clean.

"Rebecca says that I'm supposed to bring her coffee."

"Lexi, too, is what I heard," Polly said. "We can provide the coffee, but not the fluffy drinks."

"You should get one of those fancy thing-a-ma-bobs," he said. "Henry would get it for you for Christmas. Then you could always have fluffy coffees."

"Only if I hire you to come run it. I'm not going to learn how. I'd rather come here. You know, I have an investment in the place."
~~~

"The investment where you get free coffee?"

"That one. What time are you finished with work?"

He looked up at the big clock on the wall. "Half hour. Think she can wait?"

"I think that Rebecca knows your schedule as well as you do. She'll wait."

"What about you?" Andrew asked. "What do you need?"

"Coffee – the largest you can make me."

"Fancy or straight black?"

"Straight black. And I want ..." Polly glanced at the bakery display. "I want something warm and crumbly. Not too sweet, but yummy."

"You want a zebra bar. Chocolate brownie with cheesecake."

"That's exactly what I want. Then I want you to tell me anything more about that Christmas pop-up down the street."

"You mean the overly sweet and nice people who are so sugar-coated they make my skin crawl?"

"Really?"

"I shouldn't say anything. It's like they act as if they want to know people, but it's all a front so that they make nice, and people want to buy from them. They're doing a pretty good business, and no one has complained about their products. And those extra stuffed animals are long gone."

"When do they empty the dumpsters back here?" Polly asked.

"It's different depending on what company we use. Most everyone uses the same one and we get pickups every Monday, Wednesday, and Friday."

She nodded. "Black coffee, zebra bar. I'm going to say hello to your mom. Did she have a good day yesterday for Thanksgiving?"

"Mom didn't have to do a thing. Eliseo and Elva did it all."

"Rebecca didn't tell me much, but then, we haven't had time."

"Not much to tell. It was a nice day for them. Mom sat on the sofa while the girls catered to her every need. Elva and Eliseo cooked the whole meal. I think Elva was looking forward to doing something other than sling horse poop."

Polly laughed. "Okay ... me, going to talk to your mom. I'll be back."

"I can bring it to you."

"Nah, just keep it here. Do you need a ride to my house?"

He batted his eyes. "Please?"

"That's why she sent me up. Little stinker plans for everything." Polly was shaking her head as she walked away. When she hit the back hallway, she saw Sylvie trying to haul three heavy trash bags toward the back door. "Hey!" she called. "Let me help."

"I can do it," Sylvie protested.

"Or you can let your friend help you. Good grief, stop trying to be the tough girl."

Sylvie slammed her hip into the back door's crash bar and released one of the bags to Polly, who grabbed it up and followed her out.

"Did you have a good day yesterday?" Polly asked Sylvie.

"It was amazing. I did nothing. I didn't have to make a dessert or a meal or anything. Elva even put leftovers into small casseroles, so Eliseo and I have meals for the weekend. She had a ton of fun, and I had a ton of relaxation. Which I needed after that crazy trip and my dumb son getting himself into more trouble than necessary."

"Are you feeling okay about your house?"

"We wander through and make sure that windows and doors are locked. The first couple of nights I felt like I didn't belong there. Like it wasn't really my house, but it's gotten easier every night since then."

"Good. How's Andrew doing?"

"He doesn't say much." Sylvie tried to heft the first bag into the dumpster and then had to wait for Polly to grab it with her. They hauled back with a big swing and off it went, right where it belonged.

"Do you think he's okay?"

"He'll be glad to go back. He needs his own sort of normal, and when he comes home for Christmas break, he'll be okay.

They hefted the second bag. "What is in these?" Polly asked.

"Failed attempts at a new recipe. Not my failed attempts, but I'm okay with it. When people want to try things, I encourage them. Did you know that wet flour got this heavy? And the worst thing is – because it's sourdough, it's just going to keep expanding. I don't want it in the bakery."

"They made a lot."

"Thought they could rescue it. Apparently, it's been out of control for a while, and this morning, someone thought they should just incorporate it all into a large batch of flour and see if it was any good. It was no good. It was horrible.

"It's going to sit out here all weekend?" Polly asked.

Sylvie grinned. "Nope. They're coming tomorrow morning. I already called."

"I was a little concerned about the smell drawing vermin and rodents." Polly looked around. "Speaking of smell."

"Oh, no you don't."

"I don't want to." They hefted the third bag into the dumpster, then Polly leaned over and looked inside. "We disturbed it."

"We disturbed what?"

"You know what."

"Why would you do this?" Sylvie asked. "It's a holiday weekend and now we have to put up with police and rumors and speculation?"

"It's my store, too," Polly protested. "At least you aren't Jeff. How long has it been since the dumpster was emptied?"

"Wednesday morning early. Oh goodie," Sylvie said with mock disgust. "I'm leaving you here. I will act like nothing has happened and go back to work, ignoring you and all of your antics. You call Tab. I'll tell Andrew to prepare her coffee. And then you can tell me how it is you can handle finding the body of a young man and not fall apart. I need a minute." Sylvie shook her head as she walked to the back door, muttering all the way.

# CHAPTER THIRTEEN

Cold air pushed through Polly's clothing. She was shivering when she decided that this was dumb. She'd already called Aaron, who was going to call Tab. The day after Thanksgiving was one of those days anything could happen. Most of what they dealt with was theft, so a murder victim would at least put something interesting into their day. Not that they wanted interesting.

She was about to open the back door when both Andrew and Rebecca burst through.

"Polly!" Rebecca exclaimed. "You really did this today?"

"I did it," Polly said. "My fault. Uh huh. That's how this works."

"Okay, the universe decided you needed to find a body today of all days?"

"Better question. What are you doing here?"

"Andrew called to tell me that he was going to be a while and rather than make him wait, I came up to get him. Who was killed, do you know?"

"I don't," Polly said.

Rebecca started toward the dumpster.

Polly put her hand out. "Stop. You don't need to see that."

"You do?" Rebecca pushed past. "You're strong. I'm strong."

Andrew followed her over and they both peered in. Rebecca stepped back. "You know who that is, don't you?"

Polly shook her head.

"It's the kid who helped us the other day." Her voice lowered to a whisper. "You know, from the Christmas store?"

"No way," Polly said. "Why would he be in this dumpster and not theirs?"

"Maybe he saw something he wasn't supposed to see."

"What's that other smell? I know dead body smell, but what?"

"Bad batches of flour and yeast and sourdough and …" Andrew stopped. "It was really bad. Like someone mixed something very ugly into it. Mom says it's only ingredients and by themselves they're worth nothing, so it's no big deal when they have to throw a fouled experiment."

"What were they experimenting with?" Rebecca asked.

"I think one of the ladies tried making a sourdough at home. She thought it would be a great flavor for cakes and muffins, but it spoiled really bad."

Rebecca shook her head. "I'm trusting only your mother to bake for us from now on. That's my declaration. I'm never going to try it. Polly isn't ever going to try it and I will make Lexi swear that she never tries it."

"Harsh," Polly said.

The bloop of a police siren caught their attention as Aaron drove into the alley, followed by everyone else from Tab to an emergency vehicle, to Alan Dressen's team.

Aaron was first up the steps and put his arms around Polly. "You're shivering! What are you doing out here?"

"Waiting for you. You took forever."

He chuckled and headed for the back door. "We'll talk inside. Your friend, Tab, will take care of things out here. She's better dressed for this."

"We know who it is," Polly said. "He worked at the Christmas store. We met him the first day they were open last week."

Aaron nodded. "Okay. Tab will be in to talk to you." He held the door open and tried to get Rebecca and Andrew's attention, but they were more interested in all the activity around the dumpster.

Tab waved at Polly, and when Aaron pointed inside, she nodded in understanding.

"Oh, I love the warmth and scents coming from the bakery," Polly said.

"Then, go stand in front of an oven or something."

"Sylvie saw the body, too. But she doesn't know anything."

Aaron chuckled. "You are frozen, aren't you?"

"A little. I was about to come inside when the kids came out. I waited too long."

He left her in the kitchen and was soon back with a large steaming mug of coffee. Polly took it from him with a smile and allowed the steam rolling off the top to warm her face. "Mmmmm," she moaned. "That's nice."

Sylvie had come over with a warm cinnamon roll. "We are about to put these in the display. Want one?"

"Y'all are spoiling me," Polly said. "I'm fine."

"Your face is bright red, your fingers are red, and you were shivering when Aaron brought you inside. You can give us a minute to take care of you. Take her to Sal's booth, Aaron. I'll check on her."

"Seriously, I'm not a child," Polly said. "I can get to the booth on my own."

"When you stop shivering," Aaron replied.

She held out her right hand, kept it steady, then shook it in his face. "I'm fine. Now, go be a cop. I'm going to go be a customer. Tell the kids to go home. Rebecca is decorating and I need her to be on the job today."

"Uh huh." Aaron took her arm and walked with her down the hallway. Luckily, Sal's booth was the first one beyond the bathrooms. This morning, Sal was already parked there, a cup of coffee beside her laptop and a plate filled with a breakfast sandwich beside it.

"What are you doing here?" Sal asked Polly.

"You know," Aaron said.

"I don't know ..." Sal dropped her head forward, then looked at Polly who was sitting down across from her. "I do know. Really?"

"She stayed outside too long and got a chill. Make her warm up."

"On it."

Aaron patted Polly's shoulder and walked away.

"Sometimes I feel like such a kid with that man," Polly said. "What are you doing up here? Don't you have a house full of family?"

"Kathryn kicked me out." Sal laughed. "Not really. But she did encourage me to take advantage of that house full of family and take some time for myself. Not that I wasn't a slug all day yesterday. That many boys with their mother? They took over my kitchen and had the best time. I got to play with the kiddos, read books to them, and just generally be a mommy with no other responsibilities. It was glorious."

"Sounds nice."

"What about you? How was your day?"

"Insane, but you know that's how I like it. And my family helped a lot, so I wasn't in terrible shape. Just busy."

"How about Lexi?"

"She needs a day off before the Christmas season. If she thought she was busy before, she's about to find out what busy really means."

"Why do you think that?"

"How many meals do you plan to order this next month?" Polly asked with a sly grin.

"Every single one she cooks."

Polly pointed at Sal. "That right there. People have discovered what a wonderful cook she is. And if they think about it, they're spending less than they would if they purchased groceries and spent the time it takes to put those meals together. She's spending today putting together her menu plan for a week. I've told her she needs to think bigger and put it together for the entire month. Lexi believes that might be too much because what if she changes her mind."

"I'll eat anything that woman cooks. Though it might be nice if people had the opportunity to tell her what they won't eat." Sal cocked her head in thought. "Nope. That's not Lexi's responsibility. If she posts something to her menu, we have the choice to either order it or not. That's the deal we all signed up for."

"Right."

"You know that question is going to come up, though. You need to make sure that Lexi doesn't let people boss her. She's in charge of her business, not us. And if people give her trouble about anything, she can fire them. She *should* fire them."

"You're a nut."

"I'm protective. I'd be really angry if someone made so much trouble that Lexi couldn't handle it and closed her business. I'm going to be her number one customer. She has spoiled us all. My kids get healthier meals, Mark doesn't have to worry about whether he'll be cooking when he gets home from a long day, and my guilt over being the worst cook this side of the Mississippi is assuaged."

"This side of the Mississippi?" Polly asked.

"I knew some awful cooks when I was growing up. We weren't trained for it. We were trained to be pretty so we'd marry a wealthy man and could afford a cook and housekeeper. I'm very good at keeping my house clean, but the whole cooking thing is far, far beyond my ken."

"Your ken? Assuaged? Girlfriend," Polly said. "You're using the big words."

"Figured I should dig out my college degree after reading children's books all day yesterday."

Polly hadn't been paying attention and was surprised when Tab sat down on the edge of the bench and gave her a little shove. "Move over there, crazy woman," Tab said. "That was a bad one."

"What? Bad?"

"Beaten badly and someone went to town with a knife on the kid. They're going to have trouble figuring out what actually killed him."

"But it didn't happen here. There wasn't that much blood in the dumpster."

"Nope. Didn't happen here. Just dumped him right on your property. It figures, doesn't it?"

"My property," Sal said. "Polly rents the bakery."

"Okay." Tab smiled and reached for the uneaten cinnamon roll. "You eating this?"

"Not now," Polly said. "Go ahead. I was supposed to get a zebra brownie from Andrew but then he got all caught up in the murder."

"He was right behind me." Tab stuck her head out and gave a small wave. "Here he comes."

Rebecca and Andrew showed up at the booth. "What's up?" Andrew asked.

"Where's my zebra brownie?" Polly asked. "And the coffee that was supposed to be ready for Tab? And have you given coffee to all the people out back?" She smiled. "And don't forget to take coffee home for Lexi and Rebecca. You know that will get you into big, big trouble."

He took a notepad out of his pocket. "Never go anywhere without this. You never know when a genius idea or a coffee order will jump out of the air and need a place to land."

Rebecca shook her head. "I need to be home. That family of yours will lose control if I'm not there to keep a firm hand on their schedule."

"Who did you leave in charge?" Polly asked.

"Amalee promised that she'd make sure they didn't escape, but she's too nice."

Polly turned her attention back to Andrew.

"Got it," he said. "Zebra brownie." He held his hand out. "A refill, Polly? Mrs. Ogden?"

Both handed him their nearly empty mugs.

"And Deputy, coffee for you. Do you need anything else?"

"Thanks, I'm eating this cinnamon roll. Polly said I could."

"Great. I'll get those and then whip up coffee for everyone outside. Will they eat?"

"Yes," Tab replied. "Even if there is a dead body nearby. When we announced that Polly found a dead body at Sweet Beans, there was a race to see who was taking this job. We all love Sweet Beans."

"We'll feed them." Andrew pointed at Sal. "Rebecca, please wait. It won't take that long."

"I know, I know," she said. "You're taking care of everyone. When I get you to the house, you'll take care of me. It's what you do." Then she softened her smile and kissed his cheek. "That's why I love you. Don't ever change even if I do get snarky about it."

Andrew beamed as he walked away.

Rebecca slid in beside Sal. "Men are so easy. All you have to do is tell them how much you love them and they're putty in your hands."

"Brat," Sal said. "You aren't wrong, but you shouldn't have that figured out so early in your young life. Andrew isn't going to see it coming."

"What coming?"

"You directing the rest of his life."

"The only thing that I want to do in his life is make sure he does what he loves," Rebecca said.

"And feed you bonbons and bring you tasty coffee ..." Tab said.

Andrew chose that moment to walk up to their table with a tray. He placed a coffee cup in front of Rebecca, then passed out the rest.

"Like I said." Tab looked skeptically at the coffee. "He served you first."

"She kisses me," Andrew said. "I will always serve her first."

"Getting deep," Polly said. "Go take care of the people out back and then get the girlfriend home so she decorates my house."

"Are we doing outside decorations today, too?" Rebecca asked.

"You don't have to," Polly replied. "The boys will all be at the house tomorrow. As long as you have a map of where you want things to go, they'll do the rough and ready work."

"Nice," she said. "I'll work on that later today."

Andrew came back to the table. "Ready to go."

"Everything taken care of out back?"

He glanced over at the counter. "They're on it."

Rebecca handed over the keys to her car. "You drive. I have to think." She stood and took his arm.

"What if I want to think and take notes?" he replied as they walked off.

"They're adorable together," Tab said.

"Sometimes I wonder if they are too normal," Polly said. "They don't often fight. Andrew won't, even when she needs to be put in her place. He lets it roll off his back. Maybe they discuss it after the fact, but I doubt it. He treats her like a princess. It's nice to see her loving on him. She was never much for public displays of affection. I'm not sure why, but I missed a bunch of her life before they moved to Bellingwood. She's willing to hug and she says the words *I love you,* but there isn't much overt physical affection."

"Do you know anything about her father?" Sal asked.

Polly shook her head. "No, and her mother didn't say anything. Sarah gave me some information about him, but when I offered it to Rebecca, she wasn't interested. Maybe she will be someday. When that happens, I'll be right beside her, but for now, she's doing what she wants to do."

"I would be curious," Tab said.

Polly nodded. "I'd like to say I would, but I have Dad's passport and there are European stamps in there that make no sense. Maybe one day I'll do the research, but my life is busy enough right now. I don't need a ton of other people messing in my life because they're somehow related to me."

"What about your mother's family?"

Polly shrugged. "Who knows?"

"I'd want to know, too," Sal said. "I can't believe you are letting this all lie fallow."

"Someday," Polly said. "Someday." She looked at Tab who had finished the cinnamon roll and was in the process of taking a bite of her zebra brownie. "Hey!"

"What?" Tab asked. "Did you get breakfast?"

"Yes."

"Well, I didn't. I'm starving."

"Let me at least have a bite," Polly said. "It's my favorite."

Tab shoved the rest of the brownie in her mouth and stood up. "Patience, my dear. Patience. I need more coffee and I'll bring you another."

Sal shook her head and laughed. "This was supposed to be a quiet morning for me to get some work done. Instead, I've been fully entertained by all the craziness brought on by my friend."

"Me?" Tab asked as she walked away.

"Of course," Sal called after her. Then she looked at Polly. "Are you okay?"

"Because of the dead body out back? I'm fine. I'm waiting for Tab to ask questions. And the last thing I want to do is go home. Rebecca has the place in an uproar. All the kids are on task. She's in charge. Once the house is decorated, it will be extraordinary, but since I don't have to participate, I choose to be out here, doing my thing." Polly frowned. "Rats. She needs those blue Christmas lights that are in my car. I don't want to go home just to deliver those. Can I whine?"

"She just figured it out," Sal said, pointing at the side door where Andrew was coming in.

He stopped in front of Polly with his hand out.

"Keys?" she asked.

"And coffee for Lexi. How could I have forgotten that? Rebecca says you have decorations in the Suburban."

"I'll walk over and unlock it," Polly said. "You get Lexi's coffee. And take her some of those zebra brownies. That will make her happy."

He gave her a quick hug when she stood up. "You're the best."

"Remember that." Polly walked to the door, waved at Rebecca, who was paying no attention, then clicked the button twice, because once was never enough, to unlock the vehicle. Rebecca did hear that. She waved back at Polly, then got out and walked to the front passenger seat. When she saw all that Polly had in there, she waved madly and joyously, grabbing up the packages to take back to her car. If only Polly still had that much energy. Thank goodness she had young people around who reminded her that energy like this was really a thing.

Andrew tapped her arm as he walked toward the door. "See you later?"

"Maybe for dinner," Polly said.

"You should go to the library. It's open and it's quiet."

"But they serve me food and coffee here."

"What was I thinking? See you later."

She waved at Rebecca again and headed back for her friends. Tab had scooted to the inside of the booth and had purchased five zebra brownies. The thing with these brownies? They were not small brownies. Sylvie cut them into four-inch rectangles. Polly was going to roll out of here today.

~~~

A fire roared in the fireplace as Elijah played Christmas carols. He'd asked Teresa to sit beside him on the bench and every once in a while, Polly heard more notes being played than ten fingers could reach. She was much too comfortable to turn around and look, but the thought of the two playing together was enough to make her smile.

Books, games, and quiet conversations around the room as her family wound down from a long day of decorating was a good way to end this day. She knew that the warmth of the fire along with exhaustion from running around this immense house all day had a great deal to do with sleepy, somnolent kiddos.

"Where do I even come up with these words?" she muttered.

Henry looked up from his book. "What words?"

"Somnolent."

He glanced around the room. "You mean, this crowd?"
~~~

"Even Delia. She's nearly passed out over there all tucked into Georgia and Noah. But the word. Why is it in my head?"

"You learned it one day and it fit this room perfectly. Do we need to start them off for bed?"

"Nah," she said. "They don't have big responsibilities tomorrow. The ones who do know what time they need to be in bed. What time are you meeting your Dad and the rest of the crew tomorrow?"

"For what?" he asked, picking the book back up.

Polly couldn't tell whether he was teasing her or not. He had to be. Henry wasn't that irresponsible. She wasn't pushing it. "Oh, nothing. If you all aren't meeting, that's cool."

"It is definitely going to be cold tomorrow." Henry peered over his reading glasses. "You aren't going to poke at me?"

"Not really. I'm feeling torpid."

"More big words. Okay, then. We're all meeting at seven-thirty. I want to get that tree home before lunch. Rebecca texted me that we were responsible for putting the outside decorations up as well."

"I love my girl. She is on it."

"I told her to text Hayden and Heath. None of us can say no to her. They can tell me no, expecting me to bridge the gap, but if she asks, they're sunk. They'll be here. Who gets to put the star at the top of the tree this year?"

"Would you feel good about it being Amalee?" Polly looked over to where she was playing a game with Rebecca and Andrew at the card table.

"That sounds right. Her sisters and brother can help hold the ladder. She's tall enough to make it happen. You know we need to talk about her college soon. No one has said anything yet."

"What are you thinking?"

"I don't know what she's thinking."

"One of these days," Polly said. She pulled her arm out from under the blanket and patted his knee. "It will be fine."

"I'm not worried, I just don't want her to think that we're ignoring the whole thing. Is it too soon for her to leave our family?

What if she went to community college for a year or two so that she can stay home with us?"

"I love you, Henry Sturtz," Polly said. "You want her to get to know us as family, not just as a place to live while her siblings grow up."

"I want that," he said. "I don't care if she even gets a degree. I want her to know that her foundation is safe with us. Do you think she still wants to be a lawyer?"

"I wouldn't hate that. It would be nice to have one of them in the family. Okay, maybe we all talk at Christmas. If Rebecca were nearby for that conversation, it might be a good idea. Those two girls are getting closer to each other, and Amalee feels safe with her."

"Christmas it is, then." Henry took his book back up. "Anything else?"

"I love you."

# CHAPTER FOURTEEN

"How fun is this?" Lonnie Swenson asked. "It's nothing more than entertainment for you, isn't it?" She sat at one of the tables between Marie and Betty and had leaned forward to talk to Polly.

"Watching boys be boys?" Polly asked with a grin. Lonnie was right. It was hilarious to watch all the guys in her life work to heft the massive pine tree into place, smack dab between the two staircases in the foyer. Everyone had an opinion on how it should happen, and no one was really listening to Henry and Heath, who were doing the actual work. Lonnie's husband, Dave, along with Jack had figured out which group to side with and quietly helped slide the tree into place.

It had been two days since everyone was gathered here in the foyer for Thanksgiving dinner, and while they weren't overeating this afternoon, most of the entire tribe was back in place. What a terrific spot for the family to come together. Jessie and Molly weren't here today – they were out shopping. Ella Evans was working with Jason up at Elva's place. She was in the middle of training to do massage for horses. Jason wanted more exposure to that, so the two of them were making a number of horses feel much better today. Especially since Elva had brought in Buddy Ferman, their farrier, to take care of the hooves of her horses and donkeys.

"What in the world?" Betty asked, pointing to the door that led to the living room.

Agnes Hill walked in, followed by the smallest children. She was carrying Mary Elizabeth, Lonnie's youngest, but she, Cassidy, Zoe, and Kestra, had arranged the rest of the children by height. Gillian, James, Delia, Lissa, and Lauren. All of them were dressed in some semblance of elf costumes. Even Agnes wore a bright green cap with a red pompom on it.

"You never know what to expect with that one," Marie said. "She is such a treasure."

"I don't know what I'd do without her. I wonder how anyone makes it through life without an Agnes," Polly said. Then she smiled. "Or a Grandma Marie or an Aunt Betty. You all make it possible for our kids to flourish and thrive."

"That's the truth," Cat said. She put her hand on Marie's back. "I can't believe that we got so lucky to land in your family. Hay and I talk about it all the time." She smiled at Polly. "We talk about you, too. How has this become our reality? Hayden thought he'd end up in a laboratory, alone and lonely for the rest of his life. Then you took Heath in, and he didn't think much about it, except to feel guilty that he hadn't been a very good brother. You wouldn't let him get away with that and gave him space to be a brother, and a kid, and part of a big family."

"Why wouldn't we?" Polly smiled. "Hayden was easy. He was already an adult. He just needed to know that he was loved."

"See, that's what people don't understand. You make it easy to love. You tell us that you love us and that's the end of the story. Nothing changes that with you. No one feels a threat that you will take it away or change your mind. You just love us."

"Anything other than that response is baffling to me," Polly said. "If you have the chance to love, why wouldn't you choose that above all else?"

The front door opened, and Ella came in. She looked around

and whispered something to Rebecca, who was unwrapping a roll of white lights.

"I checked all of these," Rebecca said. "But look. Down there in the mess. One of the strands isn't working. Henry's going to kill me. Let's go talk to both of them."

Polly frowned. That was cryptic and Ella seemed to be in stress. Since Henry and Heath were in the well of the foyer behind the tree as they anchored the base to the wall, she stood and said, "I'll be right back."

Rebecca grabbed Polly's hand as she walked past, dragging her along. At least Polly was doing the right thing by interfering. Andrew followed. He would always be Rebecca's strength. Even when she didn't know that she needed it.

"Heath?" Ella said.

He turned to look at her and before he could open his mouth, Rebecca pushed Ella forward. "Take care of her now, Heath," she said.

He took Ella's arm and the two of them walked through the back doors into the hall.

"What's up?" Henry asked.

Polly shook her head. She didn't know.

"Bad strand of lights," Rebecca said. She plugged them into an outlet. The dark strand was obvious.

"That's what's up?"

"It's what's up with you," she said. "How do I fix this? Aren't the lights next on your agenda?"

"Go into the office," he said. "You didn't move in with a dumb man. There are boxes of lights in the top of the closet. Take your mostly-tall boyfriend with you. He can reach them."

Andrew chuckled. "Mostly tall. That's the nicest thing he's ever said about me."

"Where did Heath and Ella go? I don't want to walk into something," Rebecca said.

"Do you know what was wrong?"

Andrew shrugged. "Could be anything. I know Charlie miscarried last night. Jason could have fallen apart on her. He called Mom to tell her, and she left the house to go over to their house. Charlie's mom is weird about it since they aren't married, so she wouldn't come up."

Both Polly and Rebecca spun on him. Before he could move, Henry took his arm. "And we're just hearing about this now?"

Andrew's eyes skittered back and forth. "Honestly, I figured Mom called you, Polly. She was a wreck. She always calls you. Or she falls asleep wrapped all around Eliseo. I guess that's what she did this time."

"How far along was Charlie?" Polly asked, her heart breaking so hard that she couldn't breathe. They were only kids. This kind of pain shouldn't be happening to people she loved so much.

"Mom said it was less than two months. I don't understand any of it." He looked at Rebecca. "I promise I will figure it out before we need to understand it, but I know Jason and Charlie hurt a lot. I was surprised when you told me he was working today. Mom was going to check on her this afternoon ..."

Ella and Heath came back in. "Sorry about that," she said. "Long day. And then I had to go into the office and help euthanize a lady's dog who was dying. I hate that part of this job. It's better than letting the dog be in pain, but still. The lady sobbed and sobbed and I had to hold her until she could breathe again."

"Why you?" Rebecca asked.

"Doc Jackson is in Illinois. Gone for the weekend. And Doc Ogden was dealing with Horras Jackson's cow. I don't even know what that was about. Mom called me in a panic. She and everyone else can usually deal with the random Saturday afternoon drop-ins, but she couldn't do this. And then, I spent the morning with Jason, who would just start getting all teary-eyed. When he finally told me what was going on, that broke my heart. I should go see Charlie. He said she's alone. But I don't want to."

"I'll go," Polly said. "I need to go."

"Would you mind if I went with you?"

"Not at all."

Rebecca looked at Andrew. "You go, too. I will stay here and keep the men working on the tree. She's your sister-in-law. She needs family. I wish I would have known; I would have invited her over today."

"She probably wouldn't have come," Polly said. "This stuff hurts too much to be around people right away. And Charlie is private. Tell people where I am and ask Cat if she'd be willing to help Lexi set out the food."

"Food?" Henry asked. "More turkey and ham?"

"Nope. Delivery of barbecue is coming at four o'clock. All the fixings. No one is cooking more ham and turkey this weekend." Polly went on through the doors into the hallway. "Didn't want to have to explain myself a hundred times. Rebecca's good at it, she'll make everyone feel like they're part of life in the Sturtz household."

"How do you do this all the time?" Andrew asked. His hand slipped into his pocket. "I feel like I'm never going to be a good human like you. It would never have occurred to me that I should take care of Charlie. That's always someone else's job."

"Is your car out front?" Polly asked Ella. She pointed at Andrew. "I'm not ignoring you. In fact, I have a lot of things to say about the world ignoring what's right in front of them. Not you, but the world."

"I parked on the street," Ella said. "All I could think about was getting to Heath."

"Did he take care of you?" Andrew asked.

"Kind of. He listened and then he hugged me. He can't tell me what to feel or say or anything. That stuff confuses him, but he always tells me he loves me. That's enough for now."

They got out of the house and into the Suburban without any interruption.

"What were you going to say?" Andrew asked from the back seat.

"About what?"

"Seriously? It was like two minutes back."

"You mean the world and ignoring problems?"

"Yeah. I'm writing it down. You always get profound when emotions are high. Note that, Ella. It's what she does."

"I've experienced it before," Ella said with a smile.

"And just like that, she's smiling again," Andrew said. "See what you do, Polly? Now, go on, deliver your wise words."

Polly chuckled. "All I was going to say was that I'm tired of people talking about how society needs to fix this or that. Like society is going to do anything as a whole. The only way to fix society's ills is to do it ourselves. Society won't take responsibility for itself, but we can. We can be kind. We can be generous. We can be gentle. We can be loving. We can watch out for each other. When I hear someone say that the problem with bullies and mental health and suicides and school shootings is a societal problem, I want to ask them exactly who they believe makes up this society we live in. We do. I am the solution. You are the solution. We are the solution. Not some random *they* out there who should be doing all the fixing. You and I need to fix ourselves first. When we do that, things will begin to change."

"Like here in Bellingwood," Andrew said. "You moved into a dying town and instead of seeing it that way, you saw potential. So, you fixed a building. Then, you fixed my mom."

"I what?"

"You encouraged her to become a chef. Then you fixed another building. And suddenly, Bellingwood started fixing itself."

"You're right," Ella said. "I didn't put that all together. Polly, you're amazing."

"Not really, though I guess it looks that way. I didn't do any of it to be amazing or to get accolades. It was the right thing to do. That's something people miss. If it's the right thing to do – do it. No one else will see the problem the same way you do. So, fix it." She pulled up in front of the sweet little house they had renovated after buying it from young Wyatt Post.

Wyatt was thriving in everything once he got to a family who chose to love and support him. Polly saw his pictures on social media because she had wanted to ensure she and JaRon could keep up with his family. She was thankful for a happy boy who had learned to enjoy his life.

"I don't want to walk into this," Ella said quietly.

"Neither do I," Polly replied.

"But it's the right thing, right?" Andrew asked.

"Right. We didn't bring anything with us."

"Mom brought food and blankets," he said.

Polly nodded. "All Charlie needs is a few minutes of love. We won't stay long unless she doesn't want us to leave, okay?" She headed for the front stoop. She remembered the days when they entered through the back and everything in the house was destroyed. From the filth in the kitchen, to the passing of a drunken old lady who lived in her living room. Polly stopped to wonder how many more of those situations existed in Bellingwood.

When the words, *I wish someone would do something about that,* flashed through her mind, Polly nearly burst out laughing at her own inconsistency. She'd call the sheriff on Monday and ask about helping again. She'd been paying off people's heating and electrical bills for years to keep anyone from freezing. No one knew she did that, but it was simply money. She needed to find a better way to invest her time in the community. Lydia would know, too. The woman was all over the place with meals and extra things that families needed. That woman kept her ear to the ground.

The first knock at the door didn't get any response.

"Let me," Andrew said. He entered a text on his phone and before long, a bedraggled Charlie answered the door.

She closed it immediately. "Go away. I'm a mess," she called.

"Texting gets you further than knocking," Andrew said to Polly.

"I'm an old lady," Polly said. "Now how do we get in to talk to her if she doesn't think she is prepared for company?"

"This one is mine," Ella said. This time, she sent a text to Charlie. "I just told her that you weren't going away, and she could either let me in to help her look presentable or you'd break the door down."

"I wouldn't," Polly said.

The door opened, but there was no Charlie.

"She's gone to her bedroom. She says it's too cold to stand out here."

Polly nodded. "She's right about that. I'm not fond of standing out in the cold. You take care of Charlie; I'm heading for her kitchen to put some coffee on. Andrew?"

"I'm going to text Mom and ask what I could do that will help."

"You kids and your phones," Polly said. "I like to use mine to talk to people."

"We talk to people."

"You send messages. I like the talking thing."

"Like you said – you're old."

Charlie and Jason were still working on decorating their home. The two both loved classic decor, well, they loved to go thrifting and then re-building furniture. Charlie had a great eye for it, though she would never admit it. Jason was happy to try new things. Eliseo had spent a lot of time with them, teaching both how to use power tools, what the right finishes were for their projects, and how to find hardware that was reasonable and would last a long time.

The kitchen was painted a pretty, light yellow with golden sunflowers adorning the curtains and tablecloth. A vase with silk sunflowers sat in the middle of the tiny table set into the back nook. This kitchen was nothing like what Wyatt had lived with. They'd replaced the appliances, yet somehow Charlie and Jason had managed to keep a comfortable fifties-era vibe around it all.

The coffee pot was already set for another pot to be brewed, so Polly flipped it on and then opened the refrigerator. It was packed with food. Sylvie had been here. She took out a platter of sweet goodies and set them beside the coffee pot.

"I'm sorry," Charlie said. She was wearing a clean sweatshirt and lounge pants. "It's been a long couple of days."

"Can I hug you?" Polly asked, opening her arms.

Charlie walked right into them and before her head hit Polly's shoulders, her own were shaking with sobs. "I'm sorry. I can't stop crying."

"You get to cry. You have a lot going on. I love you, sweetie."

Charlie stepped back and wiped at her eyes with her sleeves. "We haven't been pregnant that long. I don't know why I let it get to me like this."

"Do you want to be pregnant?"

"We didn't think about it. And we're safe. Really safe."

"Really safe?" Polly lifted an eyebrow.

"Like really, really safe. I'm not on birth control because I hate how it makes me feel, but we're safe."

"Apparently, Jason's stuff doesn't believe in safe. But that's beside the point. Do you want to be pregnant?"

"If it happens, we'll be happy. If it doesn't happen for a while, that's okay, too. We want to get married, but the timing isn't ever right. Mom and Dad don't understand that we're trying to make a life that works for us. They want us to do the same thing they did and live the same way they do. They aren't happy. I want us to be happy. That's more important than doing what everyone wants. Isn't it?"

"I believe so," Polly said, "but you have to live your own life. Are you sad because you were pregnant and now you aren't?"

"I think I am. Doc Mason took great care of me. And Jason, you won't believe how great he was through it all. I know he had to work today, but he didn't want to leave me. He hurts as much as I do. He had just started talking about how cool it would be to be a dad. We were talking about a nursery and all that."

"So, maybe when you're ready to try again, you don't do any more of the safe stuff," Polly said.

"We talked about that too. Are we ready for babies?"

"And the answer?"

Charlie gave her a wan smile. "We are. I am. Jason wants to be a daddy so bad. I know he still worries that he'll be like his father, but you and I know better. He's nothing like Anthony."

"Does he hear from Anthony?"

"Not at all." Charlie looked at her counter. "You made coffee. Sylvie brought the treats over this morning after Jason went to work. I didn't feel like eating anything."

"Do you want us to stay or go? Andrew is worried about you, and he's worried about his brother. He didn't know what else to do but come with me."

"Stay for a little while? I haven't taken a shower, but at least I'm in real clothes. Andrew probably wants a Dew. We have those in the fridge for him. Jason likes having him in Bellingwood. This has been a nice week. Well, except for the broken arm and the house being broken into. Do they have anything on that yet?"

"Not yet. Can you carry the platter into the living room?"

Charlie picked it up. "I'm okay."

"I'll bring the rest. Trays?"

"Down there. First cupboard by the stove."

"Two minutes and I'll be there. Andrew wants to hug you. Ella had to put a dog to sleep after worrying about Jason all day. She needs to hug you, too."

"I can do the hugs. I can't do pity for very long, but I'll do hugs."

"You're a good girl."

Charlie jumped. She set the plate down and took out her phone. "Jason's on his way home. I'm going to tell him you're here and that I'm going to be okay. Don't leave before he gets here, okay?"

"We'll stay. Can Andrew and Ella help with anything else?"

"Like what?"

"Rebecca and Andrew got our house decorated for Christmas yesterday and they're putting up the big tree today."

"I forgot all about that. I want to get it done this weekend, so we have the whole season. I love my little house so much."

"Would you like Heath, Ella, Andrew, and Rebecca to help you tonight?"

"Maybe not everybody."

"Andrew and Rebecca?"

Charlie smiled. "That would be awesome. We haven't had dinner together yet."

"Then invite them over. I'll butt out now, except to bring drinks to the living room."

"Thank you for coming over, even if I did shut the door in your face," Charlie said. "I couldn't believe you were here. I looked like hell. I still look awful, but at least I'm in real clothes."

"You're fine. And I never care what you look like. When you need love, what you look like isn't important."

# CHAPTER FIFTEEN

Ack! Polly woke with a start. Henry was still sound asleep beside her, and the two cats jumped off the bed when she startled them.

"What's up?" he mumbled.

"I don't know. Why are you awake?"

"Better question, why are you awake?"

"I don't know. What's today?"

"Sunday. Go back to sleep."

She looked at the clock. Five in the morning? Why was she awake so early on a Sunday? Then it hit her. This afternoon was a long grind of family photographs in the foyer. For normal people, that wouldn't be a big deal, but all of those people who were here for Thanksgiving dinner and then again yesterday to raise the tree? They'd fill her foyer one more time to be part of the photography spectacle. It was a good thing that Chris and Debbie Johns had been through it all before. In fact, several times before. Her family kept growing and growing, extending the amount of time she had to keep her kiddos clean and in order.

Last night, after everyone left and the foyer was finally finished, she had opened up a group chat and everyone agreed on how today would progress. Everything with the littlest ones, including the immense family photo, would happen first. Then, those without small children would be up for their individual shots. No matter how hard she tweaked it, they would push the limits for some of the youngest.

Church would be great. They always did a nice job during the holiday season. As the first Sunday of Advent, there would be wonderful music, and Pastor Dunlap would include the children in his celebration. Hope.

It was hard for her to think of setting aside time during this season. There was so much to do, but everything told her to take the moments she could to rest and enjoy. The thing was, she did enjoy the busyness of the season.

"Your brain is not going back to sleep," Henry said and turned over. He wrapped an arm around her, pulled her next to him and said, "A half hour. Give me a half hour. Then we can start the day."

"Fair enough." Polly relaxed. Here was the reason she could enjoy the busyness as well as the quiet times. He knew better than she did sometimes what it was that she needed. How had she gotten so lucky?

Most of her friends had good spouses and their lives were in good places. But there were enough people in her interconnected world that weren't nearly as happy. She'd always hoped to have a good marriage, but she hadn't expected this.

Her body began to relax, and she allowed herself to close her eyes, breathe in the warmth of Henry, and sleep.

~~~

Because Polly had Rebecca and other highly organized people in her life, things got interesting before Chris and Debbie Johns arrived at the Bell House. You wouldn't think that Rebecca was that organized with the chaos she lived in, but she was. As soon as they finished eating, Rebecca and Andrew took charge of the kids, getting them dressed and making sure hairs were combed and
~~~

hands were clean. Polly and Henry put down tape marked with everyone's name on the stairway along the right side of the foyer. This was how they were setting up the main photograph. As long as people showed up at a reasonable time, things would be smooth. Families that showed up early were first come, first serve for individual sessions. And Polly didn't care where they chose to take the pictures. But if they needed assistance, she had ideas.

She was setting out the last taped name when the front doorbell rang. "Gotta be the Johns'," she said to Henry. He was already on his way to the door.

The couple knew their business. And they traveled with it all. Henry went through the kitchen, and the next time she saw him, he'd put his coat on and was helping carry in umbrellas and equipment. They were prepared for a long day of shooting.

Bill, Marie, Dick, and Betty were the next to arrive with Jessie and Molly Locke in tow. Molly, a third grader now, was a bit much. Jessie couldn't help herself and spoiled the little girl, making it hard for others to get past Molly's entitlement. Marie was the only adult that Molly didn't pull an attitude with. Marie had long since established that she was to be respected, no matter what. That went for Bill and the other grandparents, too. But even with Polly and Henry, the girl tended to be snotty … about the things she had, the things her mother did for her, on and on. According to Cassidy, she was impossible at school, acting as if she was smarter than everyone else, even those who were in the upper grades.

Cassidy could well be jealous of the attention Molly got from popular girls, but all the same, it was hard to have those two be in the same family and not get along. Luckily, Cassidy had plenty of her own friends. And there was no necessity for her to do anything but be friendly when Molly came to the house. Or, at the very least … absent.

The next group of people to arrive were the Swenson's. Zoe, as part of Cassidy's tight-knit friendship group, had also decided she could be friendly, but absent when Molly was being imperious. She walked in the front door, saw who was there, turned to

Lonnie and asked if it would be okay to find Cassidy. Lonnie was oblivious to the girls' private little ugliness and nodded. She had two baby girls to deal with. If Zoe wanted to spend time with her friend, that was a great idea.

Rebecca and Amalee had brought two of Delia's little chairs to the foyer and adorned them with reds and greens. They'd done the same with two chairs from the dining room. Any configuration for families would be available.

Since Jessie and Molly were here and dressed for the occasion, Marie insisted they go first. It sounded like Molly had something else to do later in the afternoon, so once she was free of this experience, she was ready to be on her way.

Dressed in a beautiful red velvet dress with white fur at the collar and black buttons and belt, she was adorable. A tiara came out of Jessie's bag for Molly's hair. They started with photos of the girl posing in all sorts of different attitudes. Molly tried to tell Debbie how to get her best side when Jessie finally shut her down, telling her that the faster she let them do their job, the sooner Molly could do something else. The problem was that as soon as they were finished, and Molly had seen initial proofs and given her approval, they then had to wait for the rest of the family to arrive for the main photograph. Trickles of people arrived one after the other.

While they waited, Marie and Bill volunteered to have theirs done. Knowing that Marie would also include Molly and Jessie in one of their photos, Polly saw that she was doing her best to keep the volcano at bay.

Jessie was an amazing manager for Henry, so Polly would put up with nearly anything, especially during the holiday season. She was only thankful that the encounters with that young family were fewer than in the past. It wasn't as if Jessie didn't see how her daughter reacted to others, it was more that she had no idea how to curb the behavior. She believed that by giving things to Molly that she'd never had in her own life would make Molly a great person. They could only hope that one day it would all come together.

"I was a little like that," Dick said to Polly in the kitchen. His voice was lowered so only she could hear him.

"What do you mean?"

"Selfish and self-centered. All it took was a beating when I was in second grade. I figured it out."

"A beating?"

"Some kid on the playground. Not my parents," he said with a laugh. "I'd been playing the entitlement game from Day One. Then Billy …" Dick looked off as if in thought. "Hadn't thought of him in years. Billy Dailey. We became best friends in high school. He died when he was much too young. But he beat the heck out of me when I pushed back too hard one day. I was a snotty little thing and I'm pretty sure he beat the next ten years' worth of mucus out of my body with two punches. I deserved it and not a single person punished him. My parents were just grateful they hadn't had to ground me for a lifetime."

"I hope it doesn't take a beating," Polly said. "You know how much I love people, but she makes it hard to like her."

"Make the distinction," Betty said, putting her arms around Dick's waist. "You can love someone and not particularly like them. It's hard when it's an eight-year-old girl. Even Marie gets too much of it and takes her down a peg."

The door opened and the last of the family, Heath and Ella, came in.

"You're here," Polly said, glad to be finished with the conversation regarding Molly. Betty was right. It was difficult for her to not want to be around a child who needed to be handled better, but today was about everybody in her immense family and she needed to let it go.

"We're late," Ella said. "Too many irons in my fire."

"Or," Heath added, "She fell asleep and then I fell asleep and we haven't been awake all that long."

"Good thing I laid out what we were wearing so we didn't have to think about anything other than coming over."

"Come into the foyer. If we're all here, we can organize the massive group, then break up and do shots. Little kids first?"

"Hay and Cat are here?" Ella asked.

Polly nodded. "Not long, but yes. And Lissa is just adorable. James is handsome as they come. I can't wait to see the results from today."

"Am I all together?" Heath asked, looking first to Ella and then to Polly.

"You know," Polly said, "except for the hair."

He shot a panicked look to Ella. "What's wrong with my hair?"

"Beanie hat on your head?" Ella said. "Take it off."

He looked sheepish and took the cap off. "Okay. Do you have your brush?"

"I've got you covered," Ella said. "You want to do it or will you allow me?"

"Will you be nice?" he asked.

"When am I not nice?"

"When you tease me. Polly, make sure she doesn't do something strange to my hair."

"I guarantee nothing. If we need humor in today's photo shoot, you're as good as anyone to provide it."

"I'll do it myself," he said and put out his hand. "Brush, please."

"Honey, I'll be good," Ella said as sweetly as possible.

"And there it is. I don't trust you." Heath snagged the brush from her and ran into the bathroom. Then, he came back, mostly put together. "Fine," he said. "Is it fine?"

Polly went to the intercom system and sent a notification through the entire system. "If you aren't in the foyer yet, now's the time! We're about to do the large family photograph. Haul yourselves, looking gorgeous, like you do!"

She hadn't scheduled any colors or patterns or matching anything today, wanting people to have the freedom to look as good as they could without her input. The beautiful thing was that all the differences highlighted the glory of her big family. She'd thought about white shirts and black pants or jeans, but that didn't allow for any uniqueness. Elijah was thrilled to have a tux. Henry was thankful to wear a jacket over a lightweight dark blue sweater. Noah had a tan suit jacket that he loved. It even had leather patches on the elbows. He was going to be a professor.

Andrew and Rebecca had intentionally matched their holiday plaid. His vest and her skirt. They were adorable. Polly had gone through her own closet filled with beautiful gowns and dresses from the number of parties she'd hosted over the years. There would be another gown this year, but she'd pulled down a dark blue dress from a few years ago and glory be, the color was similar enough to Henry's sweater that it looked as if they planned it.

Cassidy and Zoe were both in pretty black dresses. They'd made their belts from holiday ribbon Polly found at the quilt shop. Caleb and JaRon were in their most comfortable dress-up clothes – bright shirts and dark pants. Caleb had begged to wear shorts, but that was one limitation Polly wouldn't budge on. Long pants for the photo.

Delia had been the most fun to dress up. Polly had several different outfits she'd found online. The girl had an immense wardrobe because Polly couldn't help herself. Maybe she needed to be more understanding of Jessie's relationship with Molly.

Amalee, Teresa, Zachary, and Kestra were dressed in sweaters that matched in style but varied in color. Amalee wanted a bright blue, Teresa chose a deep orange, Zachary loved green, and Kestra's was golden yellow. Amalee asked to pay for photos of just the four of them alone. Polly wouldn't allow that. The photo – absolutely, payment, absolutely not. Anyone who wanted to have a small group photograph taken would have what they wanted. She'd paid for as much time as it would take. And for the kids in her family, she'd pay for any number of pictures.

When they got into the foyer, as people flowed down the left side of the steps – since Polly had blocked the right side at the top, Hayden, Cat, James, and Lissa were in the middle of their session. It was soon over, since the kids couldn't help but be distracted.

Lexi and Gillian came in. Lexi had found a gorgeous pink dress for Gillian. She, too, had gone a little crazy over the adorable outfits available for little girls. There would be several different pictures of those girls in their holiday finery. Lexi wore a dress, which was something people rarely saw. She'd done her hair into an updo with curls around her face. The teal dress was beautiful beside Gillian in pink.

Even the dogs were dressed up. Georgia had gotten a pretty holiday dress, as had Angel. Obiwan and Han weren't up for that, but they still looked festive in holiday neckerchiefs.

Debbie Johns backed up and smiled at Polly. "So far, so good," she said. "Is it time to restructure for the family picture? How many people do you have here?"

"On Thursday, we counted thirty-seven. Everyone from Thursday is back for more family torture."

"Even me," Agnes Hill said. "I see you put me on a chair by the bottom step. Do you think I'm too feak and weeble to make it up any steps?"

"No, I want you where I can keep an eye on you. Did you see where I was standing?"

Agnes was smart enough to look at the spot behind her seat. "Oh no. I have to behave. You and Henry are right behind me."

"Yep. Trustworthy, you are not. Beautiful, you are, though." Agnes was in black pants and had chosen an attractive holiday sweater with a red and green jacket. Her hair was freshly coiffed and she'd added a touch of rouge to her cheeks and a hint of lipstick.

"You likey?" Agnes asked, batting her eyes. "Photos tend to do bad things to me if I don't put a little makeup on. I wash out. Must be that wizened crone thing I have going on."

"Far from it," Debbie Johns said as she shifted Cassidy to stand closer to Agnes at the base of the staircase. "I can't believe you marked where people should stand. This makes things easy, especially with thirty-seven people. Chris, have we ever photographed a family this large?"

"No," he said with a laugh. "We've hit nearly thirty, but this tops them. We'll advertise large group photography next."

There was a lot of noise and laughter as everyone found their places. Chris and Debbie moved several people around, but they stayed close to Polly and Henry's plans. It took nearly a half hour to get the first few photos shot, what with twitching children, poking, prodding, and mischievous behavior by nearly every single person in the group. Because it was the thing to do, silly photos happened as often as serious photos. When Debbie announced that she had three amazing shots without anything going wrong, it was time to let people go about their own business.

Lexi and Polly knew that people would be hungry as the day progressed, but no one wanted another full meal, so they'd set out sliced meats, cheeses, crackers, vegetables, dips, and bread to make sandwiches on two of the long tables. The individual round tables were still set up and they'd put paper plates, silverware, and cups out to ensure that people could snack. There were also plenty of additional bibs and aprons – even for older kids and adults. Polly did her best to ensure clean outfits, but there was only so much anyone could do.

When Elijah spilled on his white dress shirt since she'd made him remove his jacket, he nearly cried. Polly pointed out that it would be covered by the tuxedo coat. He'd wanted tails to flip at the piano, so he'd gotten a jacket with tails. He was a gorgeous young man. Debbie Johns got some amazing shots of him at the piano, and then went with Noah into the library where they took fantastic shots of him in the leather chair with children on the floor as he read to them.

One of the sweetest pictures taken that day was of Heath on one knee as if proposing to Ella in front of the Christmas tree. He'd done it so many times this year, that the shot had to happen. Hayden insisted. The final picture of the day was of Polly and Henry at the top of the steps, looking down at their family in motion around the tree. It had been a fun day of photography for everyone.

~~~

Because their family had been relatively positive and upbeat
~~~

throughout the long day, Henry recommended that they have ice cream and leftover cheesecake, pies, and cakes. The kids had eaten enough of the other food that it sounded like a terrific idea.

Of course, Delia was in heaven at the thought of ice cream. She wasn't prepared to take off the pretty red sweater dress with a tutu attached. And at that point, Polly wasn't prepared to argue. It would be enough if they could get it off her when it was time for bed.

"What was your favorite part about today?" Henry asked the family at the dining room table. By now, everyone who didn't live in the house had returned to their own homes. Andrew and Rebecca were on their way to Iowa City and then back through Des Moines. Sylvie and Eliseo had picked them up as soon as they were finished with photos. Agnes was pooped. It had been a long holiday for her, so after Cassidy and Teresa walked her home, they were back for ice cream.

"It was fun taking pictures with Zoe," Cassidy said. "I wish they lived in Bellingwood. Don't you, Teresa?"

Polly peered at her daughter. This was new behavior. Either Agnes had said something to Cassidy, or she was starting to understand how relationships were built.

"I like her. She's fun," Teresa said. "Today was fun. You have such a big family."

"We are a big family," Polly agreed. "My favorite part was the silliness from you all when we were taking the big family picture."

"Caleb tried to push me off the stairs," Elijah said with a laugh. "Then everyone tried. I had to hold on!"

"To me!" Noah said. "I was going next if he went off."

"We'd have landed on all of you on the floor," Elijah said. "Luckily, I'm strong. All that working out is working for me."

"Are you really working out?" Amalee asked.

"You don't see it because you're upstairs, but I do. Right, Noah?"

"Right," Noah replied. "He's pretty good about it. Except that it happens late at night sometimes."

"I have to work out all the thoughts in my head," Elijah said. "I have a lot of thoughts. Sometimes the only thing I can do is sweat them out."

Henry shook his head and put another scoop of ice cream in Elijah's dish. "Keep eating the food and sweating out the thoughts. I'm glad you didn't fall on us."

"It would have made for a good story," Polly said.

"This is enough of a story for us," Henry said with a smile.

# CHAPTER SIXTEEN

"Oh, Mom! Something is wrong with Han. He's, like, sick or something." JaRon ran into the kitchen where Polly was cleaning up the morning breakfast mess. The kids were nearly out the door for school. What could have happened? The dogs were all here only a few minutes ago.

"Where is he?" she asked, trying not to react to the stress in JaRon's voice.

"The family room. He's shaking. His muscles are doing weird things. And he's crying and stuff. Something's wrong."

That caused her to pick up the pace. She ran into the family room, and it looked as if Henry's dog was in the middle of a seizure.

"Find the rest of the animals. Did he get into something?" she asked.

JaRon didn't move.

"What?" Polly demanded. "Move!"

"But where?"

"Find the other dogs. Caleb, Noah. Do they have their dogs? Are the cats okay? Move, JaRon. Go looking. Don't stand here."

Tears filled his eyes. He didn't often get pushed this hard. It wasn't his fault, but she needed him to kick it into gear. The boy was never speedy about anything, but today, that wasn't working.

Polly pulled out her phone and called Mark Ogden.

"Hey, Polly. What's up?"

"Where are you?"

"I haven't left the house yet. Where are you?"

"I'm desperate for you. Han is having a seizure or something. Can you come over? This is weird. Even for my household."

"I'll be right there."

She knew he would. All Polly could do was sit beside Han, hold him close, and because it's what she would do for any of her children, she wrapped him in a blanket. The shivering and muscle tremors had her pretty upset. His moaning and whining didn't help. Where was Obiwan? Was something going on with Han or had he gotten into something? She had no idea.

Noah came in from the direction of the library, Georgia in his arms. "Mom, JaRon said something is wrong with Han. Georgia is fine."

"Have you seen Obiwan?"

"He was up in Zachary's and JaRon's room all night, but he might be in with Teresa and Kestra. I don't know."

"Go look, would you? I need to see his face and I'm surprised he isn't here with Han. Hurry, please. Tell Caleb I want to see him and Angel, too. If you see any of the cats in trouble, let me know. Where has Han been this morning?"

Noah shrugged. "I have no idea. I don't usually pay attention to him. The dogs are all over the place while I'm getting ready for school."

"Go find Caleb."

What Polly wanted from her family was for them to do what she asked them to do. It wasn't fair, but it was her reality right now.

The doorbell rang on the side porch, and she looked up, then yelled. "Someone get that!"

"Come on, Han," she said. "Calm down. I'm right here. We're

going to take care of you. Please, be all right. I can't explain to Henry right now that you are gone. He won't take it well. Christmas is coming. Please be okay."

Mark walked in. "Crazy morning at the Bell House?"

"A little. Who let you in?"

"I did."

She rolled her eyes. "What's happening to Henry's boy?"

Mark walked around, knelt to his knees and checked the dog that was still having strange symptoms. "This is odd," he declared. "Has he gotten into anything?"

"I don't know," Polly replied.

"How long has he been up and moving?"

"This morning? About five-thirty, when Henry gets up."

"Was he sleeping in your room before then?"

"No," she said, shaking her head. "I don't know where he slept last night. The dogs are all over the house."

"MOM!" That was JaRon's voice.

"Do you have him?" Polly asked.

"I do. We need to get him to the clinic, though."

"Fine. I'll take him in. Let me get this next crisis under control."

"I can take him," Mark said. "It's a slow morning so far."

"MOM!" JaRon yelled again. "It's Obiwan! He's in my bed and something's wrong."

Mark shuddered. "How about you stay here, and I'll go. Han isn't having a seizure, per se; it's something else. It almost looks as if he has been drugged, but that doesn't make sense. Unless you know something you need to tell me."

"I don't, but I will find out."

He bolted out the door and she heard him thundering up the back steps, feeling foolish that she hadn't told him to go through the foyer.

It didn't take long for him to come back down the steps, this time carrying a very out-of-it Obiwan. The poor dog was too old for this kind of activity in his system.

"Cats?" she asked.

"They're rounding them up. You have a problem in the house.

The dogs have gotten into something. Looks like Georgia is okay, but Noah says she hasn't been out of his sight all night. Caleb and Angel are fine. She stays close to him. It's your wanderers. You need to find what they got into. Help me with Han and Obiwan. I'll put them in my truck, and we'll head to the clinic. Come over when you can."

"I can't let him go without me." Polly whimpered as she imagined the fear in her dogs. Obiwan was her heart. How could she let him go when he might die without her being there?

"They aren't going to die. We'll do everything we can. If we don't see you in an hour or so, Marnie will call. Don't panic, Polly. I'm here for you."

"He's my boy." She stared at Obiwan, who couldn't see her through his haze of confusion. Polly couldn't touch him without dropping Han, so she quietly followed Mark through the porch and outside to his truck. He set Obiwan into an open kennel filled with towels and then put Han in a second kennel. Once they were in place, he nodded, got in, and took off.

Polly went back inside where every single one of her children stood in the kitchen, silent and staring at the door. Their best friends were leaving and the look on their faces told Polly that they didn't expect them to return.

Lexi came down the steps with Gillian, who was dressed and ready to go to Marie's house for the day. "What's going on? The house has been quite noisy this morning."

"The dogs got into something," Polly said. "Doc Ogden just left with Obiwan and Han, who are having some weird seizures."

"Nooooo," she moaned. "Was it something they ate?"

"I don't know, but we have to find it. How much time before you all leave for school?" She knew the answer, she just didn't want to think about it. "Fifteen minutes. Everyone …"

The room fell silent, and every eye was on her. This didn't happen often, but she was using it to her advantage right now.

"Get your school bags ready first. I want all of those here in the kitchen, ready to go. Then, spread out. We have to find whatever it is that the dogs ate. Something poisoned them. Even if you think it is the silliest thing, but could be the problem, tell me. Let me decide."

"I will do the pantry and kitchen," Lexi said. "Gillian, sit on the stool. Keep Delia company."

"Elijah and I will check the basement," Noah said. "Right, 'Jah?"

"With ya, bro," Elijah said.

"We'll do this level," Amalee offered. "And our rooms."

"We'll do this level, too," Caleb said. "And our rooms. Is that okay?"

"Perfect. I'm taking the whole house," Polly said. "If you see a cat in distress, call for me."

She did leave the kitchen to Lexi and began in the foyer. They had cleaned up most of the mess from the weekend. The room was beautiful, but that wasn't what she was looking for right now. She pulled things out of trash cans and wiped the tables clear of anything that was paper or plastic. She needed a fresh idea.

"Mom?" Noah stood in the doorway of the kitchen, Georgia by his side. "I think we found it in the basement. It was in Rebecca's room. She won't be mad, will she?"

"Of course not. What did you find?"

He held up a chewed-through trash bag. Poking out of the hole were the stuffed animals that Rebecca and Andrew had brought home last week.

Cassidy walked in. "I found all the cats. They're fine."

"They don't come to the basement," Noah said.

Sure enough, the chewed-up hole was made by dogs. Stuffing and colorful furry fabric poked through.

"Is this all you found?" Polly asked.

"Elijah is picking up the rest. He dumped his laundry basket so he could clean it up."

Polly shuddered. Elijah needed to wash his hands immediately.

"Thank you. Would you ask Lexi for another garbage bag so we can cut down on the exposure? I need to find Elijah." She took off, knowing that Noah would follow through. Polly called her son's name. "Elijah?"

"I'm almost done," he yelled back.

"Drop whatever you're holding and go to the bathroom. Wash your hands. If any of it has touched your clothing, strip to your undies. You're going to be late for school today."

"What did I do?" he asked, coming out of Rebecca's room.

"Nothing wrong, just nothing good. I think that those stuffed animal remains might be poisoned."

He dropped everything to the floor. "And I've been touching it?"

"Exactly. Take another shower, bag your clothes into this trash bag, then get dressed. I'm taking you to see Doctor Mason and then we're going to visit the dogs at Doc Ogden's office."

"Poison?"

"I don't know what, but this isn't good. Hurry, okay?"

He nodded and was unzipping his jeans as he headed for the bathroom. He walked past her and took the trash bag.

"Anything special to you in here?" Polly asked.

"Are you throwing it away?"

"Maybe."

"Then, it's not special to me. I need new jeans anyway. Did you notice that I'm taller?"

"I didn't," she said with a smile. "It's time for you all to get measured again. Maybe we'll do that soon."

"I didn't wear my jeans yesterday. I got to wear my cool tux, but it won't be long. New jeans, Mom."

"You'll have to remind me again after Christmas. Before Christmas, you need to remind Santa."

"I have to write a Christmas letter this year?"

"Everyone does. You might as well get involved."

"Jeans it is." He stripped his t-shirt over his head and tossed it in the bag. "Almost clean, 'Jah," he said to himself. "Almost clean."

Polly took another trash bag, opened it, then wrapped it around the stuffing that Elijah had left behind. She looked around Rebecca's room. The dogs had done an excellent job of shredding those stuffed beasts and spreading the stuffing everywhere. This would take more than a quick morning pickup. She gathered the biggest pieces, then as she left the room, Polly made sure the door was tightly closed. No more entry. Would Henry think she was ridiculous if she put up a quarantine sign until she could get in there and purify it all? Probably, but he'd go along with it anyway.

Heading upstairs, she heard the kids all returning to the kitchen.

"We found it," Polly said.

"I forgot about that," Amalee said, pointing at the garbage bag. "Rebecca was just going to deal with it when she came home. Do you think someone poisoned it? That's why those things went into the dumpster?"

"It's something; I don't know what yet. Are you ready to go?"

With nods all around, Polly took in a breath as they put their coats on and solemnly walked out.

"No Elijah?" Amalee asked, Noah on her heels.

"He got into the stuffing. I want Doctor Mason to check him out. If he gets a day off, he'll not mind."

Noah shook his head. "He'll love it. Lazy bones. I should have touched it. Then I could stay home."

"You'd have had to get naked in front of me," Polly said. She waited for his reaction and received a look of shock. "Just kidding, though he's taken a shower and changed his clothes by now. Lexi, can I ask you to take the girls up to Marie's?"

"I have to change my clothes, but sure."

"I'm running 'Jah to the doctor's office, then heading over with all of this to see Doc Ogden. Maybe he can figure out what is going on with my boys."

Elijah came up the stairs and into the kitchen. "I'm hungry. Since everyone else is gone, can I have another breakfast sandwich?"

"Hungry, normal hungry?" Lexi asked.

"Yeah."

"Do you do this every day at school?" Polly shook her head. This boy was always empty.

"I just buy a bag of chips or something, but yeah."

"Should we be packing snacks for you?"

His eyebrows rose and his face lit into a smile. "That would be awesome! I'd be the best-fed kid in the school. Could you, like, put drinks and stuff into my snack pack, too?"

"Why haven't you asked us before?" Lexi asked.

"Because I just deal with it. No biggie. Sometimes I sneak a brownie or a couple of cookies out of the house, but mostly, I eat food at school. Like I said, not a big deal."

"Save your money for other stuff," Polly said. "You and I will plan snack bags for the week. Wow, I should probably ask the other kids if they're hungry too. You all eat really well in the morning."

"No one eats like I do," Elijah pronounced, holding himself up straight. "I'm unique."

"You are definitely one of a kind. Okay, what do we need?" Polly had rediscovered her equilibrium. It didn't hurt that her twitching, moaning animals were in good hands, better than her own, which was also hard to accept.

~~~

"We need to call Chief Wallers," Marnie said to Polly. "Something was in those stuffed animal horrors."

"Something what?"

"Something poisonous to dogs. Mark thinks it might be ketamine, but he's sent it off for more tests."

"The Christmas store is bringing drugs into Bellingwood?" Elijah asked, swinging his right leg back and forth after crossing it over his left leg. "They tried to drug me?"

"They didn't try to drug you. They didn't expect anyone to steal those stuffed animals. That's why they sprayed paint all over them," Polly said. "And you weren't drugged. Doctor Mason says you are clear."

"You're going to make me go to school, though, aren't you." He dropped his shoulders in a dramatic show of defeat.
~~~

"Not if you want to come home and help us clean the mess up from the weekend." Polly still couldn't believe how busy the weekend had been. And the next few weekends weren't going to be much better. This weekend was the Girl's Rule party on Saturday afternoon. She had tried to get out of hosting it, but finally gave up. All she needed to do was post guards at the entrances to the rest of the house. My goodness, but people crossed boundaries. Why they thought that her home was open to inspection, she didn't know, but those women acted as if she wasn't really a person, and her family was nothing more than a group of actors on set.

"I'll clean," he exclaimed, then looked at Marnie. "I'm the worst cleaner in the house. Just ask Polly."

"He's right," Polly agreed. "But he knows how to put things in trash bags."

"No I don't. You say that all the time. I don't know how to put anything in a trash bag."

Polly scowled at him. "Okay, then. Back to school for you."

Mark walked into the exam room. All Polly wanted to do was hold her dogs and take them home. She stood up.

He waved her back to her seat and hitched a hip onto the exam table. "The boys will be fine, but we're going to keep them here overnight. Pick them up in the morning. This should have passed by that point. Ketamine is a sedative, though too much does what you saw. They'll sleep it off and then they can go home."

"Will they get addicted?" Elijah asked.

Mark chuckled. "No. They'll be sleepy, but before you know it, back to normal for both of them. How are you doing, Polly?"

"I want to hug my boys. Can I?"

"Of course," he said. "Follow me."

"I'll call Chief Wallers," Marnie said. "Does he need Polly?"

"He knows where to find me." Polly practically pushed Mark through the door. "Take me to my dogs. Right now."

"Got it." Mark pointed at a large kennel off to the side where the two dogs were snuggled together. "It's okay for them to share a kennel, right?"

She turned back, her eyes filled with tears. "I want to climb in with them."

"You can, but I don't recommend it. They've had some trouble with accidents. We're cleaning up after them as fast as possible, but …"

"I know, I know," Polly said. She sat down in front of the kennel. "Obiwan," she whispered. "Han. I'm sorry that I put you in danger. I'm glad you're okay. One more day and you'll be home where everyone will shower you with kisses and snuggles." She tucked her hand between the bars of the kennel. Mark would have opened it, but she hadn't given him time. The dogs weren't making nearly the same noises they had at home, for which she was thankful. Occasionally, one or the other would twitch, but they were here and safe. Mark promised they would be fine. That's all that mattered. "I love you two," she said. "I'll be back in the morning to take you home. Until then, sleep the time away."

With a heavy heart, Polly stood. "I don't want to leave them, but I know it's the right thing to do."

"You can come back any time." Polly jumped at Marnie's voice. She had missed Mark walking out and Marnie walking in.

"I'd better not or you'll have to put a cot in here for me tonight. They have each other. That should be enough for one night."

Marnie nodded. "Someone will be here all night, too."

"I know. Okay, I need to get out before I'm out of control. Tell Chief Wallers that I should be home all day if he wants to talk to me. I have to clean up the bedroom where they ripped up those toys. I'm going in with bleach and ammonia."

"To create mustard gas?" Marnie asked with a laugh as she closed the door behind them.

"Right? But there won't be a sign of ketamine. Rebecca's blankets and sheets will be washed, and I'm scrubbing the floor and washing walls. Everything. The good news is that she hasn't unpacked all her things after moving into the new room, so what's in boxes doesn't need my attention. After Christmas break, I assume the entire room will be filled with Rebecca's organized chaos."

"I miss having Ella's stuff lying around," Marnie said. "Barrett's stuff, too, but he still lives there when he comes home. Ella is a visitor now. It feels strange, but they grow up and there's nothing we can do about that."

Polly nodded. "I don't like it. Henry and I talked about Amalee last night. We're going to figure out her college plans over Christmas break, but we want more time with her at home. We want her to feel like we're family. It took time with Hayden, and it will take time with her. The younger ones are already falling into the family's patterns. In fact, the other day, Kestra started to call me Mom, but caught herself."

"That's wonderful."

"It feels good, but in her own time. I want Amalee to feel that comfortable with me. We're going to have trouble letting her go very far away until I know she'll come back."

"They always come back," Marnie said. "Don't they?"

"Yes," Polly said. "As long as they are loved."

# CHAPTER SEVENTEEN

Sometimes calling her husband had a calming effect on Polly. Other times, she didn't want to land the horrors of the day on him. "Henry?" Polly hated having to make this phone call, but here she was.

"You sound stressed. Things okay with the kids?"

"It's Obiwan and Han." That stopped him. He said nothing for a moment. "What happened?"

"Those stuffed things that Rebecca and Andrew brought back. The dogs got into them and there was something in the stuffing. I don't know how much or what, but JaRon took me to Han, who looked like he was having a seizure of some sort. Then, we found Obiwan in the same way. Mark came over and took them to the office. The other two dogs are fine. Elijah went downstairs to clean up the mess, so I took him to see Doctor Mason, just in case he was contaminated, too."

"And?"

"Elijah is fine. He'll stay home today with me so I can keep an eye on him."

"Okay. You aren't going to work?"

"No. I'll call Kristen and then I can work in the office at home."

"And the dogs?"

"Mark wants to keep them today and tonight. Is that okay?"

"It's fine. Are you okay?"

"I felt a little murderous when I realized they were poisoned, but I'm getting over it."

"Maybe the boy whose body you found was murdered for you."

"Henry!" she said, scandalized. He never said things like that.

"Apparently, I'm feeling a little heated about the same thing. So, no big dogs in the house tonight. Would it be silly of me to check on them today?"

This was another reason she loved this man. He wasn't too macho to admit his love for his kids and the animals that lived in his house.

"It would be wonderful if you did. I'll likely go over once more before they close, just so I can take something for their overnight. Like a blanket or pillow with our scent on it."

"You're as smoochie as I am about this stuff," he said.

"No, sweetheart, you're as smoochie as I am. You surprise me sometimes."

"Yesterday was a good day. In fact, the whole week was a pretty good week. Even with a broken Andrew, and squatters in his house, and all the other craziness. I like having holidays with you. And that you have figured out how to pull thirty-seven people into our lives and make a day of photography work out, I'll never understand, but I'm grateful that you care enough to do it."

"The pictures I saw glimpses of were wonderful. I think the family's phones were all snapping away, too, so they have an idea of what things will look like when the Johns' finally get proofs to us. I can hardly wait."

"Honestly, I can't wait either."

"I've asked for the large family photo to be done first. I need to order Christmas cards."

"Won't you be sending them to the people in the picture?"

She laughed. "Probably. It's what I do. But we have other friends."

"Okay. I hear you. How are you doing now?"

"Now?"

"After downloading at me."

"I'm okay. What about you? I gave you weird news."

"It's part of my weird life. I'm not happy that you had to deal with it alone, but I'll let Mark know how glad I am that he was around for you. That means the world to me. We live in an amazing neighborhood."

"We really do. The vet, the principal, the interesting people. We're all that, aren't we."

"Just think, one day, across a field, Heath and Ella will have purchased a big lot and will need all of our kids to spend time over there. We'll just sit home in front of the fire and eat bon bons and drink wine."

"You're starting to get weird," Polly said.

"Then it's time for me to go back to work. I'll talk to you later."

"I love you. Thanks for not freaking out."

"Freaking out is for wimps and young men who are too stupid to see that the person they love the most doesn't need to be changed. She is changing the world and the best thing to do is cheer her on."

"You are your own world-builder," Polly said. "Tell me you love me."

"I love you, Doodle." He chuckled as he ended the call.

Polly turned off the Suburban. She'd been in the garage for the last few minutes of the call.

When she got inside, Elijah had dropped his head to the counter of the island where he sat. Lexi was working on something in front of him and grinned at Polly.

"Ready to go, 'Jah?" Polly asked.

"Where?" he moaned at her.

"I don't know. The living room? The family room? Your room? Whatever you want. I'm not driving you to Boone. You get a day off."

"Noah got one two weeks ago and I get one today? Really?" His head had shot up and he leaped down and threw his arms around her. "You're the best mom ever."

"I want you to check in with me," Polly said. "I worry about you and want to keep an eye on things. You know. Just in case."

"I'm high on drugs?" he asked.

"That."

"I'm high on life," Elijah replied. He jumped up and down. "And I don't have to go to school." Then, he stopped and thought about it. "I hope I'm not missing anything. I need to look at my schedule. It would be bad if I was missing out and having the time of my life doing something else."

"FOMO," Lexi said. "Fear of missing out."

"That's me," Elijah said. "I'm always afraid I might miss something. Oh well, life goes on." He flitted out of the kitchen and down the hall.

"And to the living room, he goes," Polly said. "I was hoping he'd take a little longer to get there. I have things to do, but one of my favorite ways to relax is in front of the fire while he plays. I hope he doesn't run out of energy to play for me later."

"What's on your hitlist now?" Lexi asked.

"Cleaning Rebecca's bedroom. I need gloves and whatever else will ensure that no animal comes in contact with whatever was on those stuffies."

"Bleach?"

"Maybe. Do we have extra rubber gloves around?"

Lexi gave her a scornful look. "Do I have extra gloves? Come on, girl. You know me. I have extra everything." Then, she frowned. "Except eggs. I don't think I have extra eggs. I need to go out to the warehouse and see what is hiding in that refrigerator. You know what would be wonderful? If we had a camera bot on each of the freezers and refrigerators, so I could check stock whenever I was curious."

"Because walking to them takes too much time."

"Is that comment because I mocked you about extra gloves?" Lexi asked with a grin.

"Maybe. I'll make you a deal, though. If you don't make me look for the gloves, I'll head downstairs and go out to the hinterlands under the garage and check the fridge for you."

"Gloves it is," Lexi said.

While Polly gathered cleaning supplies and trash bags from the pantry, Lexi headed for the cupboards on the porch. They met in the kitchen and Polly headed for the basement. She dropped things in front of Rebecca's bedroom door, then wandered to the old moonshiner's office and the tunnel door. It was pretty cool beneath the ground, but at least it wasn't freezing.

The amount of canning Lexi had done last fall graced shelves lining the room where Polly had discovered jars of old moonshine. The kids had once thought it would be a great playroom, but they had better things to do these days, so food storage it was. Polly opened the refrigerator and chuckled. Milk, eggs, butter, and even soda pop filled the shelves. She took a quick photograph and sent it on to Lexi with, *"What do you want me to bring in?"* as the text.

*"Eggs! We have eggs? I need three dozen and I'll take three pounds of butter and two gallons of milk. Is that too much?"*

*"I'm strong,"* Polly said. *"On it. Now you know what you need to purchase next, right?"*

*"I didn't realize I was in such good shape. I'll start the list now."*

One of the other things that Lexi was organized about was toting food throughout the house. Polly found empty grocery bags stuffed in a large open jar and filled them with the food she was taking inside. Rather than going back through the tunnel, she took the steps up into the garage and headed for the freezer and third refrigerator they had here. Henry found all sorts of things to reclaim when renovating houses. He was certain they could one day line the walls of the garage with all the freezers and refrigerators homeowners wanted to be rid of.

She took a photo of the contents of each appliance and then headed back into the house, surprising Lexi when she came in through the porch.

"I should have done this myself," Lexi said.

"It's good. You're good. You have a lot going on."

"It isn't as bad this week. In fact, I'm making beef and noodles for tonight. I want to try to make my own noodles. If they stink, I have store-bought, but this could be fun."

"I didn't bring any flour back with me," Polly said. There were at least five ten-pound bags of flour on the shelves down there.

"I have enough up here for now. What with all the baking I did last week, I overstocked the pantry."

"So, now I can leave you to it? Oh, wait. Here are photos of what's in the garage."

"I need to assign this task to JaRon. He'd love to keep inventory."

Polly smiled and headed back to the basement. She needed to clean up the mess as soon as possible because if she didn't, she wouldn't stop thinking about it.

~~~

Elijah had started a fire by the time Polly had her laptop in hand. She could have sat in the office, but it was much more pleasant to hang out while he practiced. And he didn't mind. If he was focused on something and didn't want people to hear him going over repetitive motions, he was able to tell them, but for the most part, he enjoyed the company as much as they enjoyed just being in a warm space with music in the background.

She pulled a blanket across her legs, set a pillow on them, and leaned back against the arm of a sofa. Perfection. Polly had spent at least an hour in Rebecca's room and brought all of her bedding and anything else up to go through the washing machines.

Adding machines upstairs had been a huge benefit. Sheets and comforters were done in the nearly industrial size machines in her bathroom, while the kids got used to running their smaller loads through the apartment size washer and dryer in the bathroom next to Delia's bedroom.

Since Lexi was in and out of Polly's bathroom, that meant that Polly spent a few extra minutes in the mornings, making sure the
~~~

bedroom was neat and tidy, if not always cleaned to a sparkle. The funny thing was, that by the time Lexi was finished with laundry, Polly's room sparkled and so did Delia's. Lexi was a treasure, for sure.

"What do you think, Mom?"

She looked up, startled. "About what?"

"About that motif?"

He knew the word *motif*? Of course he did. "Play it again," she said, hoping to gain some sense of what he was asking.

Elijah repeated the bit of music for her. "Do you recognize it?"

"I don't. What's it from?"

"I don't know what to call it yet."

"You composed that?" She turned to stare at him.

"That's what I've been working so hard on lately," Elijah said. "You know I told you I was working on something a couple of weeks ago."

"But you never followed up. I didn't know what you were doing."

"I talked to Mister Specek and Brandon and they're helping me. I can't tell you what it is right now or what it's about or anything, but if it happens, it's going to be so cool."

"When do you want it to be finished?" Polly asked.

"It's my Christmas present. You can hear it in pieces, but I'm not going to explain anything until Christmas morning. I really hope I can pull this off."

"Are you writing it all?"

He nodded and came over to sit beside her on the sofa with pages of manuscript paper in his hands. "See what I've done? Mr. Specek is helping me learn how to write music on paper. I can play it and record it, and now I can write it down like a real piece of music."

"You know that anything you play is real, right?"

"But I could, like, publish this."

"You could and you should. Do you want to be a composer?"

"I want to do it all. Everything. I want to write music and play music and direct music and I want to do everything. Jazz, pop, rock, classical. I don't want anyone to ever tell me that I can't do something. Does that seem unfair?"

"It seems like you. I'm very proud, you know."

"I want it to be something to be proud of. Mr. Specek says I have a good start. I just have to get it done in the next month. Brandon said the next thing we should do is write a cool duet together." He scooted closer and she moved her legs off the sofa so he could get a hug. "Mom, I have the best life. I really do."

Polly put her arm around him and let him lie across her chest. As he sank into her, his breathing slowed, and he relaxed. "I'm so grateful to be able to give you this life. You make me proud, my sweet Elijah. You have talent that never stops."

"But sometimes I need to stop, right? My teachers at school talk about burnout to me sometimes. Like I push too hard."

"Do you feel like you push too hard?"

"Maybe. I want to do everything."

"Is any of what you are doing right now too much?"

"Sometimes it's nice to take a day off from it all."

"If I thought you would be honest with me, I'd let you talk me into a few personal days throughout the year, but you have to promise to not abuse that privilege."

"I promise," he said solemnly. "When I really need it, you'll know. If I'm teasing, you can always tell, right?"

She hugged him close. Elijah ate up this kind of loving. He'd never leave if she allowed it. "I can tell when you're teasing, but if you're serious, you let me know. Let's start with two optional days before spring break. No more than that."

"Does this one count?"

"Nope, I made the decision for you today because I want to keep an eye on you. I called in a sick day for you, that's all that matters."

"I love you, Mom. Sometimes I think that I've died and gone to heaven. Then, I wake up to a dog slurping my face. It's either heaven or reality. Doggie slurps are gross, so I figure it's reality."

"You're a good kid. Tell me more about that motif you were playing?"

"I love you, but you can't get me," he said. "I'll tell you Christmas morning. You'll be the only one to recognize it and know that I've been thinking about it for a very long time. Right?"

"I love that you trust me with yourself, 'Jah," Polly said. "I want you to always feel safe with me."

"I do. This is really comfortable," he said. "If I fell asleep right now, neither of us would get anything done."

"Would it matter?"

"I don't know. What are you working on?"

"Sycamore House numbers. They're boring. Do you need a nap?"

"I'm sleepy."

That bothered her a little, but there was no reason not to let him rest and relax. "We'll take a short nap like this. If I can't wake you up, though, we're going back to the doctor."

"I didn't sleep last night," he said. "I kept thinking about the music and how I was going to write it. Doctor Mason said I didn't take any drugs."

"He also told me to keep an eye on you. But if you're right here, I can keep an eye on you, no matter what."

Elijah snuggled in a little tighter and Polly pulled her legs up to keep him from falling off the sofa. She wished she could send a picture of this to Henry, but the description would have to be enough. After putting her phone and laptop on the floor, she scooted forward so her head hit the pillow.

"Hey," he said. "Quitcher movin."

"Hey," she replied softly. "Sorry. Go to sleep."

Polly felt him relax even more. She took the music out of his hand as he drifted off, and looked at his small, neat notation. Len Specek was doing him a world of good. He'd be prepared for college and wherever this musical life took him. She set it on the table behind the sofa and then picked it up again. He'd be sad if he knew that she cheated. He'd held his finger over a note that he scratched in a corner when he showed it to her.

Of course. The motif he had played was how he perceived Henry. This was Henry's steady, loving, strength as the heartbeat of the song. Mostly in the bass clef, but some of the notes crossed into the treble, as Henry soared. Tears flowed down her cheeks. Her boy really did hear the world through music, and in so doing, he translated his life into a different world. One that very few would fully understand, but one that lived within his mind. How had she managed to capture someone with such incredible insight?

By being open to whatever was set in front of her. Each of her children had these glorious lives ahead of them. All she needed to do was make sure they felt confident as they moved forward. That was something she didn't fear. She could do this. Polly tapped the music as she set it back on the table. She could do it because of the support she cherished from those around her. Henry was her first line of strength. After that, it branched out everywhere.

# CHAPTER EIGHTEEN

Polly was up early again. Man, she hated not being able sleep until it was time to get up. This morning, all she could think of was that her dogs would come home as soon as she could get to them. She didn't care as much about work as she did about her two boys waiting for her. They were never away for any long period of time. But at least Obiwan and Han were together.

Henry had stopped in to see them before coming home from work. Polly couldn't bring herself to go back again. She would have been unable to leave and asked to crawl in to sleep with them. That might have been better sleep than she got last night.

Kids were starting to stir, and Noah was the first upstairs. He yawned. The boy hadn't showered or put on his school clothes yet.

"What's up?" Polly asked.

"It was weird without Obiwan checking on us last night," he said. "Elijah's awake, too. We didn't sleep well. Georgia thought it was weird. She was up and down on my bed all night."

You wouldn't know it from looking at her, all bright-eyed and bushy tailed. Noah walked over to the sliding glass doors and opened it. She didn't want to go outside; it was cold enough to send a chill into the kitchen. But she was a good girl and headed out. He stood and waited for her.

"What would you like for breakfast?" Polly asked.

"Three-egg omelet, hash browns, toast, and pancakes," Noah muttered.

"I can do some of that. Which would suit you best?"

"We just had pancakes last week," he said, almost disappointed.

"So you want pancakes? Sausages? Bacon?"

"Really?" he asked.

"Why not? I'm up and it's easy. Do you want to help me with the bacon?"

Georgia had come back in, and Noah padded across the kitchen floor to the pantry where dog food was located. The dog knew what was coming next and waggled her little bottom while she followed him.

"Frozen?" he asked.

Polly chuckled. "I have no idea. Let's see what I have and where we have it." She opened the refrigerator again and took out milk and eggs. "Can you snag the flour and sugar for me?"

He left Georgia to her food and brought Polly what she needed from the pantry. Being the amazing son that he was, he went out onto the porch and opened the freezer. "Two pounds of bacon?"

"Your brother is awake. Better make it three." Polly couldn't believe how much bacon her kids went through. They'd finally started purchasing their meat from a local locker. The bacon was much better, which meant that the kids loved eating it whenever it was served.

He peeled back the wrapping on the packages and set them in the oven, before turning it on to warm. Polly just watched. Whatever he was doing, it made sense to him. One by one, he set up three cookie sheets with racks, then opened the large side drawer that held spices and other small containers. He took out the baking powder, baking soda, and then the vanilla and handed them to Polly.

"Just how long have you been hanging out in the kitchen?" Polly asked with a grin.

"Dad does things, so I watch."

"How long on the bacon to defrost?"

"Not long, I need to be able to separate the pieces. Do you care if I cut them in half? It makes it easier to eat."

"You do you. I appreciate it."

Elijah was the next one to come upstairs. He had showered and fluffed out his hair. "I don't think I want braids," he said. "I want a haircut, though. I'm better looking with a close cut. Noah, you should totally grow out your hair. It's so soft."

"How do you know it's soft?" Noah asked.

"Because I just know. There are things you shouldn't ask your best brother ever."

"Why should I grow it out? I like it to be easy."

"Because you'd look good," Elijah said. "Right, Mom?"

"I think you're both very good-looking, no matter how you style your hair," Polly said. "You want dreads, do dreads. You want braids, do braids. If you want corn rows, do that. I don't care. You know who will do the work for you. Tell me when you want an appointment and I'll schedule it."

"I need a haircut is all," Elijah said. "Can I get it on Saturday? This long-hair idea stinks and I need to make it stop."

"No afro for you?" she asked.

"Not today."

Noah pushed the three trays of bacon into the oven. "'Jah, would you mind taking these out when the beeper rings? I need a shower."

"Okay," Elijah said. "I was going to …"

Polly shot him a look, effectively shutting the boy down.

"Yeah. I've got it."

"If I let Georgia out one more time, will you let her back in?"

Instead of a retort, Elijah just nodded after holding Polly's glare. "Sure."

"Thanks." Noah let the little dog out now that she had finished her breakfast and then ran down the steps.

"I was going to go play," Elijah muttered.

"You can help your brother once in a while," Polly said. "Keep an eye on the dog. She won't be out very long. He doesn't ask for much. You can say yes and not think about your own things all the time. He is always making your life easier, even when you don't pay attention."

"I know. You're right," Elijah wandered over to the sliding glass doors, opened them, and stepped back when Georgia sped inside, headed for the stairs, and ran to find her best friend. "That was easy."

"It usually is," Polly said. "People don't often ask you to do their hard tasks. Sometimes they just need a little space to get through the next few minutes. Saying yes means that they relax and you can be a hero."

"Superhero, you mean," Elijah said, flexing his muscles.

The two of them nearly jumped out of their skin when a knock came at the back door. Not a doorbell, but a sharp rap.

"Who's here at this hour?" Elijah asked. "It's not even seven o'clock yet."

"Go look?"

"What if it's a mauler?"

"Then you will be mauled, and I will call the police." Polly turned off the mixer and walked to the porch. She squealed when she saw who it was.

Mark Ogden smiled and waited for her to unlock the door, allowing two very happy dogs to race in and greet her with kisses and wagging tails.

"What did you do?" she asked him.

"I know you. I know your dogs. I had to pick up some meds at the clinic before I left for the day, so I figured that I could release them and bring them home where they'll be happier than staying in the kennel."

"And you made me happy, too." Polly stood up and gave the surprised man a huge hug. "Thank you. For this, I will do anything except bow down and kiss your feet. Those boots look like they've been through it."

"Which is why I'm not coming any further inside," he said. "The boys gave me such pitiful looks this morning that I couldn't leave them there. This is better for them anyway."

"No problems through the night?"

"None at all. They've had enough sleep that they might be very active today. Or they might need more time to sleep. Who knows with these two. Did you hear anything from Chief Wallers yesterday?"

She shook her head. "Not yet. I'll give him a call later. Are you sure it was ketamine?"

"Absolutely. Talked to the Chief and he said that one of those stuffies was soaked in it. Sounds like something broke in its belly."

"Great," Polly said. "I'm glad the dogs got a small dose, then. I couldn't handle anything more than what I saw yesterday."

"It's scary seeing them out of control, unable to tell you what's going on." Mark saw Polly give a shiver. "I'm out of here. Warm up, love the pups, we'll talk later."

"Thank you! Everyone was out of sorts without them last night. Today is a good day." She waited until he was in his truck before turning back to the kitchen. "Have you eaten, boys?"

Elijah looked at her. "I should have answered the door."

"What do you mean?"

"You just talked to me about making life easy for other people and then I argued with you. I will never learn, will I?"

"You're fine. And look who is home. What do you think about feeding them?"

"I will. And I will do anything you ask. I'm sorry."

"First of all, don't make crazy promises," Polly said. "You're okay. You are learning about how life works. It's my job to help you with that. I'm not upset, just sharing life lessons. And if you're in the middle of feeding the dogs when the timer on the bacon rings, guess what?"

"What?"

"I'll open the ovens and take out the pans. Life is shared responsibility. We all take part."

~~~

Polly was in her office at Sycamore House when Ken Wallers walked in. She stood to greet him, and he waved her back into her seat. "Surprised you're here today," he said. "I saw your Suburban and decided to stop in rather than call you. You've talked to Doc Ogden?"

She nodded and smiled. "He brought the boys home to me this morning; he's my hero. Said he was certain it was ketamine. What the heck?"

"I talked to the couple who are running that Christmas pop-up. They seem to know nothing about it. They gave me all their shipping invoices and those holiday stuffies were on none of them. Everything was in order. No extra invoices, no missing inventory. In fact, they claimed to have never seen anything like those animals."

"And the young man who was killed?" Polly asked. "The one who worked with him?"

"He was hired in Chicago and was supposed to work until Christmas day. They were complaining about being short-staffed now. The place isn't that busy, but maybe it will pick up now that Thanksgiving is over."

"Any fingerprints on any of the stuff I gave you?" Polly asked.

"Some, but they're pretty messy. However, there were prints from spray paint on the dumpster where the stuffies were tossed. All belonging to the dead boy."

"I get that he was involved with drugs, but really? Who brought this into Bellingwood? You know, Rebecca thought he was a little sketchy, but I didn't pay attention to it. Did she give anyone his business card?"

Ken frowned. "His business card?"

It was Polly's turn to frown. "Wait. Maybe I have it. We went in there the day they opened."

"I've heard about your decorating prowess."

"Rebecca's decorating prowess. That girl is amazing. I thought
~~~

I loved it, but she has turned it into some crazy passion. And she's so disgustingly happy while she decorates that it gets everybody else on board. Somehow, she managed to get Heath and Hayden, Henry, Jack, and the older boys to hang all the outside lights on Saturday, covering every floor of the house, the fence line, the garage, and the bushes out front. They just did it."

"Nothing on the rooftop?"

"Henry said he thought it was gaudy, so she agreed. The littles loved it, but he was right. He always is. We can be the elegant house without big blow-up Santas and reindeer on the rooftop."

"Your neighbors? I haven't driven down through that neighborhood yet this year."

"All of the decorations," Polly said with a laugh. "There are snowmen and Rudolphs and lights galore and it's a regular draw on the energy company every night. Pretty fantastic. What about you guys?"

"I do lights around the windows and doors. Maude loves to decorate the tree. We haven't done it yet this year, but one evening, she'll have everything ready for us to go and we'll drink hot chocolate and eat cookies and decorate. It's a party. The girls always loved it; we still do."

"I love Christmas traditions," Polly said. "I'd probably be the person who built one for every day of the season, given the chance. Then, I'd be exhausted and not want to think about Christmas again for a year. It's better this way."

"How are things going with the new kids in your family?"

"Good?" She wondered why he asked. "Have you heard something?"

"No. Maude says Zachary is a happy little boy. The older girl, what's her name?"

"Amalee in high school or Teresa?"

"Teresa," he said, nodding. "Maude says she doesn't fit in quite as well yet."

"We're working on it," Polly agreed. "I think the loss of her family has hit her hard. Zachary and Kestra are young enough that they bounce pretty well. She's right at that age – eleven –

when drama and emotions battle for control of her sanity. She lost her father, then her mother, and now her grandmother. We added Thanksgiving traditions that she asked for. They were perfect, but she needed continuity. She's mentioned family Christmas traditions, so I'll press for what those are and see if we can't blend them into the family, too."

"She seems like a sweet girl. I really miss out when new kids move into town and are older than third grade."

"It's happening more often," Polly said.

"I miss a lot by not interacting with all the kids at one point in their lives. I am grateful for all I've gotten to do with Maude's classrooms over the years. I have a better relationship with the town because of it."

"All you can do is keep doing what you do. When will Maude retire?"

"Hopefully not for many more years. Her job gets harder all the time, but she still loves the kids. And with Mr. Gordon in place, she likes the administration better than she has in a while." He nodded. "Another family from your neighborhood, right?"

"The Gordons? Yep. I like them both. He's a good man. We're lucky to have him."

"We're lucky to have a lot of good people in this town. Did you have that business card?"

Polly shook her head. "I'm an idiot. Just a second. This is about to get ugly."

"Ugly, what?"

She dumped the tote bag on her desk. "This. I'm used to it, but it still freaks me out that I'm unable to contain my world into a wallet and my pockets."

"Is that a diaper?" he asked. "You don't have anyone in diapers."

"Cat does," Polly said. "Who knows when you need a diaper." She dropped it into the trash can. "I am so sorry about this."

"It's a bit out of control."

"A bit? I'm out of control, but at least everything that should be here is probably here. This is my catch-all." Polly shook her head.

"I can't believe I'm doing this in front of the chief of police. You have been demoted from big-time cop to a dad who has to watch a woman empty her purse." Then something familiar poked its corner out from behind a stack of musical flash cards. Where did those come from? "Here we go. Mike Little." She passed it across the desk. "I don't need it any longer. It's yours."

"Not sure what I'll get from it, but thanks." Ken tapped the card on the top of her desk. "I will let you get back to it. Looks like you should straighten things up before they go back in the bag."

Polly laughed. "Thanks, Dad."

"I'm sorry. It makes me laugh."

"Let me know if you need anything else," she said, about to shove everything back into the tote bag. She stopped herself and watched him leave.

As soon as he was gone, Jeff Lyndsay stood in her doorway. "I thought he'd never leave."

"How long have you been here?" Polly asked.

"Not long. I checked with Stephanie, Kristen, and Rachel to make sure I wasn't too far behind and now I'm here." He walked around the desk and bent in to hug Polly. "Thank you for pushing me. I'm sorry that I didn't call you and let you know what was going on, but things kept moving and moving and the next thing I knew, we were on a plane back to Des Moines. Time went fast out there."

"I knew you'd let me know if there was a problem. It's good to see you. How was the trip?"

Jeff walked back around the desk and sat in one of the chairs. "It was hard. It was wonderful. It was agonizing. It was good to be there. I'm glad I went. Adam was glad he went, too. His parents have postponed Thanksgiving until this Sunday, so we're still going to do the whole celebration, but now we can do it without me freaking out because my family is falling apart."

"Is your family falling apart?"

"They've all come to terms with it. I am getting there. Mom apologized for not telling me what was going on, but I get it. It's one thing to live with it and be able to do something, it's another thing to be so far away that the only way to handle it is to worry. But now that I've been there, I'm hoping my worry won't be quite as over-the-top. Mom accused me of being dramatic." He grinned at Polly.

"She doesn't know you at all, does she? How was your dad?"

"Alert a good part of the time. But you can see how hard he works to focus. We visited a couple of facilities. One of them is within fifteen minutes of the house and looks wonderful. Mom was happy with it. Lots of caring people there and she will have unlimited access to Dad. And if she wants to bring him home on good days, they have drivers and aides who will be there for her."

"Sounds expensive," Polly said. She clapped her hand over her mouth. "I'm sorry. I shouldn't say that."

"It is expensive, and you know what?" he said, "I offered to pay anything above what they can't handle. You pay me well here and I don't have many expenses. These last ten years, I've been able to sock away enough money to get my family through this. It's nice to be able to do that without worrying. I wrote Mom a big check so she can make the decision whenever she's ready. I told my dad how much I loved him over and over. If that's all he remembers, that's important to me."

"Sounds like you had a good week," Polly said.

"It was hard. But I'm glad I went. I have you to thank for that." He pointed at her desk. "What happened here? Did Chief Wallers hold you up or something?"

"Or something. I hate this bag. I need more organization. Like a briefcase. No, that wouldn't work. I just need to be better about what I keep in here." She pulled the diaper back out of the trash can. "Why do I have this?"

"Was it one of Delia's?"

"I don't think so. I don't know where it came from, though." Then she held up the musical flashcards. "And these? I don't have anyone learning this stuff. I'm beginning to believe that my family drops random things into the bag just to see if I'm paying attention. Apparently, I'm not."

# CHAPTER NINETEEN

"Up and at 'em. Are you ready?"

Henry stood in Polly's office doorway.

"Almost," she replied. With one quick click of her mouse, she shut down the computer. "I can't believe you asked me to go with you today. You never do."

"There are two units you might be interested in," he said. "I usually find a couple of good deals to make this trek worth my while, but I don't know what you'll think."

"I'm a little nervous. I've never done this before," Polly replied. She started to put her coat on, but Henry took it from her and held it while she slid into it. "Thank you."

"They're lucky to have good weather. Otherwise, I might not go at all. I'm tired of cold and we haven't even hit December yet."

"January and February will be rough for you, then."

"Me and the plows on our trucks." Henry shook his head. "I'm going to need new gloves."

"Are you asking me to find some for you?"

He chuckled. "No. We buy them in bulk for the guys. I was just reminding myself to do something about it."

"Like send a text to Jessie so she can place the order."

"Fine. Fine. Follow me to the truck. We're meeting Gavin there. I don't want to be late." Gavin Riddle was one of Henry's foremen and married to Josie, the assistant manager at Sweet Beans.

"Really?"

"He's bringing the panel truck and several guys. If I get the unit I'm looking at, we're adding nice tools to the cabinet shop."

"Got it. Will they haul away my purchases, too?"

"If you make any, yes."

This big date was nothing more than a drive to the storage unit facility out on the highway for their annual winter auction. Clearing out before the end of the year, she supposed. Henry went every time they held an auction. He had a good relationship with Gordon, the manager, who let him know when there was something Henry might find interesting. Today, they were auctioning off four units with long-overdue rent. Henry was excited about one and thought Polly might be interested in another. The final two were wild cards. They'd see.

The weather was almost balmy. Highs in the mid-fifties made it comfortable enough to wander around a storage unit facility. If Polly got miserably cold, she'd hide out in Henry's truck.

He pulled in and walked around the truck to open her door. Polly always smiled when he did so, no matter that she told him it was unnecessary. While they were raising boys, he deemed that it was necessary. It was also important that their daughters understood the basic rules of chivalry. He ensured that the boys learned to walk on the outside of the sidewalk when with a woman. For the most part, they learned and applied it with ease. But there was always another young boy who needed to learn, so he kept explaining and teaching the children as they came into the family.

They walked to the office of the storage facility. Gordon was still inside, seated at his desk. They were a little early and no one else was on site yet.

"Good morning," he said as they walked in. "How did I get so lucky to see both of you today?"

"I want Polly to look at Unit 201," Henry said. "Those books might hold some interest for her."

Gordon nodded knowingly. "The former librarian can't stand to let a good book go, right?"

"Something like that," Polly said with a grin. "You know I used to work in a library?"

"How could I not? Everyone knows everything about you, and everyone who knows everything talks about it all," he replied with a laugh.

"Somehow, even out here, Gordon makes sure he is in the center of all the town news," Henry said. "What time do you plan to get started?"

Gordon looked up at the clock on the wall. "Fifteen minutes. I know of two others who plan to be here. You're looking at number 415?"

"A few pieces of good equipment in there. Dad would be able to use them at the cabinet shop. The other stuff … well, we'll see. Jack thought he might come over and look." Henry glanced at Polly. "I thought we could set up a small shop for him in the back of the garage at Sycamore House. He works all the time out at Dad's and doesn't go home until late. It would be nice if he was closer to his apartment. What do you think?"

She shrugged. "Sounds good to me. You're the one who will do all the work. What are you thinking?"

"There's a nice router table and a decent chop saw. I'd like to find a lathe, but at least he could get a start. Those two pieces aren't of any use at the cabinet shop right now, but Jack, or even Heath, could get a start on their shops."

"Heath should wait until he gets his own place," Polly said. "Then he can build the shop of his dreams."

"Where's he thinking of moving?" Gordon asked.

She laughed. "You don't know that yet? You're lagging behind, sir."

"Know what?"

"That Heath is looking at buying an acreage in Sycamore Acres?"

He blinked. "Sycamore Acres? Where is that?"

"It barely exists on paper," Henry said. "The land where the Sutter's organic farm used to be."

"The crazy lady and her crazy daughter?"

"That's the one. We're selling lots for homes. It's big enough that Heath can buy a small acreage. He and his girlfriend have big plans for an animal rescue."

"I want to be part of your family," Gordon said. "You have all the fun."

"With this one," Henry said, nodding toward Polly, "You have to be on your toes. She creates fun even when no one expects it."

The door behind them opened and three men walked in.

Henry strode over to them with his hand out. "Brody. Angelo. Danny. Good to see you. Are you here to bid on units?"

The first man, Brody Desalt, nodded. "I've got my eye on one. Hoping it's not the one you're here for. Number 313?"

Henry shook his head. "Not me. I'm looking at the woodworking tools and Polly is looking at the unit with books, fabric and holiday decorations. At least that's what we see up front, right? You're here to get the things from the guy who was a glass cutter?"

"Can't believe you and your family aren't taking it." Angelo said. He looked at Polly. "The wife told me to look at that unit and if I thought it was worthwhile, to bid. She doesn't need any more books or fabric, so I'm making an executive decision. It's yours if you want it. Believe it or not, I'm here for the last unit. There is some furniture in there that my wife also thought would be good to refurbish."

Polly smiled. Angelo Perez worked on one of the big farming operations west of town. He and Danny Troyer, who stood beside him were busy all year round, but harvest was finished now, and things were slow enough that it didn't matter if he took time for something like this today.

"Your wife is building a nice business," Polly said. "She and I need to talk one of these days. I have a bunch of stuff in the attic from when the Bell House was a tuberculosis sanitarium. Bed frames, dressers, bedside tables. All sorts of weird things. I should have her look at it."

"Name the time," Angelo said.

Polly took out one of her business cards, which caused him to reach into his back pocket. They exchanged cards. "How about you tell her to stop in to see me at Sycamore House or give me a call any time. As soon as she's available, we'd like to clear out more rooms in the attic. It's a little cold, but if she can handle it, you all are welcome to look." Then she shook her head. "No. Instead, let me go up and take pictures first. Then, if she's interested, we can figure out a time. No need for you all to make a useless trip."

"Never useless. If I know Maizie, she'll jump up and down with excitement. Trust me, it's good to keep her busy."

"Gentlemen. Polly," Gordon said, standing up. "We're ten minutes past the start-time. Let me look around outside to see if anyone else is here. If we can make these transactions happen here in the office, I vote we go ahead."

Polly smiled. She was going home with a pile of books, a huge amount of fabric, and some Christmas decorations that Rebecca would have fun with. After all the girl's work last week, her head might explode at the idea there was possibly more decorating in her future. She'd be home mid-December. Decisions could be made then.

Gordon left the office, even though the three who just came in assured him they hadn't seen anyone else outside. Since there weren't many units available today and it was in the middle of the holiday season, people had other things going on. Henry told Polly the late spring auction was a hopping good time with people coming in from all over to bid on items that someone gave up because they stopped paying for the unit's rent.

"Should have put on a coat," Gordon said, coming back inside. "Nothing and no one but you four. And you all want different units? Tell you what. I'll let you know what rent is due on them, you tell me what you want to pay and we'll be done."

"He wants us to do better than a dollar," Brody said.

"You know the drill," Gordon replied with a smile. "Minimum bids. You have them in your head."

"Not a dollar," Henry echoed. He took Polly's arm. "Are you sure you want that unit? It's a lot of stuff. There will be sorting and packing and unpacking …"

She put her hand up. "I'm ready. We can put it in that back bay of the garage. Then I can take it to the basement to sort if it's too cold. I have multiple kids who will run up and down the stairs."

He nodded, smiled, and stepped forward to stand in front of Gordon's desk, then took out a credit card. "If you're offering minimum bid, I'll up each unit by a hundred. Seem fair?"

Gordon shrugged. "I only work here. Fair enough. I have people chomping at the bit to get into a unit out here. Everything is filled again. Four open spaces? I'll make a killing." He chuckled. "Because today's transactions are far from making that for us. I'm only glad to have people willing to empty them."

The others came forward to pay as Henry and Polly walked outside.

"Let me get the bolt cutters," Gordon said.

Henry turned with a grin. "I carry my own. Don't trust me?"

"I trust you. But we have video cameras and a boss who wouldn't like it if I let a civilian cut away. Now," Gordon said, grabbing up the cutters, "if we can avoid Polly finding a body in one of these units, I will call this a darn good day." He chuckled. "When Henry told me he was bringing you over, you have to believe that was my first thought. Would you mind if I was the one to open your unit and walk in first?"

"Whatever makes you more comfortable. If there's a body to be found, you going in first won't change the fact that I will find it."

"That does not make me more comfortable," Gordon said. "I'll meet you at Polly's unit first, Henry. Sound good?"

"Gavin and his guys will load the other into our panel truck. Polly and I will load this into the pickup."

"I will?" Polly asked. "I didn't know manual labor was my thing today."

Henry scowled at her.

"Manual labor is my thing today, then," she replied with a laugh.

~~~

Many of the boxes they loaded into Henry's pickup weren't labeled. When Polly opened the first one, she discovered a set of Christmas dinner plates. She quit looking after that. If they had to take everything, they'd take everything. She'd sort later. And then they ran out of space in the pickup.

"I can't believe this. It's almost embarrassing," Henry said as he took out his phone. He sent a text. "We're going to have to put the rest in the panel truck. I hope they have room. The unit with all that equipment was packed. I'm guessing we'll find boxes filled with family stuff from the old man's house in the midst of it all too. Want to sort that?"

"If you need me to sort, I will. What do you usually do?"

"Let the guys take what they want and run the rest to the thrift store. If they don't want it, things go to the dump."

"Sounds like you should become better friends with Angelo Perez's wife. What did he say her name was? Maizie? I love that name."

"Jump in the truck. I'm going around to the unit. Gavin said they're nearly finished."

"Or I could stay here," Polly said.

"And get chilly? No, my dear. In the truck with you." He stood by the passenger door and held it while she climbed in. She stuck her bottom up and he tweaked it.

"I hope Gordon saw that on his video camera," Polly said.

"Give him a little laugh for his afternoon. You have a tweakable butt."

Polly relented and climbed into the truck. It wasn't much warmer than it was outside, but Henry was concerned, so she let him pamper her. They drove around the units and saw the panel truck with four of his people hauling boxes and equipment into it, stacking things as neatly as possible.
~~~

"People keep too much stuff," Polly commented.

Henry looked at her. "Uh huh. This coming from you? Today is the first time I've ever heard you consider getting rid of the furniture in the attic. You saved everything you could from your father's house. Remember Wyatt Post? He's only a little boy and you made sure to save everything, so he'd have it in the future. The Ricker's. We have stored all their family's furniture. You keep stuff because it means something. Or it could mean something. Polly, you're as guilty as anyone."

"I'm people," she protested. "Leave me alone."

He pulled up beside Gavin and rolled his window down. "Want a little help before we pack out the rest of Polly's unit?"

Gavin shrugged. "We're getting there, man. This was more than you expected. There are some great treasures, though. Way deep in the back, we found a lathe and its knives. It's been broken down, and the knives need to be sharpened. Under the tarp back there? Lumber. Hard wood. Nice stuff. There's some great tigerwood and a couple of pieces of either mahogany or cherry. Good score today. We'll lay that stuff along the side here. You and Bill can check it later."

Polly got out of the truck. She could lift boxes as well as anyone, and before long, the unit was empty. Henry took a photograph of the empty space and sent off a text. She assumed it was going to Gordon.

The truck had enough room to hold the rest of the boxes from the storage unit Henry had purchased for her, so everyone traipsed back around to finish the task. Once they were there, the guys pushed past Polly.

"We'll finish this," Gavin said. "You helped us; you get to take a break."

"What kind of deal are you trying to make, Gavin?" Henry asked. "Don't treat her like a lady."

"Can't help it," Gavin said with a laugh.

Polly shook her head and wandered off. She leaned against the door of another unit and watched as they worked. Red paint in odd patterns covered the door sill and she looked closer. Then, she looked even closer and placed her left hand above the pattern. That was a handprint. And she would almost guarantee it wasn't red paint, but instead was blood. Especially when she saw drops of the same red stuff on the ground and a brush of it against the door itself.

"Henry?" she called out.

He walked over, looked at what she was pointing at, and shook his head. "We're going to have to get into this unit, aren't we?"

"I'm calling Chief Wallers."

"Blood? Call Aaron," he said.

"I don't know if there's a body. I can't even guarantee that it's blood. Maybe someone repainted their mower or a baby's changing table."

"With blood red paint. Sure," he said. "Call Aaron. He can ask Gordon to open the unit. We can't."

Polly's phone was in the truck and she headed back that way. "The guys aren't going to believe this."

"They always look forward to spending time with you." Henry held the truck door open. Even though the temperature was tolerable, she was glad to be inside. Especially when Henry pressed a button and the truck turned on, pouring heat across her legs.

She took up the phone from the console and swiped open the call.

"Not another one," Aaron replied. "It's the holiday season."

"I don't know for sure. We're at the storage facility and there's a unit with what looks like a bloody handprint near the door."

"A big unit or small?" he asked.

"Small. And there are droplets of the same stuff on the ground. Aaron, I could be wrong."

"Or, you have the Polly-sense working on another level today. I'll get Tab on her way to you."

"Now, I'm feeling foolish," Polly said. "It is probably nothing."

"What are you doing there today anyway?"

"Finding blood and purchasing the contents of a past-due unit. Books, Aaron. They tempted me with books. And then dumped a load of other stuff on me as well. I blame Henry, but I'm as susceptible to these kinds of deals as anyone."

"I've never considered going to one of their auctions. Henry does this?"

"He just purchased the contents of another unit – all woodworking tools."

"Why would anyone let those things out of their grasp?"

"Parents die, kids live too far away, it's already too much for them to clear out their parents' houses, and then they discover Dad's workshop. They don't want it anyway, so just quit paying rent on the unit. Someone else will clean it up."

"Is that true?" he asked.

"I don't know. But it makes sense."

"What about the books? Same type of thing?"

"I'd surmise so," Polly said. "You just don't know why people stop paying. Money, death, remarriage, so many reasons. All I know is that I have boxes and boxes of stuff to unpack and sort. There are old books, so I'm hoping to find a few treasures. Apparently, I can't help myself and have decided that I should prepare Noah for a big library. Or maybe even Andrew and Rebecca."

"Maybe you can turn the library into a guest room once those two move out and you've emptied your shelves."

"Get thee behind me, you crazy man," Polly said, laughing. "I see lights at the front entrance. This should entertain the manager. He was worried I might find a body. Now, he's going to think it's real."

"Don't leave without talking to Tab."

"Like anyone here would let me get away with that," Polly said. "Henry's guys are already watching me while wondering what's going on. I don't know what he's told them, but at least they'll get a little entertainment out of their day."

# CHAPTER TWENTY

"Run away, crazy woman. You're a menace!" Gordon walked across the lot to Polly, his index finger waving at her. "I told you I didn't want you to find any dead bodies here."

She grinned. "No body yet. I promise not to go inside the unit, but I do think this is blood and I do think that the unit needs to be opened."

"Fine," he replied. "I agree with you."

"Who owns it?" Henry asked.

"Some outfit out of Chicago. They rented it in October. Think they might have something to do with that silly Christmas store in town. Called the corporate number they gave me for permission to enter the unit, and guess what?"

Henry chuckled. "Phone doesn't work."

"Oh, it works, all right," Gordon said. "It just goes to a voicemail that tells me the owners of the number are out of the country and won't check their voicemail until they return. And then it clicks off. I'm perfectly happy to open this for the deputy right now. Due diligence and all that be damned."

Behind Tab was Alan Dressen and a few members of his team.

"You didn't bring everyone?" Polly asked when Tab got out of her vehicle.

"You didn't find a body. Blood? I only need a few people. If anyone but you walks into that unit first, I'm confident that we won't walk into death. However, this is interesting." She turned to Gordon. "Did you find that video?"

He shook his head. "I've scrolled back and nothing. I'll keep looking."

"Last Wednesday or Thursday night," Polly said. "I'll bet you anything that's when it happened."

He peered at her skeptically. "How would you know that?" Then he nodded in understanding. "You found that body behind the coffee shop."

"Sylvie said that the dumpster was emptied Wednesday morning. It could have happened on Thanksgiving, since the stores were all closed. What an awful celebration that was for the poor kid."

"Polly," Tab said. She didn't often hear Polly comment on the deaths she discovered.

"It would have been. Day off, big feasts, and boom, dead body."

"You're morbid. What did you buy here today?" Tab was a little distracted, taking photographs of the door. She gestured for Alan to test the residue just in case it wasn't blood.

"Two packs of cigarettes and a bottle of Jack Daniels," Polly said.

Everyone but Tab smiled, but Tab only nodded as she took out a measuring tape. She measured everything, adding notes to her notebook. "Henry? Did you find the gambling devices you were looking for? I'm excited to start raiding your illicit gambling parties."

"The ones I found," Henry said, "will need a lot of work. You'll have to wait until this summer."

"How do you know I bought something?" Polly asked.

Tab pocketed the measuring tape, spun on her, and said, "Me big-time detective. Don't miss nuttin'. Boxes in the pickup, open unit that is now empty. Henry's panel truck and employees. You bought stuff. Regular Sherlock Holmes, I am."

"Fine, then. I bought stuff. And here, I thought you were focused on your real job."

Tab pointed at her chest. "Big-time detective notices everything around her. You promised the man no bodies. Do you want to open the door to the unit?"

"Not me." Polly backed away. "I'm holding to that promise. Is it blood?"

Tab looked at Alan Dressen.

"It's blood," he said. "All of it. Something happened here. Could be an accident, could be murder. We've got fingerprints. We'll check them against what we have back at the shop, but I'm willing to speculate that it's all related.  Now, about that video. Can I call my favorite nerd-girl, Anita, and have her walk you through the process to get video to our office?"

Gordon nodded. "Let me open this door for your team, and then we'll make the call to the nerd-girl."

The padlock gave way to his bolt cutters and Tab, with gloves on, opened the door, then reached over and switched on the light fixture.

That action gave way to gasps from everyone. Henry's entire team had gathered. Why would they miss a few minutes of Polly-entertainment? What they got instead was a murder scene like Polly had never yet experienced. With no body.

Blood splattered the floor, the walls, and haphazardly stacked boxes, many that Polly could see were slashed open. More of those hideous holiday farm animals poked out of the boxes.

"No body, but now I've got cleanup," Gordon said. "I've cleaned messes before, but not like this."

Alan slid him a business card. "Call them. Pay for it. I'll let you know when it's been cleared for entry. Okay, team. Go to work. I'm headed inside with our friend to see if we can find out who did this horrible thing."

Tab took more photographs and Polly turned to make sure that no one else was doing the same with their phones. Henry knew what she was looking for and gave her a quick nod. He'd already dealt with it.

"You really bring the party, don't you," Gavin Riddle said to Polly as he walked back past her. He touched her shoulder. "Tell Josie you need more free coffee. Anyone who walks into things like this should have all the free coffee in the world. I'm glad it's not me. I wouldn't be able to stomach it. A couple of us nearly lost our bellies today and that was only the blood. We're big, strong construction workers and you're … well …"

"Polly. I'm Polly. That's as far as you need to go with that comparison," she said with a smile.

"Polly, then. All right, guys," he said loudly. "Let's finish up and get out of here. First stop, Henry's place." Gavin gave her a guilty smile. "Polly and Henry's place. Back bay of your garage, right?"

Henry nodded and shook Gavin's hand as he passed. The panel truck had already been loaded and the unit was finally empty. Polly waved as they drove past. "If we hurry, we could get home and they'd unload the pickup too, right?"

Henry looked at Tab. "Do you need us any longer?"

"Wait," Polly said and drew Tab back. "Those stuffed animals? That's what the dogs got into. Tell your people to check them for vials of drugs."

Tab nodded in understanding. "It's going to be a task. The killers only opened the boxes on the top of the stacks. Wonder why they stopped? We would have checked anyway, but thanks for saying something."

"You're telling me I'm unnecessary."

"For moral support? Sure." Tab chuckled. "No, I was being serious. It looks like someone was frustrated with the results of a quick search. If these were filled with drugs, your young man might not have died. But slashed boxes with the stuffed animals still in them? I wonder where the drugs are."

Henry took Polly's hand. "I'm all yours, Doodle. We'll get this stuff unloaded and the rest of your day can be your own adventure."

"I'm all out of adventuring spirit today," Polly said. She touched Tab's arm. "Let me know when you know something, okay? This has been weird. Do you think the couple running that Christmas pop-up are involved somehow?"

"Not that we can tell. They're staying in an Airbnb close to Ames. Nothing weird about it. And the kid was staying in one of the big hotels down in Boone. No connection that we can find, other than that they worked for the same company. But this Monty and Linda Morris, they've been doing this for about ten years. They like to travel and enjoy doing short-term projects. We're keeping an eye on them, but who knows?"

"What about the men who tased Andrew?" Polly asked. "Do you think they're involved?"

"That's a good question, but it sounds like they'd been in the area for several weeks before Andrew caught them. Chief Wallers had several reports come in from folks who realized that somebody had been sleeping in Papa Bear's bed."

"That's enough, you two," Henry said. "I'm taking Polly. You can meet for lunch. I need to get to work."

"It's awful that murder doesn't get any more respect than that from your husband, Polly. You've desensitized him."

"It's a shame," Polly agreed. "Call me."

Henry caught her arm and she trotted along beside him, throwing looks of laughter back at Tab, who shook her head.

~~~

Polly should have gone straight to the hotel, but with all that was going on, she'd already called off that part of her day. The last thing she needed was to listen to June's gossip or face questions that she was unwilling to answer. She could log in from home and do the work. The only reason she ever went to the hotel was to ensure she was a regular part of the scenery and to assure everyone that she knew them.

The Girls' Rule group would be at the Bell House for their annual Christmas get-together and yearly wrap-up on Saturday
~~~

for lunch. The foyer was in good shape. Eliseo had probably already taken the extra tables to the house and had them set up. Tomorrow, a few women planned to decorate. Polly needed to be sure to be home so that they didn't bother Lexi or wander unpredictably through the house.

Rachel and her crew were catering the luncheon. She and Lexi had everything well in hand, so that was something Polly didn't have to worry about. The only thing left was cleaning the rest of the house. Polly had begged Rebecca for her time this weekend and since her daughter was two weeks out from finals, there would still be time for study and cleaning. Amalee was good with the younger kids, but she didn't have the personality to make them do work they didn't want to do. Rebecca did.

Instead of going to Sycamore House or starting on the pile of boxes that now took up a chunk of the garage, Polly headed for Sweet Beans. She didn't need to interrupt Lexi, who was busy with her own job. The holiday season was a great way for her to kick off a new home catering business. The girl was still learning and most of that learning was around scheduling. Polly didn't need to be involved. Lexi was smart and felt guilty every time she made a mistake. The best place for Polly to be was elsewhere so Lexi's mistakes weren't obvious to anyone but herself. She was doing great, and Polly continued to tell her exactly that.

Lexi overcame every problem that presented itself and, in the process, learned more about being a young businesswoman than she expected. She was learning to limit herself to what she could do and not worry when demands from outside conflicted with her boundaries. The friends she was feeding didn't push, but people who didn't know her thought they could direct her to do things their way. Lexi told Polly more than once that her initial response was to give in to the demands, but after a moment's thought, she asked herself what Polly would do in the same situation. That gave her the strength to protect her boundaries.

Polly parked in front of the coffee shop and glanced down the way of the Merry Times pop-up store. The lights were off. Strange. This group couldn't get any more odd.

When she opened the door of Sweet Beans, the familiar scents and sounds greeted her, a place of comfort in an odd world.

Then she saw the couple who had been introduced as Monty and Linda at a table eating lunch. Polly walked over. "Good morning."

Linda looked up, startled at being addressed. She turned on a smile and said, "Good morning. Ms. Giller, right? We hear a lot about you. You're the one who found Mike's body in the dumpster out back. That couldn't have been easy. We miss him. Now, the two of us have to work every open hour at the shop."

Polly had trouble believing that was what the woman meant to say, but it was what she said. "Yes, I'm Polly Giller. I'm sorry for your loss."

Monty stood and held a chair for her. "Join us. Would you like coffee or are you here to get lunch?"

"I'm sorry," Linda said, shooting a glare toward the man. "I should be more polite. People ignore us. They know we aren't here to create relationships, just sell merchandise."

"How's business going?" Polly asked.

"Brisk. A lot of people have come in lately. They don't always buy, but we're doing well enough to call it a success. The business comes because they want to see where the kid who died used to work. Any advertising is good advertising, right?"

This woman did not have any social skills whatsoever.

"Coffee?" Monty asked again. He had remained standing and waited for Polly to respond.

"Black," she replied. "Thank you." Polly looked at his left ring finger and when she saw a wedding band there, looked at Linda's. These two did not act like they were a couple, but given Linda's awkwardness with conversation, that wasn't surprising. "How long have you two been doing this?"

"Traveling around and opening holiday pop-ups?" Linda asked. When Polly nodded, she went on. "Not long after we were married. Almost three years. In fact, our anniversary is in May. We ran a fireworks stand in Missouri that first summer for the company."

"Have you been to interesting locations?"

Linda shrugged. "Mostly small towns. We have a small RV that we use in the nicer months. That gives us the opportunity to live in pretty spots. It's one of the first things we look for – a nice campground with peaceful vistas. Last summer, we asked for and got a spot in eastern Tennessee, not far from the Smoky Mountains. That was pretty. I didn't want to leave, but once the fireworks were sold, we didn't have a reason to stay."

"Where's home, then?"

"Wherever we land."

"Do you work all year round?"

"All seasons," Linda said. "There is always something. We even do craft shows. The company has a line of inexpensive crafting items and we set up and sell them all over. Monty and I are probably the only couple who does this full-time. Everyone else takes a few jobs through the year and lives off the money. They're retired and already have homes they paid off, you know."

"You don't have a home base?"

"My parents live in Arkansas and Monty is from southern Missouri. When we're tired of what we're doing, we'll go home to either place and figure out what to do with the rest of our lives, but for now, this is a pretty good life."

"How well did you know the kid who died?" Polly asked. "He sounded like he was new to the company."

"They get a ton of new kids for the Christmas season," Linda said. "Kids who think they'll make a killing selling crap Christmas décor." She realized what she'd said and looked down. "Sorry. Now I'll never get you in to buy anything."

"You don't need me if other people buy your stuff, right?" Polly asked. She kind of liked this woman, even though she was a bit odd. Linda didn't seem like a murderer, but then Polly had been surprised before. Not often, but it did happen.

Monty put a large cup of coffee in front of her, along with a plate of zebra brownies. When Polly looked up at him, he smiled. "They told me these were your favorites and then they wouldn't let me pay. So, enjoy."

"I own the bakery here," Polly said.

"You own a lot of things here in Bellingwood," Linda observed. "I hear you own that retro hotel out on the highway. Is it retro in the rooms or just the outside décor?"

"Only on the outside. We wanted it to keep its original look, but the rooms are remodeled and quite nice."

"The old schoolhouse? You renovated it, too? That's a lot of work."

"I married a man who owns a construction business," Polly said. "Henry Sturtz."

"His company is building the new school, isn't it?"

"That's him."

"You live a very interesting life," Linda said.

"Sounds like yours is interesting, too."

Monty huffed a laugh.

"What?" Linda asked. "We go to interesting places."

"Every podunk little town in the Midwest," he grumped.

"But that's where interesting people are from," she protested. "If we hadn't come to Bellingwood, we wouldn't have met Ms. Giller and she's interesting."

"Story is," Monty said, ignoring Linda and turning to Polly, "you found where Mike was murdered this morning."

"I found a storage unit that had blood in it," Polly replied. "No one knows if he was murdered there or not."

"If there's blood, there's a murder?" Linda asked. "Which storage facility?"

"The one out on the highway." Polly pointed in the approximate direction.

Linda frowned. "Monty, isn't that where our storage unit is located?" As if in explanation, she said. "We have more inventory, and the company provides a budget for storage. Rather than overstock the store, we store things until we need them. I wonder what Mike was doing." She grimaced. "Stupid kid. This has been hard. Monty and I usually get a little time off during the season, but the company won't let us hire anyone else unless they've put them through a rigorous interview process."

"For this job?" Polly asked. "Selling Christmas junk?"

Linda shrugged. "Made sense when they explained it. That's why we're here for lunch today, though. We decided that since the town is open late on Thursdays, we'd take Thursday mornings to ourselves. As soon as we're finished with lunch, we'll open, but I don't want to work twelve-hour days, seven days a week."

"You're open every day?"

"Sunday afternoons, not mornings, but yes, we're here every day. Not getting a lot of value out of our Airbnb, other than a place to sleep. If we'd had a good place to park the RV, we could have ..." Her voice trailed off. "Guess I'm complaining again."

Polly saw Sylvie give her a little wave from the hallway that led to the bakery. "I should let you enjoy your lunch. I'm sorry to have bothered you."

"It's no bother," Monty said. He stood again with her. "It was nice to meet you."

"Even if you don't want to buy the Christmas junk," Linda said, "stop in to see us any time. We don't get too many opportunities to eat lunch here or anywhere, for that matter, but if we're open, I'm always there. It was nice to meet you, Ms. Giller."

"Polly."

"Polly. Thank you. I'm Linda and this is Monty. Together we're the Morrises."

"I'm sure I'll see you again," Polly said. She smiled and walked across the room.

Sylvie took her arm and led her to the bakery. "Did you get caught by them or did you do that on purpose?"

"On purpose. Why?"

"Are they the murderers?"

"I don't think so. What makes you ask?"

"Because you are the best investigator the county has when it comes to murder and murderers. If you thought they did it, then I was going to tell you to call Tab and have her bring two sets of handcuffs."

Polly laughed. "No. They're just a young couple who think they've found the answer to a good life. Traveling around the country selling junk Christmas items and, in the summer, fireworks."

"Fireworks, too?"

"Yes."

"And you think they're young?"

"They're younger than you and me," Polly said. "What, early thirties, don't you think?"

"He looks older than that."

Polly stepped in front of Sylvie, so the woman didn't obviously peer at the couple who were clearing their table to leave. "Stop being obvious."

# CHAPTER TWENTY-ONE

Endless stress over this group wasn't worth it. Fortunately, having strangers in her house didn't happen very often. While Polly had encouraged the beginnings of Girls' Rule, she'd stayed away from having any part of its leadership. That was not her group of friends and leading people like that was not a strength she possessed. Right now, a passel of chatty women was in her foyer decorating away. At least she thought that's what they were doing. She didn't want to open a door to look. If they saw her, they'd catch her and ask questions or beg for a tour, or any number of things Polly didn't want to take responsibility for.

"You're quiet," Lexi said.

"Maybe I need more coffee."

"You were staring at the foyer."

"I *really* need more coffee." Polly slid off the stool and headed for the coffee pot. "One of them asked if we would serve coffee this morning. I pointed out the door toward Sweet Beans and invited them to bring whatever they wanted into the house. The nerve."

"Because we're a public facility?" Lexi asked with a laugh.

"They certainly think we are. Not one of them was alive when it was a public facility. Do you think it would be too much if I put locks on the house-side of the foyer doors?

"You don't have time before tomorrow morning. You're also out of time for today."

"Okay, I'll bar them using chairs and sofas. The floor is lava, ladies. Stay on high ground." Polly looked up. "Crap. I didn't think about them sneaking upstairs. I'll be right back."

"You're paranoid."

"I'm well-trained. You don't remember last year?"

"I remember the luncheon and all the trouble we had, but I don't remember it being a problem when they were setting up and decorating."

"I'm not taking any chances. Beat them off with a stick, if necessary." Polly pointed at the pantry. "Do you have rope in there?"

"Rope?"

"Clothesline rope or anything like that. A bungee cord? Anything that I can tie those doors shut?"

"You're serious?"

"As a heart-attack, which is what I'll have if anyone tries to explore my house."

"Let me see what I can find." Lexi walked into the pantry and came back out a few seconds later with both a bungee cord and a package of nylon rope.

Polly shook her head. "Where is my daughter when I need her?"

"Which daughter?" Lexi asked, a knowing grin on her face. "If you mean the one who will kick butt and ask questions later, she's finishing classes and packing to come home with Cathy as soon as they can. You're a very lucky mom. I hope Gillian is prepared to come at my bidding to help clean the house when she's in college."

"Rebecca loves coming home. I barely got the words out of my mouth, and she said yes." Polly took both items from Lexi's hand. "I'm already in trouble. Do you hear the footsteps upstairs?"

Lexi frowned. "Sorry. Hurry."

Polly tore for the back steps, and while running toward her bedroom saw a woman come out of Delia's bedroom.

"Hello," Polly said. "What are you doing?"

"I'm exploring this wonderful building," the woman said. "I've heard so much about it, I couldn't help myself. Don't hate me."

"I don't hate anyone, but this is a private residence and not open to the public. Please return to the foyer."

"Oh, but I must see the rest. I understand you have an old office that belonged to moonshiners. And a tunnel that led to an underground bunker? You must show it to me."

"No, I must not. I will repeat myself. This is a private residence. Please return to the foyer. We aren't open for tours. Not now, not ever."

"You could make so much money, though," the woman said. "Everyone wants to see what you've done with the building."

"I don't much care about what everyone wants. I do care about the privacy of my family. Please." Polly gestured to the doors leading to the balcony of the foyer.

"What's down here?" The woman tried to brush past her to get to the old servants' quarters where they'd built out the apartment for Lexi. "I understand the original owners had servants."

"Ma'am, I'm sorry to be abrupt, but get out of my house. You are welcome to continue working in the foyer, but you are not welcome here. That is a private apartment …"

"Oh, no one would mind if I peeked."

"I would mind." Polly was done. She dropped the rope and bungee cord to the floor and put her hand on the woman's hand just as she attempted to open the door to Lexi's apartment. "Stop. You are being extremely rude."

"Don't you know who I am?"

"I don't know. I don't care. If you're someone special, you should understand the importance of respect. What you're doing right now is not respectful and it's making a boob out of you."

"Are you kidding me?" The woman pushed Polly hand away and got her own hand back on the apartment door handle.

"That's it," Polly said and grabbed the woman's upper arm. With only a little pressure, she led her back to the foyer doors. "Go downstairs and walk out the front door. If I find that you are still in my home when I get there, I will call the police. I've had enough of your intrusion."

"I don't understand," the woman said. "This is a historical building. It should be open to everyone."

"There are historic homes in Boone. Would you do the same thing to those families?" Polly opened the door and practically pushed the woman out onto the balcony. "Leave my home. You are unwelcome here today and tomorrow, if I see you, you'd better be on your best behavior, or I will have you and any of your cronies escorted out. The sheriff's wife is part of this group as well and we won't hesitate to call a deputy for assistance."

"The sheriff and his wife need to be careful. I have the power to crush them."

"Crush away but do it from your own home. Not mine." Polly pushed the doors shut and then picked up the bungee cord, her first line of defense. The second would be the nylon rope, though it flashed through her mind that hanging the woman from the railing would be an unacceptable way to handle the problem.

The moment the bungee cord had been wrapped tightly around the door handles, she wasn't surprised to see the handles turn ever so slightly. A small push and the door opened a bit, but the woman couldn't get past the furious strength Polly had used to ensure no one could enter. She took out the rope, walked into her bedroom for a pair of scissors and returned only to find that there were fingers trying to manage the cord already in place.

"What are you doing?" Polly asked.

"You're still there?"

"I'm not going anywhere. Move your fingers before I smash them when I close the door."

The fingers left immediately. Good thing. Polly was angry enough not to care. She closed the door again, then tightly wrapped lengths of nylon cord around the handles and tied it off. Henry was going to laugh at her, but the next step was to put locks on all these doors. She'd resisted even when they had little ones who shouldn't be in the foyer alone. This was ridiculous.

Polly was breathing a little more easily when she went down the stairs into the kitchen. It was going to take time to get past this woman's attitude, but she would. Maybe by tomorrow.

What Polly wasn't prepared for was to find Lexi standing at the entrance to the basement, trying to talk two other women out of pushing past her.

"Enough!" Polly yelled and pointed to the foyer door. "Either get back into the foyer and complete your task or get out of my house. I've had it with your entitled behavior. This is a private home. You have been given no invitation and have no right to attempt intimidation of my family in order to entertain yourselves. Move it. Now.

"Ms. Giller, you don't understand."

"I do understand. You are curious. You have no boundaries. You believe you are entitled to ignore every sense of decorum. I am embarrassed for you. This is rudeness beyond anything I've experienced in a long time. To the foyer. All of you. The next person who trespasses in my private residence will be escorted out by either myself, my husband, or the police."

"You wouldn't."

"Wouldn't I? Let's see. A trespassing charge on your record. One that you can't get out of because I have a witness who will testify that I have not only asked you once, but several times to go back to the foyer. And on top of that, I have written documentation that was sent to the Girls' Rule organization requesting that no one leave the foyer for any reason other than to use the bathroom."

"That's what we were doing."

"The bathroom off the living room and library, I believe the letter said," Polly replied. "Do I have to call the police, or will you go back to work in the foyer?"

"We're going, but you really should offer tours of this beautiful home."

"I've been told that several times. It's that last word in your sentence that gets me every time. It's my home, not a public building. Please go back to the foyer."

They did and Polly rolled her eyes. "Now I have to go in there and ensure that my declarations are obeyed. Tomorrow is going to suck. And this is the very last time I invite this group here at all. I am also pulling my support. I'm done. It has changed so much since I first got involved."

"I've never experienced such a thing."

Polly laughed. "You missed out on the whole city – social – society thing. Boston was a hotbed of rules and regulations about society. The Brahmins would never behave this way."

"Brahmins?"

"The elite of Boston society, but because they are generations deep into it, they have a sense of respect for the world around them. They don't advertise their wealth and believe that type of gauche behavior to be wrong. The next tier down, though, the newly wealthy, believe that intimidation and money go hand in hand. This is what we're seeing here. The women who are part of Girls' Rule, who stay in the background? They are the ones we respect. These people are wannabes. They buy their way into things and believe that people respect their money. Nope, no respect. Don't care."

~~~

By the time Rebecca and Cathy walked into the house late afternoon, Polly had calmed down. She was calmer than she'd been earlier. The women finally left the foyer and had made it look very nice. Polly couldn't believe she'd been so rude, but she hated it when she was pushed because someone believed they could get away with it.

She'd tied off the back sets of doors to the foyer. The only way out at this point was through the doors across from the living room and one set of doors leading into the kitchen, both of which needed to be accessible.

Rebecca noticed the rope immediately. "What is this about?"
~~~

Lexi cackled. "Polly was a badass bitch this morning."

"What? Surely you jest."

Cathy quietly chuckled from the doorway where she stood beside two laundry bags. She knew the drill. Laundry facilities were always available in the Sturtz household. Especially for two broke college girls.

"I was not," Polly protested. "I did stop people from traipsing through the house, though. Thought they had the right to explore."

"And you made sure they knew that there was nothing to explore. The house isn't even clean yet, is it?"

"Exactly," Polly said. "I started in the living room, but I'm glad you're here. Ready to make some money, girls?"

"I can't believe you're paying us to clean this weekend," Cathy said. "Is there anything in the washing machine? Can I start these?"

Lexi went out to the porch to help. They didn't have much time before Lexi's weekend clients would be arriving. Hopefully the kids would be home from school by then. JaRon and Amalee were great help when it came to packing up orders.

"What's for dinner tonight?" Rebecca asked.

"You have to ask?" Lexi smiled. "You came home to help your mother prepare for an event she doesn't want to host. I'm catering to your baser instincts."

"Meatloaf?"

Lexi nodded. "With mashed potatoes, green bean casserole, and chocolate cake. I made cake pops for my clients who wanted dessert."

"You're the best," Rebecca gushed. "My favorite meal ever. How did you make so many meat loaves?"

"I didn't. I sold it by the slice."

"She still made a lot of loaves," Polly said. "Don't let her fool you. She's been cooking since she got up this morning."

"JaRon and I mixed up the meatloaves and green beans last night. All I had to do was fill the loaf pans and stick them in the oven. Mashed potatoes boiled in the pressure cooker pots, and green beans will go into the oven soon. It's all working." Lexi smiled. "I'm very thankful that I decided not to do weekend meals. I need that time to prepare for the next week."

"And you still want to do this for a career?" Cathy asked. "I'd go out of my mind."

"I have great help and I'm learning how to be more efficient. Polly talks to me about processes. When I find an efficient way to do something, I implement it across the board. I'm re-gaining time in my day. It all works out."

"But how do you take a vacation when people count on you to feed them?"

"I give them plenty of notice. They can buy meals from the grocery store. The only person who counts on me daily is Sal Ogden. The rest only rely on me to pick up the slack when they're too busy to think about cooking a healthy meal. It's usually once or twice a week for most of my clients. There are more orders today because it's the weekend. Some people save my meal for Sunday evening when all they want to do is worry about going back to work."

"That makes sense. Cool." Cathy and Lexi had entered the bowels of the porch, and their conversation grew muffled.

Rebecca tugged on the rope. "How bad was it?"

"Bad, Rebecca. Whether you're talking about the level of rudeness from the ladies who were here or about my response, it was all bad. I was furious. I nearly smashed a woman's fingers in the door upstairs. In fact, I grabbed her arm and dragged her away from Lexi's apartment down the hall to the upstairs foyer doors. She thought she had the right to enter a private apartment within a private residence. Who does that?"

"You'd be surprised," Rebecca said. "Especially when they're surrounded by others of their ilk."

"Nice word," Polly said with a smile. "Where would you girls like to start? I'll keep going in the living room and the library. That room needs to be dusted in a big way."

"What if we go out and pick up the little girls?" Rebecca asked. "That way you don't have to stop working."

"What if I want to stop working?"

"Then I'll assign you a bathroom."

Polly laughed. "I'm cleaning the living room / library bathroom. Why don't you girls start with the hallway upstairs. Mop the floor, dust down the doorsills, make sure the kids' rooms aren't terribly messy. Delia's should be in good shape. Amalee keeps a close eye on Kestra and Teresa's room. Don't worry about Caleb's room – that's his thing now. The floor in the hallway collects junk. Make sure it goes into a room." Before Rebecca could speak, Polly continued, "Not my room. Where it belongs."

"Got it. Cassidy wouldn't dare let anything in her room be out of order. What about JaRon and Zachary?"

"Not as bad as when Caleb was in there, but still, they're boys. If we have to pull the door shut, we will."

"Okay, we'll start upstairs. Who's cleaning the kitchen bathroom?" Polly grinned and Rebecca shuddered. "You wouldn't."

"I'll help you. We'll clean it tomorrow morning. That and the family room will be safer if left to the last minute. I'll shut the door to the office, and after I'm done in the library, I will start in the dining room. Are we nearly there?"

"Are you worried about the basement?"

"If I have to worry about the basement, I have Chief Wallers and Sheriff Merritt on speed-dial to escort women from the house. I've sent the warning."

"Today?"

"And to the last two months' meetings. I don't want people in the private areas of the house. The women here this morning didn't seem to think that applied to them. Most everyone else will understand what I've asked for. They don't want strangers wandering through their private lives any more than I do."

~~~

The one thing that fear of trespassers did for Polly was enforce cleanliness where before there might have been only tidiness.
~~~

After dusting and vacuuming the living room and library, the rooms practically sparkled. Even Elijah was surprised at how pleasant the living room was once everything was put away and the room cleaned. He declared it a perfect piano practice room.

Dinner was served in the dining room which gleamed. Polly had even cleaned the windows. She'd also wiped down the glass doors leading to the patio from the kitchen which were covered with doggie nose-prints and little girl handprints. How she had missed paying attention to those things, she'd never understand. Until she looked at the doors with a critical eye, she hadn't realized that things below the three-foot level were filthy – on both the inside and the outside.

The whole family talked about how the Bell House had transformed, causing Lexi and Polly to exchange almost shameful glances. If it was that obvious to the family that they'd spent the day cleaning, what must guests think when they came over. Especially these days when Lexi had people coming into the kitchen more often now.

Just the thought of that had sent Polly into a tailspin and as soon as dinner was finished, she grabbed Rebecca and Cathy. The rest of the family could clean up after the meal, but they needed to scrub down everything in the porch / mudroom. Rebecca hadn't taken any convincing. She'd recognized the need at about the same time as Polly. It was the one room they took for granted. Nothing more than a transitional space for most people, but for some, it was the first room they saw when entering the house.

The members of Girls' Rule would come in through the front door, but Rachel and her crew would come straight into the kitchen, and they'd be there early enough on Saturday that the cleanup had to happen tonight.

They pulled out piles of junk from the kids' cubbies, making piles on the floor. Rebecca went to the pantry and came back with tote bags she filled as best she could, making decisions about where things went. One by one, she walked the bags into the kitchen and gave an order to a kid to take the bag to their room and put things away. Polly chuckled when Rebecca informed them that she expected the tote bag to be returned and she'd check later to make sure they hadn't dumped its contents into a pile in the corner of their room. That girl was already a great older sister and would make a great mother someday.

For now, she was a great daughter, and Polly was grateful to have her here helping prepare for a day that would never exist in history again. This was the last time she ever wanted to be responsible for the group of ladies who had no idea what terrors they put her through.

# CHAPTER TWENTY-TWO

Polly scowled at her husband. "I haven't seen you all day."

Henry cackled. "I know when to be out of the house. Today was the perfect day to be gone."

"Where did you go?"

"I worked."

"Where, though?"

He smiled. "Well, let's see. Breakfast with Mom and Dad, then we picked through the equipment that I purchased yesterday. That was a sad day. Dad knew old Ben Martin."

"The original owner?" Polly asked.

"Yes. Really sad story there. His wife died, his kids all moved away and wanted nothing to do with their past. When Ben moved into assisted living, the kids hired an estate sales company to get rid of the household items. All Ben had left was his shop equipment and he refused to let anyone touch it. When he was able to get around, he'd go out to the storage unit and run a saw or the lathe, just to remember himself. Dad said he used to pick Ben up and drive him over there. The old man only wanted to make and smell the sawdust."

"That is sad. I'm glad you got his equipment, then."

"The kids finally cut off the rental payments. The oldest son told Gordon that he didn't care what happened to the stuff; he didn't want to deal with it."

"For as many wonderful people as I deal with every day," Polly said, "there are people I want to kick in the teeth. I think there are more good people, but stories like this make me wonder."

"Keep your positive attitude," Henry said. "It's the only way to get through the day."

She smiled. "The thing is, I'm always surprised when I hear about or encounter rotten people. You know what that tells me?"

"What's that?"

"That I expect goodness. I assume that people are good. That's a good way to approach it, don't you think?"

"I love you, too. Did the crazy lady who tried to wander through our house show up today, or did you scare her off?"

That made Polly laugh out loud. "Oh, she showed up. Lydia tells me that she calls herself a social media influencer. Her husband is a custodian for one of the buildings at Iowa State."

"How many followers?"

"You know about this stuff? About twenty thousand, so she thinks she's a big deal."

"Not approaching the hundred thousand mark for a while, then. That *would* be a big deal. But if it works in her own mind, then, good for her. How did it go?"

"She apologized, making sure she did it when a bunch of people were around to watch."

"Polly," he scolded.

"Oh, I'm not finished. She then asked if it would be okay that she did the apology again and recorded it for her insty- or tokky-channel. I didn't pay attention."

His eyes grew big. "What did you tell her?"

"I laughed and said, *No, thank you,* then walked away and out of the foyer. I have no idea what she did after that. But I'm having no part of her looking like a big deal when she was as rude as they come. That's two people we've talked about who are a disappointment to humanity."

"But then there was Ben Martin, who was a good man. And there are my parents. Dad took care of Ben. And there's Lydia …"

"See, balance. I'm back on track now."

The Girls' Rule luncheon had gone as well as could be expected. Lydia kept Polly from getting too upset at the snobbish behavior of many of the women. My goodness, but those ladies liked to show off. And the donations had transformed from caring about individuals to giving to organizations. At least they were groups that cared about people. They didn't care who gave them money, they just needed it to continue their good work.

Only three other women had tried to enter the residential area of the house, but they'd been turned around and didn't protest, so it wasn't as traumatic as Polly had worried it would be.

By the time Henry came home, the women were long gone, and the household felt normal again. Kids were free to move around, and Lexi had her kitchen back. Rachel and Lexi were friends, and that part hadn't been awkward, but it's never easy to have someone else working in your space.

Elijah was still at the music store, Noah was at the barn with Jason and Eliseo, Caleb was at the garage, JaRon and Zachary were with Bill Sturtz, while the littlest girls, Gillian and Delia had been delivered to Grandma Marie early this morning. Cassidy and her friend, Missy Gordon, were spending the day with Agnes. Rebecca, Cathy, and Amalee had taken Kestra and Teresa to the thrift store, the antique store, and then to the coffee shop. They'd gotten home about an hour ago, laden with bags.

Knowing the girls wanted to buy Christmas gifts for friends, Polly made sure that Amalee had money to share with her sisters. It had been a difficult conversation. Though they'd lived as part of the family for several months, Amalee still had trouble believing they deserved all the benefits of being Polly and Henry's kids. Polly won the debate, but it had taken time. Those kids had lived modestly for a long time. It was nice to see their gratitude, but Polly wanted them to be comfortable with their new lives.

Now, she and Henry were spending time with each other in the living room. The fireplace was lit, and she had a blanket over her lap. Four dogs and a couple of cats were sprawled out on the large pad Henry set in front of the fire. Han and Obiwan had bounced back to their normal selves after a day of good sleep in their own home. Polly was grateful for her babies' caregivers. She hated worrying about the animals. The living room was a good place to be on a Saturday afternoon. As crazy as Polly's weeks were, she loved the quiet time she could get with Henry.

"Polly?"

She looked up at the door and saw Amalee standing in the doorway.

"Hey, honey, come in. What's up?"

"I have your change from this morning."

"Keep it. Use it or put it somewhere for the next time you all want to go shopping."

Amalee looked confused, but after one argument with Polly about money, she wasn't interested in another, and pocketed the money.

"What do you need?" Polly asked again.

"Can I talk to the two of you? Are you busy?"

"Come in," Henry said and pointed at a chair beside the sofa. "What's on your mind?"

Amalee sat, folded her hands in her lap and rubbed her fingers together. "I had a meeting with the guidance counselor on Thursday. She wanted to talk to me about college. I don't have any answers. I don't even know what to think. This year has been so out of control, I ignored everything that I knew I had to deal with." Tears sparkled in the corner of her eyes. "I want to go to college, but I don't know what to do. When I said something to Rebecca, she told me I had to talk to the two of you, that you'd help me. But I don't want you to pay my way. That isn't why you took us in."

Henry put up his hand. "Stop thinking that way. We are your family. We didn't take you in because you were some poor waifs left on a cold stoop."

That made Amalee giggle.

"When Polly told me that you were going to be part of our family, it was because she knew that we needed you as much as you needed us. Do you know that there was one little boy who everyone assumed would become part of this family, but Polly knew differently? She knew that he belonged with someone else. And he did. His mother's family wanted to adopt him. When she knows, it's because she knows. That's all there is to it."

"And that means that you need to stop worrying about our money versus your money," Polly said. "We're here to help you figure out how to do whatever it is you want to do. We won't always pay your way, but because we have been around a long time, we have resources that you don't even know exist. We also know how to ask good questions and find good answers." She sighed. "If there were no limits to money or time, what is your extravagant dream?"

Amalee sat silently. "I haven't ever dreamed like that."

"You have to start somewhere," Henry said. "Give yourself a minute. What do you want to do most in the world?"

"I used to say that I wanted to be a lawyer so that I could make things right, but I'm older now and no one can do that."

"You can. The small actions that people do to make things right create a big difference as they build up. We must convince people to keep at it. Never give up," Polly said. "Is law school still a goal for you?"

"I don't know. I've enjoyed working with Lexi, but I don't want to be a chef. I'm not a musician or an artist like Rebecca. I don't want to write stories or run a business. I just don't know."

"Amalee," Henry said, "you have a home with us for the rest of your life. What if you were to stop worrying about your future for a year or so?"

"What do you mean?"

"I would surmise that since your mother died, you've spent more time worrying about your siblings' future than your own. You haven't enjoyed your high school years because of that worry, am I right?"

She shrugged. "Maybe." More tears came to her eyes. "I needed to do it that way. Grammy wasn't going to be around forever. We all knew that."

"Are you still worried about their future?"

"Not as much," Amalee said with a shy smile. "I know that if something happens to me, you'll take care of them like they are yours."

"They are ours," Polly said. "So are you. I understand this is a strange position for you to be in, but we've already started applications for adoption. For all of you. If you aren't interested, you can say no, but we wanted to take a positive step forward to make you know how much you belong to us as family."

"I didn't know that. Me, too? But I'm eighteen."

"We can still make you a Sturtz if you want."

"I want it. I really want it. Can I keep Daddy's last name, too?"

"You can do anything you want," Polly said. "What would you think about spending a year figuring out what your dreams could look like?"

"What would I do?"

"Get a job, take classes at the community college. Whatever you want to do. You have to do something, but I'm not worried. You aren't the type of girl who wants to sit around doing nothing."

"That's a bad idea. Where would I get a job?"

"Anywhere. Sycamore Enterprises always has something. The hotel, Rachel's catering company, on and on. We can look into that next spring."

"I'm always hiring," Henry said.

"Construction?" Amalee asked. "Really? I could do that?"

He laughed. "If you wanted to. Hailey likes working in the cabinet shop."

"That would be so much fun and it would be a totally new experience."

"If you want to work out there, we have room for you. First, let's get through the holidays. You can start exploring options after the first of the year."

"Rebecca was right," Amalee said. "I was so worried. I didn't know what to do. Now I have lots of things to think about. And I don't need to fill out college applications because my guidance counselor says I have to, right?"

"You don't have to do anything. At least not yet," Polly said. "A day will soon be here when responsibilities force you into all the have-tos, but not today. Today, you start dreaming. Ask Rebecca for a blank notebook. That girl has a million. I'm all about using paper to sketch out your plans, your tasks, your dreams, and your thoughts. Otherwise, they get lost in the ether. I hate when that happens. Make your dreams a concrete reality by writing them down."

"I have blank notebooks too. Everyone always thinks they're a great gift, but they are so pretty, I hate using them."

"The pretty is there to sell more notebooks," Henry said. "Ignore it and see it as a useful tool. I'm better with my tablet. Paper gets lost in my truck."

"And in my tote bag and on my desk and in everything I own," Polly said. "I usually find it later and am reminded of all I need to take care of."

Amalee nodded. "I'll start a notebook tonight. I don't know what to think now. I've ignored my future for so many years because I never thought it would be more than a dream. Now, it doesn't seem real."

There was something about giving a person back their dreams that made Polly feel good. Even when her father couldn't afford to make her wildest dreams come true, he never quashed them. He encouraged her to think outside the box to create other ways to go after her aspirations.

"Let it sink in for a while," Polly said. "No hurry. Why don't we plan another conversation after spring break. You can talk to your friends …"

Amalee rolled her eyes. "I don't have many friends. Haven't had time for them since I was always racing to get home. Now, it's like I have this big family that I'm just starting to get to know, and my brain can't focus on other friends."

"No one at school?" Henry asked.

"A few girls that I talk to sometimes. I'll eat lunch with them, but we're not really friends. I have so much schoolwork. Senior year is supposed to be easy, but I have to catch up." She shook her head. "All those years behind me were lost. That's how it feels. It's kind of surreal."

"Talk to Rebecca, then," Polly said.

"I like her roommate," Amalee said with a smile. "They're different, but they are both high achievers. They push each other. I need someone like that in my life." She stood up. "I'm going up to my room. I need to think in silence."

Polly looked at her with an eyebrow raised. Amalee always had music playing in her ear buds.

"With my music. I know. I know. Rebecca wanted to talk to you when I was finished. She's probably standing right outside the door."

"Who, me?" Rebecca asked, walking in.

"How much did you hear?" Polly asked her daughter.

"Most everything. I told you they would listen and help you figure it out."

"I haven't figured anything out," Amalee said.

"But now you know you have time. You can call me whenever you want. I have ideas."

"For me?"

"Of course for you. I have ideas for other people, too, but you don't want to hear those. They're boring."

Amalee shook her head as in confusion. "And with that, I'm going to my room. If you or Lexi need me, just buzz."

Polly nodded and waited until she was out of the room. "What does your highness need from me now?"

"Would you care if Cathy and I went back to Des Moines this afternoon? Both of us have a lot of studying to do for finals and we should get started."

"You haven't started?" Henry asked.

"I have, but not, like, serious or anything. Tonight starts the serious business."

"I don't care when you leave. Do you need Lexi to pack a food care package for you?"

"I thought you might let us raid the pantry."

"It's Lexi's pantry. Tell her what you're taking so she can re-stock."

Polly put out her hand to Henry. "Wallet."

"How much are you stealing from me now, woman? You have my heart. You want my money, too?"

"Paying the girls for helping me clean. Do you see how dazzling this house is?"

"It is nice." He shifted and withdrew his wallet, then opened it and handed over all his cash. Polly counted out some of it, handed the rest back, then handed what she'd held out over to Rebecca. "For the two of you."

"All this?" Rebecca asked. "We can eat out tonight *and* go to the grocery store. Wow. Thank you. Cathy will want to come home with me all the time to help clean."

"I'm hoping this will hold up for a couple of weeks until the staff Christmas party." Polly turned to Henry. "You know, the party with people I actually like."

"I'll be home in time to help you clean again," Rebecca said. She waved the cash around. "For money like this, I'll put in all the hours you need."

"How long until you leave?" Polly asked.

"We're waiting for one more load to come out of the dryer. Once I fold that, we're packed and ready."

"The boys will be sorry they missed saying good-bye. Cassidy and the little girls, too," Polly kicked off the blanket and stood up.

"I'll be home in two weeks."

"I know." Polly hugged Rebecca. "It's never enough. I don't mind if you travel all over the world, but I'm going to be one sad Mama if you decide to live anywhere but this area. I can live with Ames or Boone. Maybe even Des Moines. Nope, obviously that's too far away. But anywhere else? I will cry buckets."

"No manipulation happening at all," Rebecca said.

"Nope. Just a sad and morose Mama. Maudlin, even."

"Now you're getting weird."

"I'll be back in a bit," Polly said to Henry. "Keep it warm for me." She and Rebecca headed for the kitchen.

Cathy was sitting beside a pile of laundry bags and suitcases.

"You have two weeks, Rebecca. Do you really need to take all of your clothes back with you?"

"Not me," Rebecca said. She counted out three bags and a suitcase. "That's all Cathy. I've already put my other clothes in my room. Speaking of which, what in the heck happened down there? It was cleaner than the day I moved in."

"I told you," Polly said. "The day the dogs got into those ketamine-laced stuffed animals. I cleaned your room."

"It's clean-clean, though. I thought maybe you just picked everything up and then washed the bedding. You washed all my clothes …"

"Only the clothes outside of the closet and dresser," Polly said.

"That means all her clothes," Cathy said. "Rebecca doesn't believe in closets and dressers."

"I do too." Rebecca replied with a laugh. "Just for other people. Not me. But today I put my clothes away because I can't dirty up that room yet. Did you wash the walls and the carpet?"

"I used some stuff on the carpet," Polly said. "And I did wash the walls and wipe down all the furniture. I didn't want anything contaminated to be left in your room. Keep your door closed when you leave town from now on. The dogs found that it was fun to hang out in there and I don't want them getting into your things."

"Did I close it when we came up?" Rebecca asked Cathy. She was already heading for the steps. "I know. You have no idea. I'll deal with it. If the dryer dings, pull it out, okay? Now I'm in a hurry. Oh," Rebecca stopped. "I have money. Lots of money for us."

Cathy lifted both eyebrows. "Lots?"

"You and I should come home more often. Polly pays well." With that, she was gone.

"Thank you," Cathy said. "Rebecca said you sounded panicked

about the group that was coming this morning. Was it really that bad?"

"Pretty bad, but at least they didn't insist that they had a right to wander through my house," Polly said. The dryer dinged and she jumped. "I'll get that. Keep sitting. Lexi, they need a care package of goodies. What do we have?"

"We're fine," Cathy said.

"So, no brownies or cheesecake or leftover meatloaf and mashed potatoes?" Lexi asked.

"Well ..."

# CHAPTER TWENTY-THREE

One of the best things about being married to Henry was the peace that he brought her in the midst of chaos. Sitting with him for a short time was enough to return her sanity. Rebecca and Cathy were on their way to Des Moines and Polly was on her way north to pick up kids from their grandparents' house. She'd probably get a text from Rebecca that they were back where they belonged while she talked to Marie. The little girls were ready to come home, while Bill, JaRon and Zachary were done with their outing. Now that Caleb was busy with his other interests, JaRon had enlisted Zachary to be his partner in all things having to do with trains. Bill loved involving the boys in his hobby and today was a trip to their favorite store in Boone, followed by a tour of the train museum. Zachary had been to the Boone & Scenic Valley train station with his family, but he was ready for another visit.

Polly was ready to have her family around the dining room table this evening. Lexi had pot roast in the oven, which everyone loved. Tonight was a good night for games and books in the living room. Will Kellar was joining them for dinner, which was new. He didn't often come over except for special events. Maybe they had something to tell the family. Polly chuckled at herself. She couldn't help it. Everything had to be an event. It was probably nothing.

Two men wearing backpacks and carrying duffel bags were walking south toward town on the other side of the highway. She almost pulled over to see if they needed help when an old rust-red pickup did so instead. Polly didn't recognize the two men. It was not a warm day, but the high was supposed to be in the lower fifties.

A half mile later, she saw why they were walking. Their car was on the shoulder, the front driver's tire flat as a pancake. How long had they been driving on that? Illinois plates, too. They were far from home. She turned onto the gravel road leading to Marie and Bill's house, then tapped the brakes. Illinois. Two men. What in the world? Rather than stopping to turn around and check, she hurried on toward the house.

Once there, Polly headed for the front door. Marie opened it. "Hello, dear. I was about to pack up the kiddos. Is something up?"

"I have a strange question. Do you have any neighbors who planned to be away from their homes for a period of time?"

Marie frowned in thought, then turned back to the living room, while motioning for Polly to come in. "Bill? Are the Harters out of town again? I thought they planned to visit their daughter in San Diego."

"Yeah," he said. "Gone for the whole month is what I heard. Left after church on Sunday. Why? What's up."

Marie gave Polly a questioning look. "Polly was asking."

"A dead body kind of question or a different question?" Bill didn't get up from his recliner where he sat with his phone in hand. "JaRon and Zachary are in the basement. Wore me plumb out."

"He's a slug," Marie said. "What are you thinking, Polly?"

"I think I just saw the squatters that messed up Sylvie's house. I would have thought that after nearly being caught, they would have taken off."

"Are you sure?"

"No. I'm not. I'm just putting things together. I could be completely wrong. It's happened before."

"Not very often," Bill said. "You drive Henry crazy with your always being right stuff."

"That man is the one who is always right," Polly said. "I tell him so all the time. I should call Chief Wallers." She shook her head. "It's a good thing these people trust me. I must sound crazy when I call with things like this."

"You are a bit crazy." Bill hefted himself forward. "I'll tell the boys to wrap it up. I'd have thought they heard you, but at that age, they get lost in the smallest details."

"He gets lost in those same details," Marie said. "The girls are in the kitchen. I'll get them moving as well. You call the chief."

Polly nodded, stepped back into the silence of the entryway and placed the call. Before she swiped, though, she walked on through the house. "Do you know the Harters' address?"

"Mommy!" Delia cried and jumped down from her seat. "Is it time to go home?"

"It is. I have to make a phone call first. You help Grandma clean up in here and then we'll leave. Marie, you were about to say?" Polly grinned.

"I don't know the street number, but Mindy at the station will know. It's Warren and Mabel Harter."

"Thanks." Polly walked back into the living room in time to hear thundering steps racing up the steps from the basement.

"Mom!" JaRon said. "I didn't hear you come in."

Zachary smiled shyly and Polly bent down to give him a hug. "You can call me Mom, too," Polly said. "Whenever you're ready."

He nodded and relaxed into her arms. These kids were trying hard to accept the fact that they were in an environment that wasn't ever going to let them go.

"I need to make a phone call," Polly said. "Maybe you two could help Grandma Marie clean up the kitchen and get the girls ready."

Bill came up the steps, huffing and puffing, then walked to the recliner and sat down. "This old man likes those stairs less and less. Why did I ever think that putting the train set in the basement was a good idea?"

"Because it was at the time. Are you okay?"

"I'm fine. You and Marie don't need to be fussin' over me. I know what's up with my body. If there's a problem, I'll be honest. Old age is a treacherous time of life. You'd think after all these years, our bodies wouldn't betray us. Traitorous thing, you." He slapped his leg. "Ow. That hurt. Don't do that, old man."

"I know it would kick your ego's behind, but getting a lift chair for that stairway …"

"Don't start with me, young lady. You sound like your mother-in-law, and we'll have none of it."

"It's your ego, not your sense talking. You know that, right?"

"My ego still has some pride."

"We talked about a lift chair," Marie said, walking in, followed by four kids. "It would be helpful to me, too. I don't like carrying things up and down the steps, but if I could stack a pile on top of the chair, that would be wonderful."

"You think you can co-opt the idea to make me do it, huh?" Bill asked. "Try again."

"If Henry installs it, there won't be much you can say," Marie retorted. "I'm talking to him when I'm good and ready. You can use it or not, but it will be there for me. Oh, and Polly, don't worry. Bill has an appointment with the cardiologist. I have plenty of questions."

"I thought with age and wisdom, a man would be treated with more respect," Bill said. "Instead, suspicion and speculation are what I get. Harumph." He said the word out loud, rather than make the sound. He believed he'd made his point.

Polly walked across the room, bent and gave Bill a hug. "It's because we love you, you old fart. And we want you to be around for these kids a very long time," she whispered. "Stop giving your family trouble or I will lick your face."

He burst into laughter. "I don't know whether that's better or worse than cleaning a bathroom. You certainly have a way, Ms. Giller. You certainly do."

~~~

It hadn't been that long, but with all the activity leading up to their exit from Bill and Marie's house, Polly had forgotten to call Chief Wallers. She didn't think about it until she saw the car still on the side of the road. She could have kicked herself. With four very busy and active sets of ears in the car, now was not the time to stir their curiosity.

"Who had the most fun today?" Polly asked.

"We did," Gillian said. "Grandma said we're making Christmas cookies next weekend and today we helped her sort out all the cookie cutters. She showed us the sprinkles and then we got to choose which colors of frosting we're going to use. There are so many colors!"

"We're baking cookies all week," Delia said. She didn't have quite the same amount of excitement as Gillian over that task.

Polly moaned. The cookie decorating party was on her calendar, but she hadn't given it another thought once she typed the words. At least she didn't have any responsibilities, other than being there to help. Marie, Agnes, Betty, Jody Gordon, and other friends of Marie's were baking sugar cookies all this week. They'd consented to using pre-made frosting, so tubs and tubs of that were in Lexi's grocery order. Polly had a feeling they'd need to make a trip to Ames to pick up more. The variety of sprinkles and toppings had already been ordered and for the most part, were in the garage, waiting to be brought out. This party got bigger every year. Once the round tables were set up in the foyer for Thanksgiving, they wouldn't come down until after the new year because of all the events Polly and Henry hosted.

Even though Polly had groaned over forgetting that the cookie party was happening next week, it would be more fun than what she'd hosted this morning.

"What about you boys?" she asked, glancing into the rearview
~~~

mirror. "Zachary, was it fun going with Grandpa Bill to the train store?"

"I ain't never been there before," Zachary said.

Polly's head spun. Did she correct his speech? Nope. Not today. But that didn't stop JaRon. He leaned over and whispered something to Zachary, who corrected himself. "I've never gone before. It was fun. He let me buy my own engine."

"He did," Polly said with a smile. She loved her family. Sometimes her kids were as pragmatic as she was. JaRon didn't embarrass his new brother by making a public correction, but he took care of it. "What engine did you buy?"

"Santa Fe," Zachary said. "It's really expensive, but Mr. Sturtz said that it was an investment, and no one had a Santa Fe locomotive yet, so it was a good choice on my part."

"When Grandpa Bill tells you that, you believe it," Polly said. She'd had no idea that Bill's little train set was such an expensive venture. Henry did. He paid attention, but if Bill had just impressed Zachary with a purchase, that meant his basement was filled with expensive toys. It was better she didn't know. If Bill was comfortable allowing small children to mess with his train setup, it wasn't her business.

"What did you get, JaRon?" Bill never would have left the store with JaRon feeling like he'd had just as much purchase power as Zachary.

"Not much. I'm working on this cool garden. It has vegetables and I'm even going to make a grape arbor. I bought some tiny leaves to scatter on the walkway."

It was a good thing she didn't belittle this project by telling Bill that he was a crafter. They were making a tiny garden now?

"That is a great idea."

"I even have a gardener. He waves at the train conductors. Grandpa said we might move the train setup someday."

"Where?"

"He's talking to Mr. Seafold about putting up a whole building at the Christmas site that's coming to town so other people can see it. Especially during the holidays. He wants to ask Dad about it.

Wouldn't that be awesome? A model train setup in a log cabin where people can see all the fun things we've been making."

"JaRon," Polly said. "That sounds like the best idea in the world. Genius."

"Grandpa also said he wants to put a big … like those ones at zoos and stuff … train track where he can haul kids around, like at a park. He said that we could run the model train track inside. We're going to change the decorations with the holidays. So, like, Independence Day and when school starts. Then Thanksgiving and Christmas. He said he thought that, like, in the springtime when people are trying to finish all their projects, we'd close down the building and work on making more stuff for it. This is crazy, isn't it?"

"It sounds crazy-wonderful," Polly said. "Your grandpa is just like your dad. Always thinking of ways to have fun or do something that no one else has ever thought of doing."

As soon as they got home, Polly went into the office and closed the door. This was the only place where no one bothered her unless it was an emergency. Rather than call the police department, because she was so late, she called Ken Wallers directly.

"Polly, hello," he said. "Is there a problem?"

"One that I've created," she replied. "You know those two squatters? I think I know where they've been staying this week."

"Yeah?"

"Warren and Mabel Harter's place. There's a car on the side of the road just before the turn-off to Marie and Bill's place. It has a flat tire and I saw two guys walking away from it. It also has Illinois license plates, so it makes me wonder if you want to get in touch with Deputy Hudson, too."

"Because …?"

"Oh, because things seem to be leading back to a company in the Chicago area. They're the ones who rented the storage unit where I found blood on Thursday."

"I did hear about that. Gordon was fit to be tied," Ken said. "We'll discuss it later."

"We will?"

"As pure entertainment. Anyway …"

"The two guys got a ride into town from someone in a pickup truck. I don't know where they were going. I was picking my kids up from Marie's house. When I asked if anyone in the neighborhood up there was planning to be gone for an extended amount of time, she and Bill both knew that the Harters would be out of town for the month of December. If they know, everyone knows."

"And so do the squatters. I'll call Bert and we'll check out their house. Do you believe they had something to do with the murder of that kid?"

"I do, but I'm not certain. How's that for being bold with my beliefs?"

"Not the beliefs you need to be bold about. We'll start investigating. If not the Harters' house, I wonder who else made their travel plans public?"

"Bill and Marie would know, though the only name they gave me was Warren and Mabel Harter."

"Looks like you've made my job more exciting today," Ken said. "And here it was, a quiet weekend."

"I thought words like that were anathema in your line of work."

"I never said it out loud until now, when even hoping for it is ridiculous. A murder occurred, a friend of yours was assaulted, and anyone in law enforcement who thinks that quiet will occur until it is all solved is crazy. I am not crazy, though sometimes I might be naïve about the reality of Polly Giller."

"Stop it," Polly said. "This isn't my fault. But now that I've given the problem to you, I can relax. I got busy with picking kids up and didn't call right away. For that I feel guilty."

"Good. A little guilt is good for the soul. I'll contact Deputy Hudson. I'm already on my way out to the Harters' house. Thanks for the heads-up."

"Will you let me know what you find?" Polly asked.

"We all know there won't be any dead bodies."

"Stop it," she said. "If you need Henry to do anything to fix up the house, let us know. The Harters have only been gone since Sunday, so I'm hoping …" Polly paused. "No. They'd destroyed the Donovan's house and were there fewer than four days. The place will be trashed."

He huffed a laugh. "Unbelievable, isn't it?"

"That people have so little respect? It always surprises me, but then I remind myself that when we focus on the bad people, we forget that there are ten times that number of people who quietly live kind and generous lives, never saying a word."

"The news has tried to convince us that bad and evil predominates our lives. It doesn't."

"But it keeps us paying them good money to tell us the same bad news every day." Polly agreed. "I'll let you go. Thanks, Ken."

"Thanks for the call. Hopefully, we'll wrap this whole thing up soon."

"I'm working on it," she said with a chuckle.

Polly opened the door and found Henry leaning against the wall across the hallway. "'Bout time," he said.

"I had to call Chief Wallers. Saw two men walking down the road, their Illinois-plated car had a flat, and then I asked your mom who from their neighborhood was out of town for the week."

"You put all that together as a reason to call Ken?"

"Illinois plates. Items from a Chicago-based company in a storage unit filled with blood. Two young men. Andrew said two men had been squatting at his house. The Harters have been gone since Sunday and don't plan to be back until after the new year. Yes, I put it all together. Why are you out here waiting?"

"I heard you were home and when you didn't show up anywhere, I came looking for you."

He would always look for her. Polly couldn't believe how lucky she was. "And here I am."

"And here you are."

"Has your father talked to you about moving the train set?"

Henry frowned. "To where?"

"To a building you're going to build out at Ben Seafold's place for the Christmas extravaganza village he is contemplating."

"That's interesting. Especially after all the work Dad has done to make the train set move in and out of the basement of the house. And that big spool we set up for him a few months ago. That man always has a brand-new idea that puts me to work."

"He bought Zachary a locomotive today."

Henry's eyebrows went up. "My father means business. Whatever it takes to get these kids interested in his hobby."

"Smart, don't you think? At least he knows someone will take care of it after he's gone. Speaking of that, you and your mother need to talk about a chair lift of some sort to the basement. He was panting and out of breath when he came up the stairs. And he didn't get out of his recliner when I walked into the house."

"Jack mentioned that Dad wasn't feeling like his normal self. When I talked to Mom, she assured me that they had an appointment with the cardiologist."

"Two heart attacks, Henry. He's had two. His heart doesn't need the abuse of a third one. Have you not noticed?"

"Honestly, other than last weekend, I haven't spent much time with him." Henry grimaced. "Doggone it, he was doing fine last weekend. Something is going on. I need to call Mom. Unless that appointment is happening this week, they can't wait. Why didn't she notice?"

"Bill is quite skilled at making light of his troubles," Polly said. "I yelled at him in a whisper today that he needs to let his family take care of him so he can be around for the grandkids. They love him."

"I'll talk to Mom at church tomorrow," Henry said. "No need upsetting her tonight."

"Did you remember she'll be here with her friends for cookie decorating day next Saturday?" Polly rolled her eyes. "I say that I want to have a million things happening during the Christmas season. It's always so festive. And then a million things are on my schedule and all I want to do is sleep in and ignore the world. I'm useless."

"If we didn't have the foyer, you'd be doing all these things at Sycamore House. This way, you can escape to your own bedroom when it's over."

"I have the best time doing all the things we plan," Polly said. "It's the anticipation of insanity reigning in my home that gives me stress."

"Your life has been one of complete insanity. How does a cookie day impact that?"

"I don't know. Frustratingly, I think it's because it surprised me. For no good reason, too. I have it on the calendar. A print-out of that same calendar hangs on the refrigerator door. I've ignored it, to my own detriment."

# CHAPTER TWENTY-FOUR

Looking back, this had been an incredibly busy week, and today was only Wednesday. School programs, concerts, everything needing to be done before the end of the semester was happening now. Lexi was busy as people preferred Christmas shopping and having fun to cooking healthy meals. She would cook for them.

Bill's appointment with the cardiologist was today, so Polly stayed home to help Lexi with their two young girls. Betty was spending her day at Cat and Hayden's house with James and Lissa, so at least there wasn't too much disruption in everyone's lives. The morning appointment would tell everyone what was going on with Bill. At least that was what Marie hoped. She hadn't been terribly happy with her son for pushing her on Sunday after church. Henry had approached his mother poorly, more worried about Bill's health than his mother's response to it. Marie hadn't wanted to worry anyone, knowing that she was already dealing with it. His appointment had been scheduled and she knew best how to take care of her husband.

On Monday, Tab had stopped in to visit Polly at Sycamore House. She didn't have much information. Yes, the Harters' home had been broken into. Tab had hauled the broken-down automobile to impound, but the two men seemed to have disappeared. The fingerprints matched those that had been taken from the Donovan's house and those from the other homes in Bellingwood that had seen squatters. What no one knew was where they'd gone. They hadn't left much in the vehicle, except for a trunk full of blood. Anita was checking, but the plates were stolen, and the VIN number showed that the car had been stolen months ago. Their fingerprints hadn't turned up any new information, so that meant that whatever they had done or were doing, this was the first time they'd shown up in a police investigation. And somehow, they were involved with Mike Little's murder.

The conversation with Amalee about college and her future had caused no small amount of excitement in the girl's life. She spent time on the phone with Rebecca and more time talking to Polly about possibilities. She listed everything that she could possibly think of doing, from cooking to online programming, law to medicine, research, law enforcement, teaching, business management. Now that the world of possibilities was open to her, she was overwhelmed by them. She admitted it might have been depressing to think about having nothing to do, but it was exhausting thinking about a big life.

That floored Polly. While Heath had discovered the possibilities in front of him while he was in high school, he fell into the construction business early enough that he was able to focus his attention in one direction. Her other children were young enough that as they discovered themselves, they were aware of what the world could offer them. All they had to do was be themselves and do it well. She and Henry would help them find their way. Noah and Elijah were both establishing their future lives right now. They could make any changes they wanted to along the way, but their joy was found in the things they loved. Caleb had discovered a place for himself with engines and motors. He could do many things with that as he grew up. JaRon was still exploring possibilities, from food to the world of creation. He had plenty of time. Cassidy was still a little girl, and as long as she wanted to play in that space, Polly wanted her to know freedom.

Now that the Ricker children were part of the family, she had to transfer that love of exploration to these children. Kestra and Zachary were young enough that they could be children for as long as they wanted to be. They'd grow into themselves. Teresa was still trying to figure out who she was within the family as well as within herself. The next two years would be a struggle as she entered the worst years of adolescence. Even when Polly was in the midst of dealing with hateful behavior from young Rebecca, she'd tried to remind herself that puberty was short-term. There had been quite a few bathroom cleanings for the girl, as there likely would be for Teresa.

Because the four kids had entered as a unit and were part of a loving family, it required different treatment to incorporate them. The three girls had each other. Zachary was venturing into a deeper friendship with JaRon, giving him more access to Caleb and the other boys, but when Kestra and Teresa were upset, the first person they went to was Amalee. It made sense, but it meant that Polly found out about things second-hand unless she stepped right in and confronted a problem. After only a few months, though, she could hardly be worried. There was plenty of time.

Delia burst into the family room where Polly had been tidying up. "Mommy, Gillian is bad."

"Is she now," Polly said, plumping the last cushion on a sofa. "What did she do?"

"She won't let me play."

"How is she stopping you?"

Delia put her clenched fists on her hips. "She is a bad girl. She won't share."

"What do you want that she isn't sharing with you?" This was likely more about Delia wanting something than Gillian being a bad girl.

"Tator."

"I see. And you can't play with something else?"

"I want to play with Tator!" Delia's voice rose. The next step would be a tantrum. Reasoning with her at this point was out of the question.

"Let's go upstairs," Polly said. "I need to do laundry. You can help, and we'll talk more about Tator." Tator was a Mr. Potato Head they'd found at the thrift store. It fascinated the two young girls and pieces could be found on every level on any given day.

"Gillian in trouble?" Delia asked hopefully.

"We'll see."

"Good. She's a bad girl."

Polly took Delia's hand, hoping that Tator and Gillian were in the kitchen and not in the foyer. If Gillian was playing with Tator, that meant she knew Delia wanted the toy. She'd soon tire of it, and by that point, Delia wouldn't think about it any longer. Right now, though, getting Delia out of the way was Polly's best option. How did Marie do this every day? The woman was a hero.

The tables in the foyer had been stripped of all their decorations, though boxes filled with tablecloths and more decorations lined the front of the room. This weekend was the cookie decorating party and the next weekend was the big Christmas party for Henry's and Polly's companies. Everyone that could be here, would be here. She loved that party. It was the only time of the year that she saw everyone together with their families and it brought her such joy.

They made it up the steps and Polly stopped in the doorway to Delia's room. "Should we wash your sheets? Just think, Delia, if we did, you'd feel all fresh tonight when you go to bed."

"Bed now?"

"No, tonight."

"Bed now," Delia demanded.

"You can climb into your bed for a few minutes while I work in my bathroom. When you're finished, come find me." Polly was tired of arguing already. Raising toddlers was different than school-age kids. Cassidy had been a problem for years until she finally began seeing how other children responded to each other and to their families. Growing up was a learning experience. For everyone.

Polly pulled sheets out of the washing machine and transferred them to the dryer, then loaded it with Henry's work clothes. She enjoyed having the machines in the bathroom. Henry was good about getting his clothes into the laundry hamper, and to be honest, was thankful that Lexi no longer needed to see his underwear. If Polly had realized that was uncomfortable for him, she'd have changed patterns a long time ago, but now that she knew, she made sure that his clothing was her responsibility. Could it have been his? Of course, but this was something she could do for him.

Her phone rang as she was in the process of sorting his clothes. Polly stopped, looked at the face of Rebecca and smiled. "Good morning, sweet princess, what's going on in your world?"

"Andrew had to go to the police station today."

"Arrested?"

"Polly," Rebecca could affect the tone of the disgusted with very little effort. "No, it's about the accident. They know who did it and she was arrested. He took his roommate and a third-year law student to the meeting."

"Because …"

"Because there's going to be a settlement. Her daddy is rich like no-one's business, and he was pissed off at her behavior. So, since he's afraid that Andrew might sue them …"

"That doesn't sound like Andrew," Polly interrupted.

"No, but it sounds like that man would sue the pants off someone, so he thinks everyone else would do the same. He's going to pay Andrew a ton of money to not drag them into court."

"Because Andrew was going to drag them into court."

"Right. Andrew just wants to be done with the whole thing, but Polly, he's getting, like, fifty-thousand dollars. Plus, the guy is paying for all his medical bills, plus the man will pay for his senior year of college. That's a lot, right?"

"That's a big amount of money for a young boy. What does Andrew think?"

"His mom told him that every single purchase he makes will be scrutinized by her. She's happy that he has some financial freedom, but he better not think for a minute that he can stop working at Sweet Beans and he better keep editing those papers."

"I love that woman," Polly said with a laugh.

"It's funny. Andrew hasn't yet thought about how he could spend any of it. He was just going to put it in the bank. But Sylvie was all over him."

"When did this happen?"

"Yesterday afternoon," Rebecca said. "He called me late last night and we talked forever. We dreamed about good ways to spend the money. You know what he said?"

"What?"

"He wanted it to be there when we got married so that we could live wherever we wanted."

"That's sweet. You still want to marry him?"

"Polly." Rebecca was disgusted again. "You're messing with me."

"A little bit." Polly looked up to see Delia come into the bathroom, dragging her blanket and top sheet behind her. "Look what you did, Delia. Thank you."

"What did she do?"

Polly put Rebecca on speakerphone and said, "Delia, tell Rebecca what we're doing right now."

"Sheets," Delia said.

"I'll go get your bottom sheet," Polly said. "Talk to Rebecca. We'll put fresh ones on after we're done chatting with your sister. What about the pink ones?"

"Pink sheets," Delia said in agreement. "Rebecca!" She took the phone from Polly's hand and walked over to Henry's chair. It was cute to watch her mimic adult behavior. After setting the phone on the table, she clambered up into the chair and then took it back, staring at the image of Rebecca. "School today?"

"I have a class in an hour. How are you?"

"Mad at Gillian."

"Ooh, no. Why are you mad?" Rebecca asked.

Apparently, Delia wasn't finished with her anger over Gillian playing with Tator. That was some long-term memory. Polly left them to their conversation and went into Delia's room. She'd been meaning to do this for the last two days, but things had happened. Oh, she could say that, but every time she thought about it, something else distracted her and she allowed it to happen.

Polly was putting the last of the pillows on Delia's bed when the little girl toddled in with the phone. "Rebecca gone."

"Did she hang up?"

"She left," Delia said.

"Did she say good-bye?"

Delia was frustrated with the conversation. "She left. Here." She shoved the phone at Polly, who took it and smiled.

"You are a pesky thing this morning, aren't you?"

"What pesky?"

"You are pesky. Life is annoying you today."

Delia screwed up her lips and nose into a strange face and then said, "Bad Gillian."

"The one in a bad mood is Delia. Come with me." Since Delia was always interested in something new, Polly had her attention, but when they got to the bathroom, Delia was suddenly nervous. This could mean two things. A bath, which Delia wasn't ready to have, or Polly was about to teach her how to clean something else, which Delia hated nearly as much as a bath. That meant she was being punished.

Polly closed the door behind them and tripped the lock, just in case. Now Delia knew she was being punished.

"I not bad!"

"No? What have we told you about not taking toys from Gillian or anyone else?"

"I not take Tator. Gillian wouldn't give me Tator."

"Because she was playing with it. You can play with Tator another time, but you have chosen to be in a bad mood about it. Bad moods are a bad idea."

"Bad Gillian."

"Bad Delia." Polly took a clean rag from the top cupboard and set Delia on the countertop. "I want you to wipe and clean until it all sparkles. I'll do the toilet and the bathtub."

Delia threw the rag on the floor. "Not bad Delia."

"You are now, little girl," Polly said. She patiently picked up the rag and set it, not in front of Delia, but on the other side of the sink. "You can either choose to do the cleaning and be good Delia or not. I won't choose for you, but I will continue to choose your punishment. It can get worse."

That made Delia's eyes grow big. "What mean, worse?"

"My choice when you make yours. If you want to see what worse can look like, you choose to continue your bad behavior. Otherwise, wipe the countertop clean." Polly turned back to the toilet. There was no movement for a few moments, but then she heard wiping and snuck a glance in the mirror. Delia was fervently wiping the countertop. She didn't do much in the way of cleaning, but that wasn't the point today. The bathroom was already cleaner than it used to be because Lexi and Amalee ensured that this was the cleanest of all the bathrooms. With the small apartment-sized washer and dryer in here, people were in and out regularly.

By the time Polly had the rest of the bathroom as clean as she liked it, Delia was ready to leave. She took off down the hallway. Polly stopped in Cassidy's room and buzzed the kitchen to let Lexi know that she had another one on the way downstairs. It was nearly lunchtime and just like the animals in the house, the children knew when it was time to eat. Polly needed to move laundry through the system again in her bathroom so headed back to her bathroom before following Delia.

Her phone rang again. This time it was Marie, so Polly shut the lid and sat on the toilet for this conversation.

"Hi, Marie," she said.

"Hi, yourself," Marie replied. "We're fine. Everything is fine. Your father-in-law hasn't been taking his meds like he should, so he got himself in trouble. With his heart, his doctor, and his wife. Stupid man."

"Hey," Bill said in the background. "I got busy."

"That's no excuse, old man," Marie said. "He's going to take it easy for a week and I'm going to monitor everything he puts in his mouth. The holidays have him off track, or so he says. I think he's just lazy and I'm putting an end to that behavior. How are my girls?"

"Whoa, whoa, whoa," Polly said. "That's it? Bill gets a scolding and you're ready to talk about the girls?"

"Bill has been scolded and berated for the last hour. He's feeling plenty shameful. If he's not, I have more to say about the subject. But we miss our kiddos."

"I don't know how you do it with those four children," Polly said. "I am in charge of one little girl and she's enough to send me off the rails. We just finished cleaning a bathroom because she was mad at Gillian for not sharing a toy."

"We've been seeing that at my house more often lately," Marie said. "I haven't subjected her to a bathroom cleanup, but if that's the training you've started, I can do it. She thinks everything should be hers the minute it crosses her mind. It's the age. She'll get past it. Gillian did. By the time they're in kindergarten, they learn soon enough that everybody else has the same attitude. I remember one family with two children Henry and Lonnie's ages. They had to buy two of every toy or book because they refused to insist that the children learn to share. Wonder whatever happened to them. Bill, do you remember?"

"Remember who?" he asked.

"The Mansurs. I don't remember the parents' names, but the kids were Barty and Julius."

"Names like that, they would already be mad at their parents. I don't remember them."

"They were gone by the time Henry was in third grade, I think. Hadn't thought of them in years. But I do remember the shock of seeing duplicates when we took the kids over to play."

"Oh," Bill said. "The Mansurs. He got a job with UP out of Chicago. I remember now. The house was never really clean either. For me to notice, it had to have been bad."

"That he remembers," Marie said. "Taking his pills every morning, he can't be bothered. I swear, this man better straighten up or I will take to straightening him myself."

"That sounds dangerous. Have you called Henry yet?"

"I tried, but he didn't answer. He'll call soon enough. I wanted to let you know that, according to his doctor, the old man would live. According to his wife, the jury is still out."

"I love you, too. And Delia will be glad to see you tomorrow. I suspect she's tired of me. How about Betty? How's she doing?"

"Hands full of little ones. I talked to her first. I will take Bill home, then run over and spell her for the afternoon. Or I'll keep her around so that we can double-team the sweet babies who have threatened to take over the world."

"I love you, Marie Sturtz. And tell Bill that he needs a poke in the brain. We want him around for a long time. He isn't only responsible for his own health, but his kids and grandkids need him."

"He rolled his eyes."

"Marie!" Bill said. "You aren't supposed to tell all my secrets."

"Then, be good and I'll start keeping them again."

# CHAPTER TWENTY-FIVE

"Love you! Have fun today," Polly said.

Caleb waved at her and Henry as he headed for the front door of the garage. This was truly his happy place and was across the street from one of his other favorite places – the comic book store. As far as Polly was concerned, she didn't care if her kids read *War and Peace* or *Avengers,* just so they read words on a page. Caleb preferred his motor magazines, but he still enjoyed wandering through the aisles of Doug Randall's store, Boomer's Last Stand. He generally came home with a comic book or two, but often, he was there over the lunch hour and his comics ended up at the garage.

Next stop was breakfast. It was early; Marie and Betty had shown up an hour ago and told Polly and Henry to have breakfast together somewhere without all the children. They were setting up for the cookie decorating extravaganza and needed no extra help. Those women were braver than Polly.

They'd engaged people all over to bake five dozen cookies – about a batch per baker. Those cookies would arrive this morning while the two women, their friends, along with Lexi, made colored frostings for each table. The decorations and toppings were already in containers and ready to be set out. They'd purchased tablecloths that could be thrown away and had been saving containers of all shapes and sizes for the last year. This was a big deal for them and for the kids. As long as Polly could stay away from the spectacle, she was happy.

"Joe's or Sweet Beans?" Henry asked.

"I love that you asked, but you want breakfast at Joe's, don't you?"

"I prefer it, but I know you."

"I'm at Sweet Beans every single day of the week," Polly said. "I can afford a morning with my favorite waitress ..."

"And your favorite ...," he interrupted.

"You're looking for the word *husband,* but I don't have a favorite husband. I only have one and he's the best thing that ever happened to me.

"Good answer." Henry pulled into a spot just down from the diner. They looked busy this morning, even if it was before eight o'clock. Polly rarely saw the outside world at this hour, having sent the kids off to school before driving the little girls out to Marie's house.

She always had fun with Henry when they went to the diner. Everyone there knew and liked him. He and his father had been part of the community so long, the old guys knew what best to tease him about. He was good-natured and played their game, as long as they stayed positive. She remembered watching him take out an old codger one day and was surprised at how efficiently he'd achieved the man's downfall. But the next time Henry saw him, he was polite and cordial, thereby eliminating the old guy's need for anger or revenge. She really had married the best guy in the world.

Because he was in the middle of training his boys to be chivalrous, no matter what culture said about women being able to do it all themselves, Polly was learning to be patient. Henry was going to open her door and make sure she got out of his truck safely. She didn't say anything when he held the diner's door open for her and she only smiled when he held the chair out for her to be seated.

"Good morning," Lucy Parker said as she walked past them carrying a large platter of food. "You're here early, Polly. I never see you at this hour, especially on a Saturday. Henry, I see at this hour a lot."

Polly shot him a glance. "Breakfast is more fun with the pretty waitress and the homeboys, right?"

"Aww," Lucy said. "I'll take it. Good for the soul. Miranda? Coffee by the pot for this table."

A young waitress, new to Polly, scurried over with a pot of coffee and two menus. She must have recognized Henry, because her next words were, "Your usual, Henry?"

Polly lifted her eyebrows. "Wrong pretty waitress."

"They're all pretty in here," he commented. "Good morning, Miranda. Let's have chicken-fried steak and eggs this morning. It's Saturday. I made it through the week."

"Yes, sir. Do you need a moment, ma'am?"

"I'll have the same. Why not? And it's Polly. Henry's wife."

"Oh, I've heard of you," Miranda said. "You own Sycamore House, where Rachel works. I went to school with her. Tried to get hired at Sycamore Catering, but she didn't need any more help. I'm kinda hoping that someday …" She shrugged. "This is a good job, just on my feet a lot. I'm not used to that."

"Rachel's on her feet all day, too," Polly said. "Keep applying. You never know when a job will open up. We're hiring all the time."

Miranda smiled and walked away.

"Not the top of her class," Henry said in a whisper as he leaned toward Polly. "But a sweet girl. This is as good a job as she'll probably ever get, unless you decide to hire her and make her life better."

"That's on Rachel. If she doesn't want Miranda, she doesn't have to hire her."

"Did Miranda get your orders?" Lucy asked, holding the platter at her side. "She's Joe's great-niece. He has a soft spot for family. I hope she'll work out. She wants to do well, so it should be okay. Joe will have anybody's head if they give her trouble."

"She did fine," Polly said. "I have my coffee and that's all that matters."

Henry nodded. "That's the most important part of what matters."

Lucy took off and he said, "Do you mind?"

"Mind what?" Polly asked.

"If I check in on the guys. It's kind of what I do in the mornings."

"I'm stifling you?" she asked with a grin. "Go ahead. I'll enjoy my morning coffee without the man of my dreams sitting beside me."

"Really?"

"Go," she said. "Chat it up. If you aren't back when the food arrives, I'll eat yours, too."

"Sounds fair." Henry scooted his chair back and walked to the rear of the room where a large group of men sat drinking coffee, laughing, and chattering. These people filled up the mornings at Joe's Diner and Henry was in his element.

Their food had just arrived when Henry sat back down. He lifted an arm and waved Miranda over. "We need a couple of to-go boxes."

She nodded and walked away as Polly gave him a curious look. "Now I don't get to eat at Joe's either? It's bad enough I can't get barbecue in Ames. What's going on?"

"Joe Steffens. He hasn't been in the last couple of days. He's like clockwork – in here at seven every morning. We're going to check on him."

"Why us?"

"Because I'll do it and none of the other idiots around here think it's important. I haven't seen his pickup in town either. I'm worried."

Polly shuddered. "What color pickup?"

"It's an old rust-red colored truck."

"We need to go now," she said. "You know where he lives?"

"Southeast side of town. Almost in the country. Why do you think it's urgent?"

"Because that's the color of the truck that picked up the two guys I believe are the squatters."

Henry took cash out of his wallet when Miranda brought the empty takeout containers.

"Is everything okay with the food?" she asked.

He handed her the cash. "This should take care of the bill and the tip. We had an emergency come up. I'm sure the food is fine. We'll eat it later."

"Do you need coffee to go?"

Polly shook her head and drained her mug. "We're good. Thank you for taking care of us today." She scooped her food into the container, then took Henry's when he was finished. "They're going to love us at home," she said. "This was the good stuff, but it would be too much for me in one meal."

They were in his truck before she knew it and headed to the highway.

"Should I call Aaron or Tab?" Polly asked.

"It could be nothing."

"Andrew said those two have a taser and a gun. We have to be prepared."

"I have none of that."

"What do you have?" Polly asked.

He shot her a glance. "I have you. You are a dangerous weapon. And I have tools in the back. What about a heavy wrench, a maul, a claw hammer? Anything sound appropriate?"

"I'll take the hammer. I can throw it, right?"

"Scarily enough, I think you could. I'll take the maul and the wrench. Make sure your phone is in your pocket. Once they're down, we'll call the cops."

"I love you, Henry. Who else but us is making jokes about wading into a possibly dangerous situation? To top it off, you assume that we'll be able to take them down."

"Who else but us walks into dangerous situations without foreknowledge and still come out on the other side? At least this time, we'll have weapons. Poor Joe, though. I hope they haven't done to him what they did to Andrew. The old guy doesn't have the strength to manage something that awful."

Henry drove out past Davey's steakhouse, then took a gravel road south. He pulled into an old farmstead. The house had seen better days. Sure enough, the old rust-colored pickup was parked in front, along with a blue sedan with Story County plates. Either Joe Steffens had company, or the two had stolen another car. Henry pulled in behind the two vehicles and said, "Wait for me. I'll bring the weapons."

"I'd take a small wrench, too," Polly said. "Anything I can heave."

"With your aim, you'd probably take me out. Maybe just use them in self-defense, okay? I'll throw what needs to be thrown."

"Unless I hit the one I'm not aiming for. Then it's a win, right?"

"Whatever."

"I'm calling Tab," Polly said. "This doesn't feel right."

"Intuition?" he asked.

"Something. She'll tell me to wait …"

"But we both know you won't do that."

"Not if the old man is in trouble. Would you?"

"It's why I'm packing heat."

She chuckled and took out her phone, then swiped open a call to Tab.

"What are you up to now?" Tab asked.

"I think we found the squatters. Do you want to back us up?"

"Who is the other part of us and where are you?"

"I'm with Henry. And it's at Joe Steffens's house – southwest of Bellingwood. Go past Davey's, then take the first right to the south. Just down the road a piece. I think he's the old guy that picked them up on the highway and he hasn't been into breakfast at the diner this week. When Henry heard that, he dragged me away from our breakfast and we're here checking. It could be nothing, but I'm guessing it's something."

"Your guess is better than most. Should I bring the ambulance, too?"

"Bring everyone. If you hear from me in a few minutes that all is okay, fine, but all is not okay. Henry says you can set your clock by Mr. Steffens's morning routine. He's either here under duress or he's been hurt or maybe something even worse."

"Dead," Tab said quietly. "That's what you're telling me."

"I don't think so. But I do think he's got a problem."

"We'll be on our way. I could tell you to wait, but you won't. Please be safe."

"Henry is handing me a hammer and a wrench. He has a maul and bigger pipe wrench. Don't tell me we aren't dangerous."

"You with anything in your hands are dangerous. Just be safe."

"Come rescue me," Polly said.

"On my way."

"She doesn't even argue with you anymore," Henry said. He held out his hand for hers as she climbed out of the truck.

"Have we given them enough time to notice that we're here?" Polly asked.

"Do you mean will they have their guns and tasers ready? Yes, unless they are truly morons."

"What do we do?"

"We could stay outside until reinforcements arrive."

Polly was already moving toward the door. She couldn't bear to think that there was an old man on the other side, either in pain or distress. Not when she could do something about it. It was times like this that she wondered where her sense of self-preservation had gone. Maybe it was all the times that she wandered into semi-dangerous situations and managed to come out either unscathed or only slightly scathed. She chuckled at her own use of the word.

"What are you laughing about?" Henry asked.

"Better you don't know. I will tell you later if it is still appropriate."

She didn't bother to knock, but opened the back door, hammer at the ready and her left hand holding out the wrench. Henry was holding up an immense pipe wrench. He pushed her aside and went in first.

"Brat," she muttered.

He called out, "Joe! It's Henry Sturtz. We've been worried about you at the diner. Where you been, man?"

Polly heard the sound of electricity and then the swing of a something before she heard Henry curse. The next sound was a thud. She rushed forward through the tiny back porch and saw her husband standing over a young man, who still had hold of the taser. Its tiny prongs had attached themselves to Henry's heavy jacket, not affecting him in the least. The kid lay on the floor, holding a knee and whining about how it was broken and hurt so badly.

Looking up, she saw Joe seated in a chair with a gun to his head.

"Back off or he dies," the other young man said.

"No bullets," Joe said, his voice thick with fear and emotion. "Empty."

The young man smacked Joe's head with the gun, causing the older man to slump in his bindings. He'd been wrapped with duct tape and tied with rope to one of the old vinyl kitchen chairs, facing the doorway. That he'd given that information to Polly and Henry was enough, though.

As blood dripped down the side of Joe's face, Polly tossed the wrench. She only cared that she missed hitting Joe and she did by several feet, but the abruptness of her movement caused the young man to lose his focus.

She rushed him with the hammer high in her right hand. At the last minute, rather than using the claw, she rapped his upper arm with the side of the hammer as hard as she could. He released the gun and fell to the floor moaning.

Henry reached into his coat pocket and pulled out two lengths of rope. "Do you want to help me with this?" He had kicked the taser out of the kid's hands and across into the dining room after pulling the prongs out of the front of his own coat.

Polly reached down and pushed the gun away from the other kid who was now whining and crying, while holding his arm.

Rather than deal with him, she opened drawers until she found a pair of scissors and a dish cloth. Wetting it with warm water, she went back to Joe and patted his head with the cloth, trying to stop the bleeding.

He blinked his eyes, then let them close again. "Thank you for coming," he whispered.

"I'm sorry it took so long," Henry said.

The back door opened; this time it was Deputy Hudson along with paramedics Adam Masterson and his partner, Jean Meade.

"You didn't wait," Tab said.

"Did you expect me to?" Polly asked. "Adam, he was cold-cocked with that gun. Can I release him from all this?" She gestured to the over-the-top bindings they'd used on him.

"We'll take care of Mr. Steffens. Is he alert?"

"Kind of," Joe said. "My head hurts. I'm tired. I haven't slept in days because they kept me tied up."

"You okay taking a trip down to Boone?" Adam asked.

"They won't let me sleep in the hospital either," Joe complained, "but I should get checked out. At least they'll be nice to me down there."

"Let me bring in a gurney." He turned to Tab. "Looks like we have some possible broken bones. I'll call for another unit."

"Those two can wait," Tab said. "We have questions."

"Can't you do anything for the pain? He broke my knee. I'm going to sue." That came from the young man lying on the floor beside Henry.

"See how far that gets you," she said. "Did you attack him first? Henry, was it self-defense?"

Henry pointed at the two tiny holes in his coat. "See that taser? It met Carhartt. Carhartt won. So yes, he attacked first. And Polly only went after the other when he hurt Mr. Steffens. I'd say, we're on the side of the righteous."

"That's my assumption, then. Young man, can you sit up?"

"Not with this rope on my hands."

"Henry, you really should start carrying zip-ties when you travel with Polly."

He grinned. "That's a good idea. Maybe I'll get a pack and

keep some in the truck and some in the Suburban. We'll be prepared for anything."

"You all think you're so funny," Polly said. "While my breakfast is cooling in the truck, we're rescuing Mr. Steffens while taking down a couple of murderers."

The young man who'd wielded the taser spoke up. "I didn't do no murder. I'm not going down for that. Mac did that one."

"Why are you two still in town?" Polly asked. "After all this, why didn't you just leave?"

"Because we're supposed to find the rest of the drugs. If we go back without them, they'll kill us."

"Shut up, you moron," Mac, the other young man, said. "Just shut up."

"You two really are morons," Tab said. "Those drugs you were looking for? We have them. We've also reached out to the Chicago police to take down those who hired you to come to Bellingwood. This wasn't going to be your last stop, but because you are idiots, well, here you are."

"Where did you find them?" Mac asked.

"You took the top layers of the animals out of the boxes you opened, but you didn't dig down deep enough. There were three animals at the bottom of each box with the vials sewn into their bellies. And you stopped looking after the first row of boxes. What a lazy bunch of morons," Tab said.

Adam had brought a gurney. He and Jean helped Mr. Steffens onto it. Joe relaxed as soon as his body lay flat on the bed.

"Joe," Henry said, "don't worry about your house. We'll make it better than before. You just heal and try to get some sleep. I'll be down to pick you up when it's time to come home. Right, Polly?"

"I'm sorry you had to face this at all," Polly said. "I have friends who will help me clean up the mess these boys made. We know how sloppy and filthy they are. We cleaned the Donovan's house and we'll do the same for you. Just take care of yourself."

Joe took her hand. "You're good people. Thank you for the rescue." His eyes filled with tears. "This is almost as good as Christmas. I'm glad you were here today."

"Me too, Joe," Henry said. "And the next time I see you at breakfast, you can buy my coffee. How's that?"

"I'll buy your whole breakfast." Joe tapped Adam's arm. "Now, get me out of here before I blubber like a baby."

Polly turned back to the two squatters. "Why did you kill Mike Little? He certainly couldn't have been a threat."

"He wouldn't tell us where the drugs were. He told us that everything he had was already gone," said Mac, the taller one who'd had control of the gun when they walked in. "He lied. He knew he was lying. I knew he was lying. And my boss would have known he was lying. Mike Little wanted all the money. Once he met up with the Midwest distributor, he tried to pull a fast one. He was going to sell it all by himself, telling us that the only shipment that came in was the one he had unloaded at the Christmas shop."

"Did Monty and Linda Morris know that was happening?" Polly asked. She glanced at Tab for permission to continue. Tab shrugged. Polly's innocent questions were always better than an interview. As long as it was Polly asking, Tab could get enough information to interrogate the boys later. Tab's hand flew across her notepad as she wrote down what was being said.

"They didn't," Mac said. "Just two morons who think they're living the good life traveling around the region selling stupid stuff. They don't want to work that hard. Mike was their little servant. He hated them, but did what he had to so that the drugs could come in. They wouldn't let him put those ugly Christmas animals out for display either. So, he emptied them one night, then realized he needed to totally destroy them. We all came back to spray paint the lot. Didn't need that stuff getting out."

"Why take his body back to the dumpster?"

"Throw off the cops. If you hadn't found the storage unit, we'd have gotten away with it. We were going back there this weekend to go through more boxes. We'd have found the drugs, but we were in a hurry."

"How about the video from the storage facility?" Polly asked Tab.

"Video shows them coming in the front and then leaving again. We found Mike's blood in the trunk of their car. They must have done something to the camera in the lot near the storage unit. Gordon didn't notice it, but it's been shot out."

"Mac did that, too," the shorter one said. "Came up on it from behind. It took a couple of times, but he shot it out so we could do what we had to do."

"How are you out of bullets?" Polly asked, pointing at the gun in an evidence bag.

"Old man must've stole 'em. We didn't have any extras. Stole the gun and the taser off the guy whose car we took. He had a loaded gun in the glove compartment, but no extra ammunition. Idiot. What good will that do you when you run out?"

"Maybe you get more from your house," Polly said. "Most people don't need to carry around a box of ammunition in their car just for the heck of it. You guys really are dumb. Which of you practiced using the taser until you figured it out?"

The shorter kid laughed. "I tased him. He had the gun. I got the taser. He went down like a rock. Pretty good weapon."

"Need anything else?" Polly asked Tab.

"I have enough to arrest them and start the process. As soon as the other ambulance shows up, we'll take them in to get fixed up and then to jail they go. Looks like they have things to answer for here and in Illinois. Gonna be a tough go for a couple of young men who didn't have anything on their records before this. Gotta start somewhere, though, don't you?"

Will Kellar and Stu Decker walked in with another pair of EMTs. "Deputy," Will said in acknowledgment. "Where do we start?"

Tab pointed at Henry and Polly. "Let them get out of here. They've had a big morning. Maybe we'll keep their weapons for a while though." She laughed. "That okay?"

"I have more," Henry said.

"He's pretty dangerous with a maul and a pipe wrench," Polly said.

# CHAPTER TWENTY-SIX

Yearning for a few moments to collect her thoughts after the morning's adventure, Polly and Henry walked into the kitchen, expecting to find chaos. Though it was messy, and the sink was filled with trays and mixing bowls with leftover colorful icings, there was no one to be seen. However, happy squeals of delight and chatter came from the foyer. The kids were having fun.

The door opened and Marie came in, carrying a trash bag, tying it off as she walked. She stopped in surprise. "I didn't expect to see you two so soon. What about breakfast?"

Polly held up the takeout bag. "We detoured before we started."

"With what?" Marie handed the trash bag to Henry. "Will you take that outside for me?"

"Yes, Mother," he said.

"What detoured you?" Marie asked Polly again.

"This time it was Henry's fault. Joe Steffens hadn't been at breakfast for a few mornings. No one else thought it important to check on him. Henry thought differently. So, we checked."

"And?"

"And we captured the squatters. They were also responsible for the murder of the young man who had worked at the Christmas store."

"You did not," Marie walked into the pantry and took out three trash bags. Holding them up, she said, "Kids can make a mess. But us adults, we're good at it too. You should see the production we have going on in there. More kids than I've seen here before. All the neighborhood kids, some of their parents, and even more friends of the neighborhood kids. I'm thankful we baked so many cookies. Lexi keeps coming out to color more frosting. We'll have enough toppings and decorations, but the kids are doing a beautiful job. Come see."

Polly shook her head. "Not yet. I just want to sit and be still for a few minutes."

"Still coming down from the experience? I understand. Was Deputy Hudson there?"

"She came after we confronted the two young men. Henry got zapped by a taser, but his coat refused to let it through to his body. The other kid had a gun on Mr. Steffens, but Joe told us there were no bullets in it. He was cold cocked for that, so I smacked the kid with a hammer."

"No need for bullets when Polly is on the case, eh?" Marie gave her a quick hug. "I am always afraid for you, but I am also proud of you. Most people won't choose to walk into a difficult situation. They run away and hide. But not you. If someone needs you to be their strength, you wade right in."

"How's Bill, anyway? I know you said he wasn't taking his meds. Is he better now that you're in control again?"

"He's back to himself. Stupid old fool. You really shook him up when you told him off. I don't think he always considers how important he is to more people than just me. We had a long talk about how the kids need him in their lives. It's hard for him when they grow up and start living their lives without his daily input. Caleb was hard to let go. I told him that we would come into town on Saturdays more often so he can stop in at the garage. I know that's when JaRon and Zachary and young LJ Mellado like to come out, but we might start coming in to pick them up. Just so Bill gets to see all his boys. He misses Caleb."

"You need to tell Caleb that he's missed. The boy is as bad as Bill. He doesn't think anyone cares about where he is or what he's doing. He's been a lone wolf in his own mind for so long that it's hard for him to trust that people really want to spend time with him."

"I'll do that," Marie acknowledged. "Bill will never say anything because he doesn't want to take the boy's independence away. Grandmas are made for saying things that open up a heart, don't you think?"

"*You* are made for that," Polly said.

"You should heat up your breakfast and take it into the dining room. When you're ready for all the action, come visit the foyer. We'll be done around noon. Moms know we aren't feeding the kids lunch, so they'll be picking up about that time."

"We should create a driveway for all the cars that go in and out of here during the week," Polly said.

Henry walked in and shook his head. "I heard that. What's the newest idea that you have?"

"A drive-through driveway. Open up the other end of the hedge, so people can come and go without having to back out. How much work would that be?"

"I don't know," he said, sounding only a little put out. "We can talk about it. Now, what are we doing about breakfast?"

"Your mother says we should warm it up and eat in the dining room. She'll keep the hordes at bay until we're finished, and I've settled down."

"You should have seen her, Mom," Henry said. He opened the plastic bag containing their takeout. "This woman has mad skills with a hammer and wrench. Who needs a gun when Polly is packing construction tools."

Marie smiled. "You two are perfect for each other. Eat your breakfast and come see the extravaganza when you're done."

Henry set out two plates and scooped food onto them. "Polly, you want your whole meal?"

"Half," she said. "It's all I would have eaten at the diner."

He nodded as if he knew that to be true. "I'll split one with you."

The noise in the foyer was filled with laughter and loud conversation from all ages. Polly smiled as she poured two cups of coffee and took flatware and napkins into the dining room. They rarely used the room for small meals, but a corner of the table would be perfect for her and Henry.

He followed her with two plates of steaming hot chicken fried steaks with scrambled eggs and hash browns. White country gravy covered the steaks and when she sat down, she smeared more of it over the potatoes. A yummy warm breakfast to start the day, even at this hour.

"Does it bother you?" Henry asked.

She blinked. So many things were running through her mind. "Does what bother me?"

"The amount of drugs we've seen in Bellingwood? It seems overwhelming. How do we protect our kids?"

"Our kids personally, or …" Polly waved her hand as if encompassing the whole world. "… Or all the kids in the world."

"Ours specifically. The world generally."

"We pay attention to our kids," she said. "With all the adults in their lives, I'm not too concerned. We watch them close enough to notice personality changes. Not that I'm naïve. Anything can happen. We almost lost Caleb to Ariel Sutter's crowd last year, but again, so many people are part of his life that we were able to catch it before things went bad."

"I hope all our kids and their friends know they are safe and loved inside these walls," Henry said. "That was the one thing I always knew when I was a kid. Home was safe. We argued and complained and whined and moaned about how tough it was, but it was safe. We were loved without question. I wanted my home to be like that." He chuckled. "I didn't expect to live in a place this size, but here we are, and you've filled every room with love."

"*We* have," Polly said. She took his hand. "I'm a lucky girl to have found you."

"We are both a couple of crazy people," he said, giving her hand a squeeze. Henry picked up her empty plate. They'd been hungry and it had taken no time to finish their breakfast. "Should we see how much recovery it will take to bring the foyer back to normal? The big staff party is next weekend. How many people will we hire to clean and prepare it?"

"Stop worrying," Polly said with a laugh. She stood with her coffee cup in hand. "More coffee and then I'll be ready to face the onslaught. The house will be fine. We'll be fine. We have friends that take care of us when we're overwhelmed. We have family that steps in when we need them to run an event like this morning."

"This was always Mom's event. You gave her a location where she could turn it into something bigger than she could have foreseen. She is in her element right now."

"I'm glad. I worried that we wouldn't be able to give her grandchildren. And when we were first married, Lonnie wasn't intending to ever have children. Your mother is made to care for little ones."

They set their dishes in the sink, alongside so many others. As soon as she could, Polly needed to get started on that, but first, it was time to see the children's work.

She opened the foyer door and at first no one noticed her, but then, young Kestra looked up and yelled, "Mommy! Come look!"

Polly felt tears come to her eyes. It hadn't taken as long as she worried it would. While the older of the four children might not hurry to call her mom, that was okay.

Amalee stood up from the table where she was decorating cookies with Kestra and several other children, some Polly only recognized from seeing them in the classrooms at school. "Polly! They are having so much fun. Come see."

Polly and Henry walked around the room, stopping at tables where the kids were making big ol' messes and having the time of their lives. Marie, Betty, Sal, Agnes, Andrea Waters, Francesca Mellado, Jody Gordon, Rachel and Anita, Jessie, even Charlie and Cilla were moving between tables, cleaning up the worst of the messes, righting bowls that tried to tip over, filling frosting bowls, generally keeping an eye on the fun.

Her friends were here in force. Hannah McKenzie had brought her kids in, Joss Mikkels was there with all six of hers. Eliseo had brought his nephews and nieces to the party. Even Stu and Mandy Decker had brought their children up from Boone. They were seated with the McKenzie kids. Wherever she looked, Polly saw kids of all ages having fun.

Christmas music played over the speakers, the tree was lit, as were all the electric candles. The festivities were extraordinary.

Kestra hugged Polly when she got to the table. "This is fun. I love living in your house."

"Our house," Polly said. "This is your house. Always."

Kestra nodded and Polly glanced at Teresa, who ducked her head. She walked around the table and put her hand on Teresa's back, startling the poor girl. "Are you having fun?"

"It's okay. I should have invited Keri. I didn't think it would be this much fun."

"You can invite her next time," Polly said. She bent and hugged the girl's shoulders. "I love you. I'm glad you're here."

Teresa couldn't look at her. She was one of the children that Polly wanted to keep an eye on. Teresa was so afraid of loving another family and then losing more people that she loved. It would be hard for her to get past that, but she was already talking to Alistair Greyson. One day she'd learn to trust.

And if Polly had anything to do with it, Teresa would soon learn that the more people you loved, the more love you felt. It was a perfect equation. Though loss was part of life, so was growth and transformation.

Marie came up beside Polly and took her hand. "Thank you for this morning. Look at the joy on these kids' faces. You allowed me to give this to them."

"'Tis the season for joy," Polly said.

"'Tis the season for love," Marie echoed.

# THANK YOU FOR READING!

I'm so glad you enjoy these stories about Polly Giller and her friends. There are many ways to stay in touch with Diane and the Bellingwood community.

You can find more details about Sycamore House and
Bellingwood at the website: http://nammynools.com/
Be sure to sign up for the monthly newsletter.

For news about upcoming books:
https://www.facebook.com/pollygiller

There's a community for you!
Bellingwood Readalong for discussions about the books
Bellingwood Cooking & Recipes (free recipe book PDF download)

For information on Diane's other writing projects,
https://www.facebook.com/dianegreenwoodmuir

Watch for new releases at Diane's Amazon Author Page.

Recipes and decorating ideas found in the books can often be found on Pinterest at: http://pinterest.com/nammynools/

And if you are looking for Bellingwood swag,
https://www.zazzle.com/store/bellingwood

Printed in Great Britain
by Amazon